S0-ABC-973

Praise for *Eye of Vengeance*

"King adeptly imbues his hard-boiled narrative with a real-life context . . . a brisk, riveting read."
— *Entertainment Weekly*

"The word has been that Jonathon King is the future of crime writing. *Eye of Vengeance* proves that the future is now."
— *Michael Connelly,*
New York Times bestselling author

"As fast as a bullet and as accurate as an atomic clock, *Eye of Vengeance* will keep you awake, entertained, engrossed, and in general stuck like glue to its story."
— *Rocky Mountain News*

"An inventive and suspenseful tour de force."
— *The San Diego Union-Tribune*

"This is terrific, edge-of-your-seat storytelling . . . will leave you gnawing your knuckles. Rings with a gritty authenticity because Jonathon King has walked the walk."
— *Denise Hamilton, author of Savage Garden*

"Jonathon King writes the thinking reader's thriller. In every one of his gripping and intelligent novels, he manages hot-as-hell pacing and an engaging style with a sure hand. In *Eye of Vengeance,* he again demonstrates his ability to create unforgettable characters and to immerse us in their world. A great read."
— Jan Burke, national bestselling author of *Bloodlines*

"King writes with the eye of a reporter, the instincts of a cop, and the heart of a champion. I enjoyed every page . . . poignant and thrilling at the same time."
— T. Jefferson Parker, author of *The Fallen*

"Edgy, brooding . . . unusual." — *Publishers Weekly*

"Strong characters, complex tensions, and fascinating details about crime reporting should have readers lining up."
— *Kirkus Reviews* (starred review)

"Harrowing. . . . masterful plotting . . . a winner."
— *Booklist*

continued . . .

Praise for Jonathon King's Other Novels
Shadow Men

"King's writing is gritty, vivid, and suspenseful."
— Harlan Coben

"In *Shadow Men*, King captures the intrigue, lyrical beauty, and darkness of the Florida Everglades better than any other writer I know." — James Lee Burke

"King evokes locales with such vivid descriptions that the reader can't help but picture them like a movie in the mind." — *The Boston Sunday Globe*

"Max Freeman may be the most thoughtful, well-read, and multilayered private-eye hero since Spenser . . . haunting and evocative." — *Booklist* (starred review)

"Just about as perfect as a crime novel can be."
— *The Independent* (London)

"King writes with lean and supple prose that captures the region in vivid and ominous detail . . . hurtles forward with steadily rising tension. *Shadow Men* excavates new and fertile terrain in Florida thriller fiction and finds nuggets of pure gold." — James W. Hall

"Entertaining, quirky characters." — *People*

"A good, lean, fast-paced story with enough suspense and twists to keep any mystery lover turning pages."
— *The Miami Herald*

"[A] stellar outing. . . . King strikes a deft balance between his extraordinary South Florida setting and an engrossing tale of inhumanity and greed."
— *Publishers Weekly* (starred review)

"*Shadow Men* has all the requisite ingredients for a good thriller. . . . South Florida comes alive."

— *South Florida Sun-Sentinel*

A Visible Darkness

"Well into James Lee Burke territory . . . top class."
— *Independent on Sunday*

"Shot through with burgeoning suspense and rich, brooding atmosphere." —*Booklist* (starred review)

"[An] engaging thriller. In much the same way James Lee Burke uses the bayous of south Louisiana in his stories, King's Florida has a distinct, character-revealing personality." —*The Albany Times Union*

"It's the characters in this book that make it irresistible." —*St. Petersburg Times*

"[King] weaves a powerful plot into this volatile mix, provides a credible hero and a memorable cast. All this plus a subtle love story and some superb detective work." —*St. Louis Post-Dispatch*

"A compelling story." —*Rocky Mountain News*

The Blue Edge of Midnight

"Takes us far deeper into the Everglades and much closer to the hard-core survivalists . . . [Freeman] turns into an impressive action hero."
  —*The New York Times Book Review*

"King's . . . insight into character and his evocation of an exotic landscape will remind readers of Michael Connelly and James Lee Burke."
  —*The San Diego Union-Tribune*

"A tough, compassionate novel."
  —*The Boston Sunday Globe*

"Stunning . . . superb from cover to cover."
  —*Pittsburgh Tribune-Review*

"Excellent." —Randy Wayne White

"King's descriptions of Florida's backwaters put him right up there with James W. Hall and Randy Wayne White—excellent company, indeed." —*Chicago Tribune*

"A terrific book. . . . King adds new dimensions of depth and substance to the modern crime novel."
  —Michael Connelly

"The atmosphere is as thick as the humid summer nights . . . a talented writer, one who obviously knows the territory." —*South Florida Sun-Sentinel*

ACTS OF NATURE

JONATHON KING

A SIGNET BOOK

SIGNET
Published by New American Library, a division of
Penguin Group (USA) Inc., 375 Hudson Street,
New York, New York 10014, USA
Penguin Group (Canada), 90 Eglinton Avenue East, Suite 700, Toronto,
Ontario M4P 2Y3, Canada (a division of Pearson Penguin Canada Inc.)
Penguin Books Ltd., 80 Strand, London WC2R 0RL, England
Penguin Ireland, 25 St. Stephen's Green, Dublin 2,
Ireland (a division of Penguin Books Ltd.)
Penguin Group (Australia), 250 Camberwell Road, Camberwell, Victoria 3124,
Australia (a division of Pearson Australia Group Pty. Ltd.)
Penguin Books India Pvt. Ltd., 11 Community Centre, Panchsheel Park,
New Delhi - 110 017, India
Penguin Group (NZ), 67 Apollo Drive, Rosedale, North Shore 0632,
New Zealand (a division of Pearson New Zealand Ltd.)
Penguin Books (South Africa) (Pty.) Ltd., 24 Sturdee Avenue,
Rosebank, Johannesburg 2196, South Africa

Penguin Books Ltd., Registered Offices:
80 Strand, London WC2R 0RL, England

Published by Signet, an imprint of New American Library, a division of Penguin
Group (USA) Inc. Previously published in a Dutton edition.

First Signet Printing, June 2008
10 9 8 7 6 5 4 3 2 1

Copyright © Jonathon King, 2007
All rights reserved

 REGISTERED TRADEMARK—MARCA REGISTRADA

Printed in the United States of America

Without limiting the rights under copyright reserved above, no part of this
publication may be reproduced, stored in or introduced into a retrieval system, or transmitted, in any form, or by any means (electronic, mechanical,
photocopying, recording, or otherwise), without the prior written permission
of both the copyright owner and the above publisher of this book.

PUBLISHER'S NOTE
This is a work of fiction. Names, characters, places, and incidents either are the
product of the author's imagination or are used fictitiously, and any resemblance to actual persons, living or dead, business establishments, events, or
locales is entirely coincidental.
    The publisher does not have any control over and does not assume any re-
sponsibility for author or third-party Web sites or their content.

If you purchased this book without a cover you should be aware that this book
is stolen property. It was reported as "unsold and destroyed" to the publisher
and neither the author nor the publisher has received any payment for this
"stripped book."

The scanning, uploading, and distribution of this book via the Internet or via
any other means without the permission of the publisher is illegal and punish-
able by law. Please purchase only authorized electronic editions, and do not
participate in or encourage electronic piracy of copyrighted materials. Your
support of the author's rights is appreciated.

For my brother, James D., Semper Fi

CHAPTER 1

I have my arms around her, my chest pressed into her back, the tops of my thighs against her hamstrings, and I can feel a vibration from deep inside of her. Or maybe it is my own trembling. She has been quiet for what seems like an hour now, but time is hard to judge. There should be heat building from our shared body temperatures, so close together. But instead of a trickle of sweat between my shoulder blades there is a feeling of coldness on the back of my neck. It is a reaction that I recognize from too many police ops and I don't have to ask Sherry if she is feeling the same thing. Clinging together against the kitchen counter in this unfamiliar Everglades encampment, we are about as physically close as a man and woman can be but it has nothing to do with love at the moment and everything to do with fear.

"Jesus, Max," she says when yet another violent crack, louder and more menacing than a rifle shot, rips the air inside the one-room cabin and we can only assume another piece of the structure has peeled off the roofline or the southern wall. Another gust of unholy wind attacks and the entire place shudders and the creak of wood twisting against its own grain sounds like an animal's whine.

"Jesus."

I squeeze Sherry harder, the muscles of my arms starting to ache from holding her so tightly but I cannot help it.

"She'll hang together, babe," I say yet again, maybe trying to convince myself as much as Sherry. We have already heard parts of the second building or maybe the deck planking itself come ripping off, hard-bitten nails screeching as they were yanked at an angle from the trusses. We have heard sheets of the tin roofing being peeled off by the fingers of the wind and sent flipping away with the almost musical waffling sound of an old flopping saw blade and then the cymbal crash of it smashing against something.

"She'll hold together," I say again.

But it is not the sharp collisions or heavy cracks that make me doubt my own words. It is that humming, the low throb of the wind that makes it sound like it comes from the deep bowels of an enormous beast. It has been getting deeper for the last hour and I know that we are in the middle of one hell of a hurricane.

I have been stupid before, but never so blissfully.

For the past week, Sherry Richards and I had been treating ourselves to a late fall of isolation and escape that most South Floridians and perhaps most of civilized North America would think impossible in the first decade of the new millennium. Sherry's a cop. Some might say too obsessed, too dedicated, and too hard-edged. Some might fall back on that knee-jerk explanation that a woman has to be that way to make it in her profession. Those some are the ones who don't know her. I know her.

"I'm taking ten days off starting the eighteenth of October," she announced one morning at a staff meeting of the major crimes division of the Broward County Sheriff's Office, where she is a detective.

Heads turned. Eyebrows rose. Questions spilled forthwith. Her answers were curt and simple:

"Vacation."

"Can't tell you where."

"No. I'll be unavailable by phone or radio."

"Diaz has my back on ongoing cases."

"None of your business."

She left the care of her home in Fort Lauderdale to a young woman named Marci whom she had managed to rescue from a serial abuser and killer several months ago. After that case Sherry took the woman in and worked hard at making a friendship out of what was meant as rehabilitation. I finally talked her into taking the time off.

"Give Marci some space and yourself a break."

"I'm not going on some cruise, Max."

"Never entered my mind. I was thinking of something much more therapeutic."

I'd worked Marci's case from a different angle, and although the ending was perhaps acceptable, Sherry and I had been at odds while searching for her stalker and hadn't come together until the end. In the dark nights that followed, sitting in the turquoise blue light of Sherry's backyard pool, we had decided that if we were going to make it as lovers and friends we were going to have to do some mutual discovering. The idea of a short hibernation, in that sense, was shared.

So six days ago Sherry gathered enough clothing and oddities for a week in the wild. At my river cabin on the edge of the Everglades I had packed in as much additional food as I thought necessary. I had been living out here on and off for four years and although the amount of work I was now doing for my lawyer friend, Billy Manchester, put me out into the world more than when I first arrived, I still kept the place provisioned enough to get by for at least a few weeks if I had the need or desire. The cabin can only be reached by small boats; in my case, a canoe. To the west are the wide-open Everglades, more than four thousand square miles of flat land, most of it covered in sawgrass, and it often looks like a million acres of prairie grass running to the horizon. But instead of rich soil, the surface of the Glades is a moving layer of water that quietly follows the pull of gravity and runs south from Lake Okeechobee to the sea. Some find it forbidding, others naturally and uniquely beautiful. For the first few days anyway, we were members of the latter.

Sherry is tall and long-legged and can whip my ass in a distance run. I've seen her hold an excruciating yoga pose longer than I'd thought humanly possible and I have also seen her kill a sexual predator, pulling the trigger on her service weapon at nearly point-blank range. Her toughness is unquestionable. But isolation in someplace like the Glades takes a different degree of mettle. I have no running water in my cabin, just a hand pump at the old cast-iron sink where botanists used to wash away the detritus and entrails and stomach contents of whatever species they were studying in the late 1800s. I have a rain barrel at the roofline to which a gravity showerhead is attached. In a small corner closet I have a chemical toilet like the kind used on board a small seagoing boat. I cook mostly on the pot-bellied, wood-burning stove though there are a few bottles of propane and an ancient green Coleman stove under the kitchen cabinet. I read by kerosene lamplight. It is not paradise, but you know that going in.

For the first couple of days we were satisfied to fish lazily on the southern area of the river that is wide and flat and bordered by sedge grasses and tupelos, red maple and bald cypress. Sherry had fished here before with me and it's an easy enough activity that fits most people's sense of normality in the wild.

"You know, Max. This thing about incentive, motivation, greed . . ." she started on the second morning when we were sitting in my canoe on a wide and open stretch of river, near a green edge where the color of the water goes suddenly dark and the bigger fish lurk. "Does a fish have that? Maybe we just have to figure out how to jack that up somehow. Make 'em more greedy."

Her line had been dormant for about an hour, lying like a single silvery string on calm water.

"They aren't much different than people, love," I said, encouraging this little banter thing we'd become comfortable with over the years. "They'll always want more. Dangle stuff in front of them and wait till they want it bad enough, they'll take it."

She might have been pondering the thought, or figuring out a way to tell me I was full of shit, when a big tarpon hit her line and bent the pole like a whip.

"Wooooo haaaaa!" she cried out, and the instant enthusiasm and joy on her face caught me so off guard that I was slow to react to the sudden shift in the boat's balance and nearly let us roll over. The tarpon immediately turned from the edge where it'd taken her bait and shot toward deep water. Sherry spun with it, her arms high, waist revolving, butt properly planted. I jammed my reel under my own seat and grabbed the gunwales with both hands, steadying the canoe. I'd learned from a dozen dunkings that fishing from a canoe is a different sport, a challenge of balance and concentration between shifting weight and anticipation of a strong animal's moves.

Sherry's reel was grinding with the sound of an electric can opener but the tarpon's strength still turned her end of the boat and started it moving. I countered the shift with my weight. Sherry let the big guy run, let it wear itself out a bit. She was working it like a pro. The line was tight as a guitar string, sizzling with water spray, but suddenly went slack. Sherry nearly fell back off her seat, her face shocked. Furrows started in her forehead, and bordering on disappointment, she started to look back at me. All I could do was point out where the fish was doubling back and yell out a warning.

"Reel!" I shouted, and she turned back and started cranking just as the silver-sided tarpon broke surface, flashed in the sun as it violently twisted its body in an attempt to throw the pain of the hook, and then crashed back into the river.

"Holy, holy!" Sherry yelped with delight. She got a dozen spins on the reel to take up slack when again the line zipped taut and the fight was on.

Three times over the next ten minutes I had to reach out and grab a handful of her waistband to keep Sherry from standing and going overboard as she battled the fish, her determination sometimes overtaking pragmatism.

Twice I said, "Don't let her get to the mangrove roots in the bank. She'll try to swim into them and cut the line."

The second time I said it Sherry took her focus off the fish, shot me a "shut up" look, and slapped my hand away after an offer to take over.

She finally reeled the exhausted fish to the side of the canoe and I reached over with a net and scooped it aboard. She let me hook my fingers into the gill slits and hold it up like a trophy. The tarpon seemed to be smiling and she mocked it with her own.

"Tough little bastard," she said.

"She's not so little," I said, removing the hook from the tarpon's mouth and then easing it back into the water. "And she's gorgeous."

When I looked back up Sherry was watching me.

"She, huh?"

Those first days while the iced beer was still cold, we sipped and ate onion and tomato sandwiches and napped in the quiet roll of the boat or stretched out on the small dock landing at the foot of my stilted shack. Sherry listened to the sounds of the animals that always surrounded us. When she started asking me to name them I was surprised that I could guess only a few. Splash of a red-bellied turtle. *Kee uk* of an osprey. Grunt of a mating gator. During the day we sat in the speckled light that passed through the tree canopy as though it were green cheesecloth. At night I read to her aloud from Cormac McCarthy's *All the Pretty Horses* and we made love on the mattress I'd pulled from the bunk bed down onto the floor.

But by the third morning, I detected a twitch in Sherry's ankle or a couple of extra sighs while we were lounging on the dock.

"How you doin'?" I asked.

"I'm fine," she said. But I knew the difference in tone between "I'm fine" with half a glass of beer and "I'm fine" and getting more bored by the minute.

"Hey, I've got a friend, Jeff Snow, who has a place out farther west in the Glades and down south a bit," I said early in the day. "It'll take a three- or four-hour paddle in the canoe, but it's out in the wide-open marsh field and very different than here."

She cut her eyes at me, a look of interest, maybe in a change of scenery, maybe the challenge of a good physical workout.

"I mean, it's October, a perfect time out there because the temperature, even in the full sun, is pretty tolerable. In the summer I won't even go out there."

"Oh, not even you, eh? Mr. Tough-Guy Gladesman." She was smiling when she said it, but I had been right about the challenge. Sherry did not thrive long without a challenge.

"And the stars are amazing," I added, just for incentive. "Horizon to horizon without any of the city lights to muck it up."

She took another sip of late morning coffee and acted like she was pondering the possibilities.

"Sold," she finally said, stretching out her long legs, flexing and showing the hard cut in the muscles of her thighs. "Let's go."

We packed up a cooler of food and plenty of water. The plan was to stay a couple of nights, maybe three, at the Snows' fishing camp and then make it back for a final day at the shack before returning to civilization. I was digging around in my duffel bag for the small GPS unit on which I had recorded the coordinates of the Snows' place. I wasn't that good of a Gladesman to be wandering around in that open acreage without some help. While I sorted through some old rain gear and special books that I kept in the duffel, I pulled out the leather bag that held my oilcloth-wrapped Glock 9mm service weapon from my days on the Philadelphia Police Department. I hefted it in one hand, feeling the weight of it, but as soon as the memories of its use started leaking into my conscience, I pushed it back into the duffel, deep to the bottom. Don't go there, Max, I said to myself. I finally found the GPS, left the gun inside the duffel, and shoved it back under the bed. New time. New memories.

In a waterproof backpack I stored the GPS and extra batteries along with some camping tools, including a razor-sharp fillet knife I kept in a leather sheath for the fish I hoped we'd catch, and the small steel first aid kit I always took with me on trips. I thought of myself as a careful man. I knew enough about alligators and water snakes and poison vegetation, and after four years out here, how one never underestimates that shit can happen, even without the source of its usual progenitor: people. We were ready within an hour's time and though I thought about it twice, given the pristine vision of where we were heading, I decided to take my cell phone. Sherry said she'd left hers at home because she didn't want to talk to a soul or get called into work on some damned so-called emergency. I didn't want to spoil the sense of just she and I, the way I'd planned it, so I tucked it deep into the bag, out of sight.

Just after noon, with Sherry settled in the front seat of my canoe and me in the stern, we pushed off.

CHAPTER 2

Edward Christopher Harmon looked into the muzzle of the man's blue-steel Python handgun and took a step forward. Adrenaline was swirling into his bloodstream as it had so many times before and with a pure force of mind he stopped it before it reached his eyes.

You don't show fear in such instances. You don't show panic, or emit even the scent of wildness. You bring your heart rate down with deep, measured breaths. You consciously keep the irises of your eyes from growing wide. Harmon's wife once described him as having "safe" eyes. He tried to achieve that look now. When they think they have you, when they think they're going to make you beg, you must present yourself as being the one in control. And at the moment, they definitely had him.

"Colonel, you and your men are presently on private property. I am a representative of the oil company that owns this land and I am here to retrieve certain items belonging to my company," Harmon said to the small dark man holding the gun on him.

"Silencio!" the man hissed, his own eyes giving away the wildness that Harmon was working to avoid. The little colonel had already achieved one goal, taking Harmon and his partner, Squires, by surprise. The rebel militia officer and his six-man squad had embedded themselves among the dozens of locals from the town of Caramisol and the surrounding Venezuelan mountains who were looting oil from a spigot that had been tapped into the company pipeline. A dozen old, rusted tanker trucks snaked in a line that ran down the roadway, waiting their turn to pay cash to the bandits, a third of what they would pay through a government outlet, for loads that they could easily resell on the open market. The armed rebels were the paid protection for the bandits who gave them a percentage and an occasional fresh group of teenagers from their villages for their antigovernment militia. The little colonel matched Harmon's step forward and lowered the beautiful .357-caliber revolver just so, turning it sideways and bringing it forward so that the end of the six-inch barrel must have been scant centimeters from touching Harmon's throat.

"Come on, man," the colonel said quietly, abandoning his Spanish for perfect American street English. "Don't diss me in front of my crew, oil man. We can work this shit out."

Now all Harmon could see was the rear sight of the Python and the burled walnut grip in the young man's hand. The Colt Python truly is the finest in American arms design and it pained Harmon to see the colonel holding the beautiful gun sideways, its grip turned parallel to the ground like some gangsta movie amateur, which went totally against the firearm's function. The thing was engineered to fire straight up, butt end level with the floor, barrel sighted along the line of vision. Idiot couldn't hit the side of a barn holding it like that. Harmon could also see that the gun's hammer mechanism was not cocked. Maybe the kid simply didn't know the difference between a 9mm and a revolver and how much time it would take to roll that hammer back and fire.

Harmon's own version of the Colt, the smaller one with the easier to conceal two-and-a-half-inch barrel, was in his hand tucked deep into his jacket pocket, the trigger more appropriately cocked and hot.

"Interesting accent for a Venezuelan rebel, Colonel," Harmon said, not moving his eyes off the other man's.

"University of Miami 1998. Business administration major. Go 'Canes," the colonel said, leaning in, smirking this time. Being a smartass. Losing focus. Harmon knew that Squires would be watching the others. All six of the colonel's men were carrying Kalashnikov rifles, weapon of choice for paramilitary around the world. But none of them would be as experienced and comfortable with killing as Squires was. It takes a few times before you get used to shooting the hearts out of other men. Squires had been there more than a few times.

"I will take whatever it is that you have in the briefcase, Mr. American Oil Man, and then we will see

what we can work out in the way of a negotiation,"
the young man said, now a bit louder so his comrades
could hear.

Harmon could sense rather than see what his partner
was doing behind him. They had been in situations that
varied on this theme before, though it had been a few
years. They'd both been in hot zones. Lawless wars.
Military actions as soldiers themselves as well as being
the hired guns on the other side. They had both faced
the possibility of death. Now that they were considered
to be "security executives" on a corporate payroll did
not mean that their world was all about passing out
business cards and making contacts. They'd been sent
down here to retrieve a computerized analysis device
from the pump room across the way. This zone was becoming far too hot with all the paramilitary action, and
the diminishing political landscape between the United
States and the new Venezuelan government dictated
that a bit of company creativity be used. They usually
called Harmon when it came to such creativity.

An hour ago, Michael Mazurk, their helicopter pilot,
had done a perfect dust-off and Harmon and Squires
had simply jumped out of the side doors while the
local oil thieves and their customers guarded their
eyes from the blowing dust. They had then walked a
straight and purposeful line to the pump room. They
were dressed in casual attire: Dockers and collared
knit shirts. Harmon was in his spring jacket, as always,
and had a briefcase in his hand. Squires had the MP5
slung under his arm and carried it in a nonthreaten-

ing way, but a good study would see that the big man was as comfortable and proficient with the weapon as if it were a natural appendage. They were two fiftyish-looking Yankees with professional eyes on the pump and seemed to have little interest in the group stealing oil. If Venezuelan government troops showed up, the thieves and their customers would scatter. But under the eyes of the crowd, two American oil men were no threat and subsequently of little interest. Harmon had keyed the big padlock on the pump room and in minutes had found the computer recorder on the control panel and removed it. He then opened his brief-case. Inside were a satellite phone, a block of plastic incendiary explosive and a trigger switch, and fifty thousand dollars in cash.

While Squires watched their backs through the par-tially opened pump room door, Harmon took a few extra minutes to search through some file cabinets and look for any other recording devices, laptops, CDs, anything that might hold information. He'd been at this corporate game long enough to know that informa-tion was valuable, especially those bits of intelligence he wasn't supposed to have. Harmon and Squires worked on a need-to-know basis and it was not just an old television line when their bosses said they would disavow any knowledge of their actions. The corporate boys could do a lot to free you up if things went bad and you ended up in a foreign prison or worse, but not without some motivation. Harmon was always on the lookout for his own private insurance or leverage and he'd collected a lot over the years, copied documents and computer files. He was a careful man in that sense. But there was nothing in the pump shack worth sticking around for. He gave up and set the explosive and checked the switch. He then made a call on the phone to Mazurk that they were ready for pickup. When they stepped outside, Harmon turned, carefully and obviously, and relocked the big padlock on the door. He knew the crowd would be watching. He wanted him and Squires to be described only as company men, carrying out nothing more than what they carried in. They were employees doing their jobs, nothing more, without care for the activity around them. See no evil. That's the way Harmon liked these operations to go. He might have even had a satisfied look on his face as they walked back to the roadside field where the chopper would now be inbound. He would be back home by tomorrow. Maybe even take his little boat out on Biscayne Bay, do some fishing with his wife, split a bottle of Merlot, and watch the lights of waterfront Miami sprinkle on at sunset.

But now he had the barrel of a beautiful American gun at his throat, and he was about to blow the heart out of a young University of Miami graduate with a homeboy lust for excitement. The more things change in this world, he thought, the more they remain the same.

Without taking his eyes off the other man's, Harmon extended the briefcase and dropped it at the little colonel's feet as he had been asked.

"*De pinga!*" the colonel said with a smile and then motioned one of his rebel gunners up to his side. "*Abre el maletín!*"

The soldier shouldered his Kalashnikov and bent to one knee to open the case. Another one Squires would not have to worry about, Harmon registered. The soldier laid the case down, flicked open the unlocked latches, and flipped the top up. His face registered the delight of seeing the stacks of banded American money, and as his confederates read it, all took a step forward to gain a look.

"Fifty thousand in cash," Harmon said to the colonel, who had not looked down but could no doubt feel the excitement in his men. Greed comes in every language. "It's yours. I only need the phone and the black box. You take the fifty grand and go party with your friends or whatever you do and we'll trundle on out of here. Consider it a visitation fee, eh?"

The little colonel held his gaze but Harmon could tell he was not just considering the proposal.

"Well, of course it is mine!" the colonel finally said, tipping the muzzle of his Colt Python, touching the soft skin hanging under Harmon's chin. Harmon hated it when they actually touched him.

"But I will have to perhaps make a call on your phone to my commandant to see what to do with you and your black box, Mr. Oil. You must know that the political climate has changed down here and bribes are not the only way it works any longer. You don't just walk into my country like you're the fucking Miami police and tell the *chulos* what to do with your high and mighty. Here, we are the power!"

It was then that Harmon picked up the distant sound, at first faint, like the hard purring of a cat. He knew it would grow louder into the whumping of air on a blade. He still had his hand in his pocket. In Miami even the gangbangers would have had him put his hands on his head by now.

"There are many lessons here for you, college boy," Harmon said and for the first time there was a slight growl in his voice. Harmon knew that Squires would begin firing as soon as the soldiers' eyes went up and away to search the sky for the helicopter.

"Number one is that no, we aren't the Miami police. You see, they wouldn't just kill you in the street and not stay to fill out the paperwork. And two, the more things change . . ." He began pulling the trigger on his own little Colt before finishing the thought. Three rounds in quick succession pierced the fabric of his coat pocket and ripped up and through the heart of the UM business major. The young man did not react enough to even tighten his grip on his own weapon and Harmon slapped it away and went to one knee as the air above him ripped with the automatic fire of Squires's MP5 on full auto. His partner drew a line across the chests of all five standing rebels. They dropped, some with short spins as the bullets slapped them, and not one got off a shot. The last man was still on his knee over the briefcase, eyes still full of American greenbacks and maybe a vision of what the money was going to buy him and his family. A pleasant place to be when you die, Harmon thought after quickly taking the Colt from his torn pocket and shooting the stunned rebel in the side of the head.

The chopper was banking in low now, the pilot perhaps seeing the bodies still twitching around the men he was there to pick up. He reacted the way he should, coming in fast for a dust-off, keeping the landing rails off the ground, keeping the pickup side tipped up so the blades wouldn't decapitate his employers. In the distance Harmon could see the oil thieves reacting to the action. They were probably used to gunfire when the paramilitaries were around. They probably were not used to seeing those same men fall to the ground while strangers backed away, watching them intently, weapons still at the ready. Squires was in his position for cover fire, walking backward in a low squat with the MP5 sweeping for movement. Harmon snapped the briefcase closed and picked it up, his Colt still out in his hand, but useless at this range if anyone from the pipeline should start firing. But men were not his fear and the fact that he was again walking away from a dead man who just moments ago had had a gun barrel at his throat only reinforced that odd mentality. He turned his back to the group of curious men gathering at the pipeline and walked to the chopper. Passing Squires, he nodded at the big man with a look that said "our work is done here," and in seconds they were in the aircraft and away.

In three hours' time they were winging their way north on a commercial flight out of Montevideo to Miami.

Sitting in first class, Squires was folded into the seat next to him sleeping easily after consuming several brown bottles of Cerveza Especial at the airport bar and then reading some Cuban novel he'd purchased called *Adios, Hemingway* and passing out. Harmon, though, was nervous, but his anxiety had nothing to do with the bit of trouble they'd had at the pipeline. He and Squires had been in such situations before. It would pass. When they were still in the helicopter on the ground at the airport, Harmon had said his good-byes to the pilot by handing him a brick of ten thousand dollars in bills from the briefcase. There would be no mention of what he may have witnessed during the routine ferrying of the Americans. Harmon knew the pilot was a player by the way he'd stared straight ahead after banking into the quick pickup and then quickly lifting back out of the clearing, never hesitating over the fact that Squires was still hanging out of the open side door with his MP5 covering the increasingly agitated group of fuel thieves, some of whom by then had magically produced weapons of their own. The extra cash in his pockets in addition to his professional fee would ensure that no report or even a vague memory of the incident would remain. Harmon's only regret was that in the interest of the company's unwritten policy—what happens there stays there—he'd had to instruct the pilot to sweep low over the middle of an inland lake where he and Squires wrapped their used weapons in Harmon's bullet-pocked jacket and tossed the bundle out the door. He hated having to do that with the little Colt. He only had one more like it at home.

No, Harmon's nerves were twitching because while Squires had been drinking at the airport bar he'd been watching a satellite news station, concentrating on the reports of a tropical storm that was moving westward from the open Atlantic through the southern Caribbean. It was expected to strengthen to hurricane status within the next twenty-four hours and continue on a path vaguely in the direction of the Yucatán, but as a longtime resident of Miami, Harmon knew you couldn't predict these bastards. A hurricane had an eye, but you could not read it, and it never showed reluctance or hesitation. And unlike most human dangers, Harmon was scared as hell of it.

CHAPTER 3

The kid still had his eyes closed when the collar of his shirt was yanked back, the first button pulled up into his throat until it popped and went skittering onto the girl's dresser top.

"Dream about the panties on your own time, son. I brought you up here to steal stuff, not sniff it," Buck said, releasing the fistful of collar and then lightly backhanding the boy's head.

"OK, OK, man. Jeez, chill," Wayne said, tucking his head down into his shoulders. When he turned, Buck was already focused on the jewelry box on the pink and white dressing table. He flipped open the top and while Elton John's "Tiny Dancer" plinked away, he pawed through the necklaces and earrings. "Junk," he snorted and then started toward the bedroom door.

"If you're not going to do me any good in here, Wayne, next time you stay outside with Marcus," Buck said and then stopped to toss the big-handled screwdriver at the kid. "Now go downstairs and check the guy's study. And if the desk drawers are locked, pry 'em open. That's where the good shit will be."

"Yeah, all right," Wayne said, turning his back and straightening his shirt. But Buck stood and watched him for one more second, saw him take the teenager's panties and stuff them into his jeans pocket. He shook his head and wondered again why he ever thought of using these kids on these burglary gigs. The fact that they would do almost anything you asked without hesitation was their only redeeming value. That plus he needed someone to help do the heavy lifting. But one day they were going to put him in the weeds, he thought as he moved down the hall toward the master suite. Then there'd be no more Miami-Dade Correctional Center for him. He'd be riding straight up to Raiford Prison. He looked at his watch again. They'd been in the house for twenty minutes already, first stripping the wires on the big plasma television in the living room and loading it into the van. Then the other electronics: CD players, stereo components, the Xbox computer games. You take the heavy stuff first in this kind of work. Buck had again borrowed a friend's white van, slapped the magnetic FreezeFrame Air Conditioning Service sign on the side, and come probing for the right house.

The two boys had been useful because they got a charge out of sneaking over the walls of these gated communities and then scurrying around from house to house with the laser intercept Buck had put his hands on. They'd hide in the bushes like they were playing a kid game and soak up the garage-door laser signals of home owners coming in after dark from work. It was another benefit of these far-out suburbs. The commute into Miami took these office workers forever and they rarely got home until after sunset this time of year. They'd hit the button to open their garage and the boys would be right there to record it with the intercept.

Then Buck would return with them a week later and scout the possibilities. If things looked cool he'd simply hit the garage door, back the van in, snap on the surgeon's gloves, and in broad daylight they'd clean the place out. When they had what they wanted, they'd just open the door and drive away. In the past he'd left the two boys outside as lookouts, giving them a Nextel so they could beep him if anyone approached or things got hinky outside. This was the first time he'd given Wayne a shot at working the inside and he'd done it mainly so they could load the big stuff that he couldn't hoist alone.

While Wayne went back downstairs, Buck did the master suite. He'd lied. The best stuff was always in the bedroom. He went to the walk-in closet first, the boxes up high and then behind all the hanging stuff, looking for a wall safe. You never knew, especially in these new suburban places. Folks had jewelry passed down, coin collections, shit that was valuable like Granddad's antique fishing rods were to him. He dug an old gray metal lockbox out from a spot back on the floor. Take it with, there will be time later to bust it open. From the closet he moved to the dresser. There was unopened mail to someone named Briand A. Rabideau tossed on top but nothing like a credit card app or something he could use. Inside the drawers he found the lady's jewelry box, under some silk nighties. Why did they always think that was a place to hide valuables? Like some burglar is going to be shy about rooting through their underwear. Young Wayne already proved that theory wrong and he wasn't even seventeen yet. Buck went through the box, took the necklaces and the rings, some good-looking stuff there, and then stripped the pillowcase off the bed and tossed the jewelry and the lockbox inside. Then he moved to the bedside night-stand drawers: lip balm, bottle of aspirin, warming jelly, and a wad of one-dollar bills. Buck pocketed the cash and muttered something about the lucky bastard. He pulled the drawer out full. They were always stash-ing stuff in the back. That's when he saw the old-style .38 revolver. He stared at it a minute. Bobby the Fence always liked to deal guns. Good as gold, he always said. Acid off the numbers, they went like cash on the streets and among the woodsmen out in the Glades. But Buck disliked guns. Too many idiots without an idea how to use them. Gave them bullshit false cour-age. Fools rush in; he remembered that one from his grandfather. Buck was a planner. Guns made shit hap-pen too fast.

Bleep, bleep. The sound of the Nextel decided for him. He shoved the drawer closed and left the gun behind.

Bleep, bleep.

Pissed, Buck snatched the phone off his belt.

"Goddamnit, boy. I tol' you one signal was enough," he said into the instrument.

"I know but I think it's the lady, Buck," came the excited voice from Marcus, who was keeping watch outside. "I think it's her car just came in down at the east end. Y'all ought to kick on outa there."

Buck was already at the top of the stairs and taking them two at a time.

"Let's roll, Wayne," he called out but the other one was already ahead of him, with an armload of stuff from the den and heading through the kitchen for the garage door. Both of them dumped what they had into the open van doors and Buck jumped into the driver's seat, keys still in the ignition. Soon as the engine cranked, Wayne hit the garage opener alongside the entry door and skipped to the passenger side and slid in. Buck eased the van out of the garage while the door was still rising, and just like they'd planned, Wayne turned in his seat and pointed the stolen signal back and flicked it. The door rolled back down and its seemingly undisturbed look would give them a few more minutes of getaway time before the owner discovered the burglary.

Buck drove slowly out into the street and hung a left. Wayne looked sharply at him but was smart enough not to question why he was going in the opposite direction from the development's entrance.

"We'll run us a circle. The lady's gonna drive the shortest route, straight home. Better she don't even pass by a white van today," Buck said to answer the question that hadn't been asked. They took another left and another and then paralleled the street they'd been working on for four blocks before Buck used the Nextel to get Marcus, who'd been instructed to use the backyards to make his getaway if they ever had to bail out of a house.

"Meet us out on the main road," Buck said into the handset.

When they took another left at the entrance road, they both peeked down to the west to see if the woman's car was in her driveway, but it was too far to tell.

They were silent and drove out to Eighth Street and spotted Marcus sitting on a bench under a bus stop shelter. He jumped in back when they pulled over and then squirreled his way up until he was hunched between them.

"It was her, dudes. I watched her go right up into the garage." His voice was excited, like he was describing some kind of sports play he'd watched in the game while they'd been out pissing.

"Man, you guys were just around the corner."

"She see the van?" Buck asked.

"Didn't see you pull out, no. Maybe seen your ass pull 'round the next street if she was payin' attention."

"Doubt that," Wayne said.

"That's why we switch the tags. Every time, boys."

The two young ones nodded. Learning from the man.

"So what'd ya git? Huh?" Marcus said, taking a quick inventory behind and around himself but wanting to hear it.

"We might get a thousand out of it," Buck said dryly.

"What? With this big screen? And that's a brand-new Bose with the multiple changer, dude. That's like nine hundred retail," Marcus whined.

"What we do ain't retail, boy," Wayne said, deepening his voice to mock the phrase Buck always used on them. Both of them laughed and even Buck let a grin tickle the side of his mouth.

"An' what's this?" Marcus then said, reaching out to pull at a piece of turquoise silk that was now sticking out of Wayne's side pocket. "This here somethin' valuable, Stubby?"

Wayne looked down and slapped at his friend's hand, blood flushing his cheeks and then cutting his eyes to Buck, who'd glanced over and then lost the grin.

"No, but this is," Wayne said, recovering and leaning forward to reach under the seat to pull out a bottle of Johnnie Walker Black he'd found in the den while Buck was upstairs.

"All right! Stubby. Lust and liquor, dude," Marcus said. "Crack that dog."

Buck heard the childlike tone in their voices and probably could have found some of his old self in there if he'd had a mind to. Instead he kept driving along the Tamiami Trail toward the west coast home. Get back to where they belong. Safe. Fuckin' teenagers, he thought. Gonna get me killed.

CHAPTER 4

There is no specific way to know how old the river is that I live on. We know the larger cypresses that define the place have been growing for more than two centuries. The long, gauzy strands of Spanish moss and strangler fig that wrap themselves in those trees could be three to ten years. The bright green pond apples, each slightly larger than a golf ball, that hang on branches at the edge of our first bend are only from this season. The tea-colored water, opaque and sometimes sluggish, sometimes swift depending on the rain amounts in the Glades, is only today's.

In the area near my shack the river runs through a shady tunnel of green. The cypress and water oak boughs mingle and meet and often form a roof above. When the water is high it floods out into the surrounding vegetation and the place looks more like a forest that is hip deep in dark water than a river. You have to watch the current closely, see where the strings of bubbles and the ripple of moving water are most obvious in order to stay midstream. My first several months here, when

I was paddling hard and trying to burn the street images of Philadelphia out of my head physically, I must have looked like a madman bouncing off nature's walls as I tried to make my way from one end of the river to the other, careering off felled tree limbs and bumbling into dead ends of marsh and giant leather fern. In time I learned the route by memory and then started paddling it at night in the moonlight until I knew it by feel.

Sherry used a strong paddle in the front, her back and shoulders flexing each time she reached out and grabbed at the next purchase of water and pulled it back, the strings of muscle in her triceps and forearms tight as cable. But she was still a novice. She steered the canoe like she was on the inner-city streets or in a pursuit chase, looking ahead to the next obvious turn in the river and then heading the bow in a direct, point-to-point line. I could tell her a dozen times to watch the current and just let the boat flow with the water, sometimes down the middle gut of the stream, sometimes in the deeper water running stronger near the edge. But it was like telling someone how to drive, a strong-willed someone. She had stopped glancing back at my suggestions and now simply ignored me. Her action had its intended effect. I shut up.

Now, only at times would I quietly call out "turtles to the right" when I spotted a crop of yellow-bellies sunning themselves on a downed tree trunk or "snout on the left in the pool" when I saw a gator's arched eye sockets and nostrils floating on the mirror-flat surface of a pond of water off the main channel.

Sherry was also becoming adept at spotting the herons that kept pace in front of us or the rare afternoon appearance of a river otter on a sand bank. She would simply extend an arm and point in the direction and then look back at me, smiling, to see if I was paying attention.

After an hour of hard and fairly synchronized paddling, we slid out of the wooded part of the river and into the open. Here sawgrass started to dominate and before long we were at the mouth of the river—an open acreage of lowland bog and a feeder aqueduct that ran through a ten-foot-tall berm that served as a man-made border to the true Everglades. We got out and hauled the loaded canoe up the incline and then from the top looked out over the sea of water-soaked grassland.

The sky was Carolina blue and cloudless. The sun was high and even without shade I still guessed the temperature was only in the midseventies. There was a slight breeze out of the west that smelled of damp soil and sweet green cattails. The sawgrass ran out to the western horizon like a ruffling Kansas wheat field. The texture would change and shimmer as acres of grass tops moved and danced with the shifting winds.

Sherry had her profile in the breeze, her nose turned up and eyes wide.

"It's really gorgeous, Max."

"Yeah. Not a tiled roof or billboard till you hit Naples."

She didn't turn to me or even indicate she'd heard

my crack but I was watching her carefully, her eyes, the lack of tension in her shoulders. We had known each other as investigators working cases together and as lovers in the way that couples with a special chemistry enjoy. But she had never seen me in this environment, in a lonely place, in a place this natural. Over the past few years I'd taken this wild and open expanse as my home and as a sanctuary from the past. Would she be willing to adopt even a part of it? Would I be willing to give it up? You make those choices when you're on the edge of something, Max, I thought to myself. Maybe she was making them too.

I checked the GPS even though I knew the direction to start off in. We took a few extra minutes to admire the view and then slid the boat down the backside and refloated it.

Though I hadn't done any extensive planning for this week, and certainly none for this spur-of-the-moment trek to the Snows' Glades camp, I silently congratulated myself for near perfect weather. It was the end of the hurricane season, late October. We'd had some recent rainstorms that kept the water levels in the Glades fairly high. In fact late last week the far outer bands of a tropical storm that was probably the last of the season had pelted us pretty good and replenished the evaporation and runoff that constantly rules over this place. But the last I had checked that named storm was rolling well south of Key West and heading toward the Yucatán peninsula. Its passing had helped create the high pressure and the accompanying clear sky and low humidity that now blessed us. At seventy-five degrees I could paddle all day and in high water we could keep a nearly straight course on the GPS reading. For the first hour I kept us moving due south in the open channel alongside the berm. As we neared the Loxahatchee Recreation Area, we struck out west onto the sawgrass plain and into what author and conservationist Marjory Stoneman Douglas made famous as "the river of grass."

We ran through about a quarter mile of six-foot-tall sawgrass and around some outcroppings of melaleuca until we came upon an obvious airboat trail. The flat-bottomed airboats cruise regularly across the close-in Glades. With their propeller airplane engines mounted on the back to provide the push, the boats can glide across the water and over even the thickest patches of grasses and small-diameter trees. Having slapped down the vegetation on the most frequently used trails, they have effectively created six-foot-wide waterways cutting through the grasslands. We took advantage. The open-water strips make canoeing a simpler task but beware if one of the wind machines catches you on its freeway at high speed. The safe part is that the raw, ripping sound of an airboat engine at full throttle can be heard a quarter mile away, which gives you plenty of time to ease your canoe off into the sawgrass to avoid being swamped or run over. Today, it was silent.

There is something of a physical hush in the tall grass here. I believe it is the heat, the slow simmer of the Florida sun trapped in the quiet water, and the smell of wet stalks and green lilies. On occasion the wind will pick up and there is a brushing sound just above our heads and then the call of an anhinga or wood stork passing on wings above.

"What is it that you like so much about being out here, Max?"

Sherry's voice was no louder than the bird calls above. I pondered the question for a few seconds.

"I'm never in a hurry out here," I finally said. "All those years on the street, always in a hurry, even when you were doing nothing but surveillance, the anticipation made you feel like you were in a hurry. Maybe it was just my nerves."

I took a long, hard pull on my paddle and looked up at Sherry as I followed through with the stroke. "Why? You don't like it?"

She looked back with that grin that shows more in her eyes than it does on her lips.

"It's way different from anywhere I've been," she said. "Maybe a little too innocent."

"It does have that quality," I said, thinking of the term as a positive whereas I was sure she was still unsure of her own definition. We lapsed into silence again. If you took a deep breath down here, the must of growing grass and decaying humus was sweet and ancient. If you stood, just the altitude of a few feet changed the aroma like a lingering perfume that only interests you when the woman wearing it passes by but intrigues you as it drifts away.

"I think Jimmy would have liked it out here too. He liked innocent. That's what got him killed."

If it were possible to sound both wistful and bitter at the same time, Sherry had captured it. Her husband, also a cop, had been killed in the line of duty. He'd answered a robbery in progress at one of those convenience stores every cop hates and often call the Stop & Rob, letting the humor cover the anxiety. Jimmy had caught a glimpse of someone running from the store as his partner pulled the squad car up, and he bailed out of the unit and then chased the subject into a dead-end alley.

"You really think that, Sherry?" I said. "He was a good cop from what I've heard. A holdup. A routine traffic stop. You know the statistics. It wasn't like he was cowboying."

She took another two strokes before answering.

"I'm not saying he wasn't careful, or that he was naïve, really. But he had a certain trust in people, especially kids."

When Jimmy had closed in on the runner trying to scale a ten-foot wall at the end of the alley, he realized it was just a kid, a skinny-armed eighth-grader wearing sneakers too big for his feet. He relaxed. His weapon was still holstered and he was giving the boy one of those "come here, kid" gestures, his fingers bent, palm up like he'd caught him sneaking candy from a bowl. That's when the child pulled a 9mm from his baggy shorts and fired a round into Sherry's husband's heart. Freak tragedy. Never should have happened. It's something you never forget if you're the loved one left behind. All that crap about closure and moving on doesn't remove the memory cells that live in a human brain. I'd seen Jimmy return in Sherry's eyes a few times since we'd been together and I was still at a loss for how to react. Maybe she was thinking of him, what she was missing. Maybe she was thinking of what it would be like to be with someone who was the opposite of him. So I stayed quiet. Let her enjoy it, or shake off the vision on her own. Some things we handle alone.

I nodded when she looked back at me. The grin was back in her eyes and for the next hour we talked about our favorite bakeries, about Tuscany cannoli and key lime pie and why nobody in the country can make a Philly cheesesteak sandwich the way they do in the city because of the bread from Amoroso's. We were on to the delights of fresh stone crabs straight off the boat at the docks in Chokoloskee when we suddenly broke out of the high grass and slid out onto several acres of open water and the change caused Sherry to stop midsentence. On flat water the sunlight was pinging off the reflected blue of the sky and for a moment the scene was like a still life painting, the colors too perfect, the lack of movement too unreal. Sprigs of marsh grass spiked up from the sheet of glass before us and I actually watched the small ripple of wake from our bow move out for ten yards ahead of us until its offensive disruption was absorbed. For a full two minutes, neither of us spoke, maybe afraid to break the spell.

"Humans don't belong here, Max," Sherry whispered from the bow and I let the statement stand until a breeze rose from the west and rustled the grass and nipped at the water and life moved back in. I knew that once you got over the immense feeling of the place you could focus down and see the scarlet skimmers working the water surface and if you closely inspected the sawgrass you'd find the apple snails working the stalks. Then up in the sky we watched the dark body of a low-flying snail kite swoop in from the south and utter a low grunt as she went into one of the grass out-croppings.

"All we would do is fill it in and build suburbs on it," I said, and it may have been the last environmental statement I would make throughout the trip.

Spotting an outcropping of tall grass that cast a slab of shade on the water, we paddled over and broke out some lunch. While we ate I tried to point out some of the vegetation and insects that lived here and we counted three alligators that showed themselves in the distance, exposing only their snouts and the humped orbs of their eyes as they cruised across some open water. They made no attempt to come our way, which seemed to ease Sherry's distress a bit. Then I made the mistake of bring-ing up the story of rangers from Everglades National Park who last month came upon the aftermath of a fight between a thirteen-foot-long Burmese python and a six-foot gator out here. The snake, probably released by some owner because it was getting too damn big, had tried to swallow the gator and ended up bursting open at its sides after it had the reptile midway down.

Sherry stopped and put half of her sandwich down and stared at me.

"Sorry," I said.

She just shook her head and looked out in the direction of our last gator sighting and after a long silent treatment asked: "Didn't you say this boat is thirteen feet long?"

By three in the afternoon I was sweating. We'd moved well west and the sun was high and there was no shade. Sherry had peeled off her long-sleeved shirt and was paddling in one of her simple runner's jerseys. She'd done her hair in a ponytail that was sticking out through the hole in the back of a baseball hat. I kept on the broad-brimmed, plantation-style straw hat and had gone bare-chested but still built a sheen of sweat on every exposed inch of skin.

We were working toward a gathering of pigeon plum and strangler fig trees that had started off looking like low bushes an hour ago but had now grown to a thirty-foot-tall hammock. Jeff Snow used the outcropping as a landmark to take a clear shot north to his fishing camp. Although the sawgrass and other vegetation was always changing and shifting, this season the GPS setting from this small island ran through a fairly open-water trail due north to his place and would be easy canoeing. He had explained to me, as I now did to Sherry, that inside the thick hammock we now approached was a cabin that had been built by one of the early Gladesmen. The owner had brought in most of the trees as small saplings with the idea of someday providing himself with shade. He had been more prescient than he could have imagined. Now you could not even see the structure inside and the root systems had eventually trapped enough moving soil to establish a foundation and the seeds the first trees dropped had proliferated.

"Snow says he's only seen an airboat slip into the place one time in all the trips he's taken out here. Usually folks are pretty friendly, swapping fish stories and helping each other out," I recounted to Sherry. "But he says he's never met anyone from the place."

As we slid by some one hundred yards from the northern edge of the small island of old growth trees, the place looked deep green going almost black in the interior. An entrance stream actually looked cold to me and not in a way that beckoned one out of the heat. I kept paddling.

"Shame to be out here and not take advantage of the view," Sherry said as we passed. I checked the reading on the GPS and dipped an oar, catching a back current and spinning us north.

"That's not going to be a problem at the Snows' place, I promise," I said, changing the mood. "We're about an hour and a half out."

Maybe having a specific time to the journey's end challenged the athlete in her, but Sherry began to dig her paddle in earnest and I tried to keep pace. We made the fishing camp in sixty-eight minutes.

Now here was Eden. The low buildings, three in all, were joined together by a dock, wide porch, and walkways. One building held a great room with a fold-out couch that made up into a full bed facing big windows and a freestanding fireplace. The kitchen was against one wall; the cooking and living spaces were separated by a standing island. The next building was a sort of bunkhouse for guests with bathrooms attached. The third was a small equipment shack for the generator and water storage and tools and such for on-site repairs. Most of the encampments out here were so constructed, Jeff told me, so that if a lightning strike or other accidental fire started, the flames would not automatically take out everything at once. This place had only been built in the last few years and the honey blond glow of the new wood in the late sun made it look warm, inviting, and almost magical sitting in the midst of the low grasses and shimmering water.

"Wow," Sherry said as we got close. I was pleased to have brought her on a venture that coaxed such pleasure from her twice in one day.

We were about fifty yards out when we both saw the resident horned owl appear from his nesting spot under the bunkhouse eaves and soar out over the Glades with our interruption of his personal space.

"Look. We chased the mousetrap away," Sherry said. She had not been pleased after spotting a mouse in my riverside shack but I had promised that there were no such mammals out here. Too wet. Too lacking in food source. The animals in the Glades, even on the isolated land islands, lived a curious existence out here where a totally different environment shaped them. During a visit to an island on the edge of the Glades in Florida

Bay, a friend showed me the knee-high osprey nests
that the legendary fishing birds had built in wide-open
fields. "They don't build them in trees out there because there aren't any four- or two-legged carnivores
to threaten them."

Sherry was quiet for a few beats when I finished the
story. Maybe she thought I was making it up to mollify
her. Then she turned, interrupting her stroke.

"But he'll be back, right? The owl?"

"Yeah. It's close to hunting time for him anyway.
He'll be back by morning."

With the high water we were able to paddle right
up to the dock and tied off. I used the Snows' hidden
key and opened the great room and unloaded our gear
and the cooler and food. I showed Sherry the gravity
shower and she didn't hesitate. While she was busy
I made up a dinner of cheese and stone wheat bread
with sweet butter and sliced tomato we'd brought and
then stole a bottle of wine from the Snows' counter collection and chilled it in our iced cooler.

By the time I'd taken my own shower Sherry was sitting back in one of the Adirondack chairs on the open
deck. Jeff had set up a half-dozen chairs in a semicircle
facing west. There is no theater like it and the falling
sun was already spreading crimson rays into the tops
of the far sawgrass and into Sherry's blond hair.

"Is that Wally out there?" she said to me and nodded
out to the east. The question threw me and I looked out
in search of a boat or a plane or anything that might
contain a man.

"There. On that mound."

I looked again and in the low light could make out the hump and curled tail of a good-size alligator taking in the last warmth of the day. Sherry then quietly whistled the opening stanzas of a television cartoon from both our childhoods I recognized as Wally Gator, "the swingin'est alligator in the swamp. See ya later, Wally Gator."

"You do have a memory, girl," I said.

"For frivolity."

"No. Not always."

"Then sit with me here, Max, and we'll get serious," she said, and in her voice was more than just an invitation for sitting.

While the sky turned shades of pink and then deepened to orange and finally a purple shade of plush velvet, we sat and ate and let the wine leak into our abused backs and sun-soaked heads and when the air finally started to chill I got out the sleeping bags and covered Sherry's legs with the flannel side.

"Very gentlemanly, Max," she said. But when I crouched to kiss her she hooked her wrist around the back of my neck and she, the flannel-lined bag, and I slid slowly to the deck.

"Well, I guess I don't have to be quite so gentlemanly," I said and rolled over on top of her. Even in the darkness I could see the flicker of green in her eyes. And tucked in a depression next to her collarbone, the sparkle of the necklace she always wore, the two jewels, an opal and a diamond, joined together. I knew it was a present from her husband. I had ignored the reminder in the past, and despite the way it picked up the light this night, I ignored it again.

We made love under the stars, a canopy of glitter that out here in darkness spread incomparably from horizon to horizon with no city lights or building corners or even high tree lines to obscure it. The sight was so stunning and rare I was fooled that first night: when I looked down into Sherry's eyes I thought that glorious look on her face was my doing. Then, on a whim of suspicion I looked up behind my shoulder and beheld the real reason for her radiance.

"Oh, I see," I said. "The real stars in your eyes."

She laughed, caught, at least partially, by the truth.

"Oh, all right," she said, reaching up and pulling my face down to the crook of her shoulder and neck where she could still see the sky past my head. "Tomorrow night, we can switch places."

CHAPTER 5

"**S**hut the fuck up, Wayne."

"Oh, you got a better idea? We're sittin' here with no smoke, no cash, and no chance of scoring any more deals. What? What else we got, dawg?"

Christ, thought Buck, tipping the sweating bottle of Budweiser up and taking a long slow drink off the beer. Even out here these guys are picking up somebody else's bullshit lingo, watching some MTV shit or listening to the hip-hop radio crap out of Miami.

Dog. Hell, he could still hear his daddy's voice saying if you had a good dog and some shotgun shells you could eat forever out in the Glades for free. But that didn't last, did it? Didn't even last for the old man, did it?

"You tell him, Buck. Tell him he's full of shit," said Marcus, the younger one.

Buck took another pull off the beer and the two watched him, each waiting for a yea or nay from the man. He took his time at it.

"Wayne might have hisself an idea," Buck finally

said. "He ain't thought it out yet, but there might be some possibilities there."

Wayne sat back in his wooden, straight-backed chair, balancing on the back legs, smirk on his face that made him look even more like a cartoon balloon with his features drawn on with a marker, his face all pudgy and white and hairless with his baseball cap turned backward so it yanked his eyebrows up and out of shape. Marcus kept his eyes down toward the tabletop.

There's your dog, son, Buck thought, slapped on his snout and chastised like some mutt.

"We're gonna have to get somethin' goin' soon unless you boys want to go on up the road and get a job at the Wendy's," Buck said.

"Shit. Ain't doin' nothin' at no Wendy's but a ten up," Wayne said. The reference to an armed stickup raised Marcus's head, floating on a smile. He and Wayne snickered and both reached out and tapped knuckles.

Buck shook his head. His father had warned him about getting involved with chuckleheads like these two. But it wasn't like Buck had a lot of choices these days. After his last stint up at Avon Park Correctional for burglary and possession of stolen property he was looking at a three-strike rule and after he was released he'd come home to the Ten Thousand Islands thinking he might try to live straight for a while, stay the hell out of trouble. But none of his old running buddies had stuck around to ride with. The place was still a shithole if you wanted to do anything but scrape boat bottoms or hire on with a commercial fishing crew or work in the stone crab warehouse. You could try to make some extra cash by catching gators and selling the skins that, yeah, was illegal but really hadn't been considered that by anyone who grew up here because their daddies and their daddies' daddies had always done it. You could pilot an airboat around the Glades and the islands, taking tourists from New York or the Midwest out on the water trails and point out the hyacinths and gator holes and give tutorials on the flora and fauna. But someone was always askin' some stupid-assed question and you couldn't just yell at 'em to shut up, or if you did, you got fired by the tour operator.

Buck had called Bobby the Fence about the electronics and such that they'd got the other night over in the suburbs but Bobby was working a deal with a guy he said had hijacked an entire eighteen-wheeler full of big-screen televisions and would have to get back with him. Or maybe that was just bullshit to set him up for the lowball price that Buck was already expecting. Things were tight, but this wasn't a place where ingenuity let a man down. Buck was only a kid when things were tighter and they were doing a lot of surviving in the Ten Thousands on what seasonal stone crabs you could catch and living on the fish you pulled for your own consumption. But then the state of Florida put a couple of brains together in Tallahassee and came up with a cap on the amount of fish each commercial rig could catch. They called it conservation but the locals here in the southwest corner of the peninsula called it money out of their pockets. It was during these slow 1980s that the best cash crop coming off the Gulf of Mexico was in the form of bales. Marijuana suppliers bringing product up from South America were constantly trying to find a new pipeline to avoid federal authorities. Buck's father, one of the best guides in the Everglades, had already come across a few lonely bales out near some access roads where the small plane pilots either got scared and dumped their loads or simply missed the dirt strip by a few hundred yards with the last one out the door. He had also come upon some water-soaked packages out on the fishing grounds and the scuttlebutt would be that boaters trying to bring in loads to land had dumped them while being chased by the Coast Guard. Buck's father was never one to waste, no sir. Knowing people, he got the word out and was able to conceal his finds until someone contacted him. He didn't get full price, but the cash was American and he didn't want to smoke the shit anyway.

Soon after, what had once been occasional found money became a business. The suppliers were looking for boat-handling middlemen to unload the pot off the big smuggling ships offshore and then use their native knowledge of the hundreds of small inlets and rivers through the thick and unmapped mangroves to get the product to land-based drivers. Buck's father was one of the best and was recruited. His mistake, as he told Buck later, had been bringing on the chuckleheads when the demand became high and when the word, as it always does in a small community, started get-

ting passed around on the docks and down at the Rod
& Gun Club. Where Buck's father was careful, hoard-
ing his newfound money, planning a retirement, the
chuckleheads were spending. They'd taken trips up to
Tampa and over to Miami to buy four-by-four pickups,
projection TVs, jewelry for their wives and girlfriends,
and new outboards for their boats. They paid cash, but
sometimes the businesses that sold the goods still kept
records. One hot, muggy August afternoon more than
three dozen DEA and IRS agents backed up by the Collier County Sheriff's Department and the State Forestry
Division swooped in with their hands full of arrest and
search warrants and probable cause statements and a
fistful of plastic flex cuffs.

Nearly every man in town over the age of eighteen
was taken by Department of Corrections buses to the
county courthouse. Those who turned state's evidence
and helped the feds make a tighter case cut themselves
deals and got county jail time. Others, who simply refused to talk, did eight to ten in the federal penitentiary. Those identified as the leaders, including Buck's
father, weren't offered much of a choice: lead us to the
suppliers or do twenty-five years.

Buck remembers the three men in sweat-stained, but-
ton-down shirts coming down to the dock. All of them
had holsters tucked up under their arms, the butts of
9mm handguns sticking out where a stitched name-
plate might normally show on a man's work shirt.

His father was sitting in his boat, a fishing line flung
out the back where Buck knew you couldn't catch

nothin' but a lazy longnose garfish at best. But his father's eyes watched out over the gunwale, focused placidly on the glimmer of early sun on the water. The men asked him several questions to all of which he simply replied, "I'm just a fisherman, boys. I ain't got the slightest notion what you're talkin' about."

Eight years later Buck's mother would receive a piece of mail in a long brown envelope with a Department of Justice seal stamped in one corner. She signed for it and slit it open with a kitchen knife, read a few seconds, and then crumpled it up and tossed it in the trash with a look so cold and stoic it even made Buck shiver. He fetched the letter out after she left the room and read the line where "Ernest T. Morris has been pronounced dead of injuries sustained during an inmate-related altercation at the Federal Penitentiary in Hibbsville, Georgia."

By the time Buck got busted for his own forays into the drug business, then the sale of stolen property business, which mostly involved boats and boat parts, and then the flat-out stupid business of hijacking and delivering semitruck containers of everything from stereos to microwave ovens to, once, a thousand boxes of MP3 players, his name and state records were far too well distributed along the west coast of the state from Orlando south.

Only thing to do was to make some occasional raids on the other side of the state off the Tamiami Trail where those new suburbs had sprouted up like weed pines. But them folks did have some money and did buy some awful nice merchandise to put in them pink box houses that were easy to get into. Making some contacts with inmates who knew people on the outside was probably the only good thing that happened to Buck up in Avon Park. That was how he met Bobby the Fence and even though he knew Bobby was getting too big of a cut on the stuff that Buck stole, he was a line to fast cash. But even with all of the precautions Buck took, he was smart enough to know that the new neighborhoods would eventually get their shit together and hire extra security to patrol and supplement the regular cops. He had to look for other ways to make a living.

"OK, give it to me again, Wayne," he said, snapping open another beer, this time pushing it over to the kid, not offering any to the other one.

"Yeah, well, like I said," Wayne started, now not as bold as when he'd just been throwing the idea out there, "this guy I know, a guy who does a bunch of dock work and sinking foundation poles and such to build fishin' camps out in the Glades, he done a bunch of jobs up in the north round Palm Beach County and Broward.

"There are folks up there spending big *dinero* on these camps just to come out and stay in because they're sick of the city or somethin'. Anyways, he says they got all kind of fancy shit they bring out to their places so that on the weekends they can party and have their families with them and fish and shoot."

"Fancy shit?" Buck said, looking at the boy, trying to catch his eyes, which were avoiding his. The kid, Wayne, looked up quick at the question and then over at his buddy, hoping maybe he'd get bailed out with an answer.

"Well, tell him," Marcus said and then answered the question himself, earning his way back in.

"Says they got stereos and TVs and radio systems and such. Bunch of generators for power and brand-new tools that ain't hardly been used." Both boys were now nodding their heads, making a case.

Buck had not let down the front legs of his chair while he listened. Wayne was determined to make that happen, force Buck to be interested.

"And the guy says he once seen a computer. A laptop," he added and thought some more. "And guns."

Buck's hooded eyes came ever so slightly more open, exposing the tint of yellow in their corners caused by years of sleepless nights and bad prison food.

"Guns?" Buck asked. Just the vision of them made him nervous. He could well remember the tower guards at Avon Park, always looking down on the inmates in the yard, their faces dark in shadow but the long muzzles of their rifles in clear sight, intimidating, just daring someone to screw up big enough.

"Yeah," Wayne stammered on. "Says one day he's out there workin' on a roof when the owner comes out with some friend and they got some new shotguns and they ask this guy does he want to take a look. Guy says sure and takes a break and the owner shows him this brand new sixteen-gauge over-an'-under. He's tellin' 'em about shootin' curlew back in the olden days and then these two, the owner an' his friend, take turns firing out at some squawk that come flyin' overhead. Guy says they can't shoot for shit but them guns is real nice and he never seen 'em pack them back to the city when they leave for the next week or two."

Buck moved forward, setting the front legs of the chair down with a *thunk*. He reached down and brought up another beer, opened it and pushed it across to Marcus. Now all three drank together. Guns, Buck thought. Bobby the Fence had just asked him last night if he'd had any guns to turn over. Much as Buck hated them, they were cash money these days.

"So does this friend of yours know where these fishing camps are?" he said, raising his eyebrows, being conspiratorial with them, which he knew got them going.

Wayne crossed his arms in front of him, turned his head in a playful way, like he was holding good cards in a game and wanted to savor the feeling for as long as he could without pissing Buck off.

"He got a map," he finally said. "The boy ain't got the balls to do a job himself. But he'll sell us the map with all the locations. GPS and everything."

At that moment a wind came up and pressed against Buck's stilt house and a shutter rattled and swung open on the kitchen window. He got up without a word and went to the sink and looked out. He'd heard some of the boat captains talking about a 'cane stirrin' up

things south near Mexico. He'd have to check the forecast later. Right now he was concentrating on a possible score. The boys' eyes followed him and Marcus
gave Wayne a "what the fuck you doin' " look. Finally
Buck came back and looped his leg over the back of the
chair and sat down.

"Tell it to me again, son."

CHAPTER 6

They sat in the office at noon, Harmon at his desk in the middle of the room, alternately watching the unlighted incoming lines on the phone and the TV mounted high in the front corner. He used the same cynical and disdainful eye for both. Squires was at the desk behind him, against the back wall, his short-cropped, blond-gray hair poking out on occasion from behind his computer monitor. When Harmon cut his eyes to the left, he could see his partner's hand cupped over the mouse on his desk like it was a cigarette you didn't want to expose or a clump of something you spilled on your mother's table linen and didn't want her to see. Squires's finger twitched and Harmon could hear the constant click of the machine but he knew the guy was just acting like he was working.

"Black eight on the red nine," Harmon said over his shoulder.

Squires hesitated, clicked once and then said: "Fuck you, Harmon."

Harmon grinned, knew the guy was playing solitaire

back there and then reached across the desktop for yet another toothpick, and looked up over the top of his wire-rimmed glasses at the Weather Channel.

"This drag-ass hurricane is going to kick Cancún's butt and then shoot right up the middle of the Gulf," he said. The sound on the television was muted and the bubble-headed bleach blonde had obviously just finished her spiel and was silently staring at the black guy sharing afternoon anchor duties with her like she was paying attention to him. Harmon was waiting for the blonde to get up and go to the wall map to point out the various "computer forecast tracks" for this new storm, Hurricane Simone.

"You just watch. Crandall's going to yank those rig monkeys off the platforms in Section C-seven and C-eight and we'll be out there three days later going through their lockers and the rig bosses' files trying to figure out what they've been screwing with for the last ten weeks," Harmon said, glancing again at the phone like his boss was going to call the orders in any minute.

"Better they're on leave than having those greasy Cajun fuckers on the deck giving you the voodoo eye while we're doing inspections," Squires said from behind his monitor. Harmon grinned. He was listening.

"You're a racist, Squires. Admit it," he said, just for something to do, poking at the man.

The glass door on their office said Martindale Security, stenciled on with some cheap paint by some cheap sign painter they'd found in the Hollywood, Florida, yellow pages. Martin Crandall, their biggest, hell, their only client these days, had ordered them to rent the space and label it up like a legitimate business. Probably had something to do with a tax write-off for the oil company but Harmon had liked the old days when he and Squires simply worked out of their homes or apartments, got a call from some contact, set up a meet at an obscure diner somewhere, and went over a plan. The only advantage now was the way things like the shooting in Venezuela seemed to disappear. When you do work for the corporations, matters like a few dead paramilitary smudges in the outback can disappear under the heap of more "important" and income-producing affairs. Harmon had rented this place because it was cheap and he could pocket the rest of the expense like he'd done with the extra forty grand he'd split with Squires from their latest trip. He knew Crandall would never ask for verification. It was a corner space in an old-style strip shopping center. The east wall was theirs alone. The west wall they shared with a Chinese restaurant and take-out place. Every time the Chang Emporium brought an exterminator in to spray, the cockroaches and monster-sized palmetto bugs would migrate through the cracks to Harmon's side of the wall. The infestation had scared away two receptionists already but Harmon didn't care. He just went ahead and pocketed her salary as well and never bothered with a replacement. It wasn't as if they were busy.

"I ain't racist. I like the black folk just fine," Squires grumbled from the back. "Least they ain't so stupid to bring a knife to a gunfight."

Last time they'd been sent out to do a security check on one of GULFLO's Gulf rigs he and Squires were doing a routine search of the workers' lockers, pawing through their personal stuff, knowing from years of experience what to look for. These guys were never too creative when it came to hiding their dope—the meth that kept them going at the dangerous and boring-as-hell jobs they held, the coke that gave them something to dream about, and the downers to keep them level enough not to lose an arm in the drill works. One day Squires came up with a handful of some kind of animal teeth the size of a tiger's all strung out on a leather cord.

"Pop the tops!" he'd told the big Cajun rigger whose footlocker he was searching.

"Don't know what you askin', me?" the old roughneck said, staring into Squires's eyes like a dare.

Squires had seen all manner of hiding places for the workers' chemical stashes including the one like this where they hollowed out the bones they used as jewelry, filled them with cocaine, and then capped them with a silver attachment that looped onto a chain or cord to form a kind of necklace.

"You carrying a little nose powder here, boy?" he said to the pair of unblinking, swamp green eyes.

The man just spat a string of tobacco juice to the side but when Squires selected the largest tooth on the string and started twisting at the clasp, the dark-skinned rigger raised his right hand as if to wipe the spittle from his chin and then in a blur of movement and a spin of elbow so quick it caught Harmon flat-footed, the man had stepped chest to chest with Squires and had a blade to his neck.

"You don't touch a man's prayer beads, you, less you preparin' to bleed," the rigger said through his clenched teeth, and Harmon was amazed to see the bundle of teeth back in its owner's possession.

But there was no hint of fear in Squires's face, even as the knife edge pressed hard against his jugular. The Cajun seemed only mildly baffled by the security man's stoic response until everyone in the silent bunkhouse heard the muffled snick of a gun hammer being cocked and the rigger must have felt the hollowed pipe of an HK Mk23 special ops handgun muzzle being pressed up into the rounded notch at the bottom of his breastbone. During the man's pirouette, Squires had come up with his own practiced sleight of hand.

"You might cut me, boy. But I'll blow your heart through a hole out your back before you see a drop of my blood hit the floor," Squires whispered.

They stood eye to eye for three seconds and an eternity before the rigger finally backed off.

"Ain't no powder in these," he said, holding the teeth out. "You look yourself. I ain't no doper, me."

Now Harmon was shaking his head at the memory, looking across the office at the back of Squires's computer. They'd found plenty of stash that trip but not in the tiger teeth. Squires had been wrong on that one account, but almost before the incident was over it was as if he'd already forgotten it. That was the beauty of the guy. No memory, no conscience.

Blessed are the forgetful, some old philosopher once said, for they get the better even of their blunders. It was a way of living that suited warriors and lawyers, and Harmon could never understand it.

"You gonna get that, boss," Squires said, snapping Harmon out of his flashback. "Line two?"

Harmon looked down at the blinking light on the phone. They'd disabled the chirping noise of incoming calls the day the last receptionist left. Only the boss ever called on line two. It had to be Crandall. He would be alerting them to get ready to travel after the storm passed. But Harmon knew from experience the man wouldn't say where until the day they left. He picked up the phone and swiveled his chair away from Squires.

"Harmon," he answered. "Yeah. Sure. Yeah. We'll be ready. Have we ever not been ready?"

CHAPTER 7

"**W**hat are we going to do, Max?"

I hear the question, but with only half of my attention. I thought Sherry had been reading, her back settled in the bow of the canoe, ankles crossed on top of the cooler, which held the last of the beer, a book of Ted Kooser's poems I'd lent her in front of her face. I was at the other end, a hand line dropped over the side, daydreaming. Like the gentleman that I am, I'd kept the eastern sun to Sherry's back and pulled down the brim of my baseball cap, the one stitched across the front with the reversed script letters that perplexed most people unless they figured out that it was simply "FOCUS" spelled in mirror image. After three days my eyes were getting used to the starburst glitter of sun off the slow-moving water.

"Huh?" I said, full of elocution.

"What are we going to do about us? When we get back, I mean, to civilization?"

It hadn't all been small talk since we started this odd vacation, but tackling the future and the meaning of our relationship was not something we'd poked at. I'd decided the reason was because we were both, fundamentally, cops. We'd been trained, I suppose, to be more reticent than most people. Trained also, I believed, to be more careful with the people we met, be they citizens or suspects or potential trouble or all three at once. If you ever sat down in a diner with a few of us you would immediately feel it as an outsider. We're trained to evaluate you, give nothing up until we've got some kind of take on where you're coming from. It's a broad ripple effect of the way we're taught to approach a driver during a car stop when we're all rookies: search the mirrors, look for hand movement, assess with your gut and let it tell you if you should have your own hand on the butt of your sidearm.

I had been on the force in Philadelphia for more than a decade. I'd grown up with the cop rules and what they brought home with them and had seen it turn my parents' relationship ugly and violent. But I had also known my grandparents to be a loving and respectful couple despite the lifestyle.

Sherry and I had been dancing for a couple of years now. Granted, some of it had been very close dancing, but like the school chaperone, an emotional hand had always been measuring a space between us.

"I like you, Max."

It wasn't the words that got my attention. Sherry's eyes always had this ability to subtly change color depending on her mood—a green when she was loose and happy, but decidedly gray when she was being fierce and suspicious. I was trying to see them now, in the shade of midmorning sun.

"I think you might have said that last night, when it was my turn to look at the stars," I said, stalling.

I could see her narrow those eyes, but still couldn't pick up the color.

"I want you to move in with me, into the house in Fort Lauderdale. But I don't want to ask."

It was a statement. Clear and matter-of-fact, but I knew how much it had taken for her to let the words out of her mouth. I was trying not to overthink what my response should be. It has always been my burden, rolling questions and answers around in my head, probing them, searching for the rough edges, grinding the sharp spots, the dangerous possibilities, and trying to smooth them. Maybe she sensed my hesitation because I could see her face begin to change, like she was going to take back the invitation. Before she could say anything I leaned forward and gripped either side of the canoe gunwales and rocked forward and stepped to her. Now her look turned to a wary smile but before she could come out with anything I led with my mouth and kissed her fully on the lips, holding my body weight above her like doing a push-up.

"Oh, is that an answer, Max?" she said. "Because it's very nice, but . . ." I know she did it. Because it sure as hell wasn't me who suddenly threw my weight to the starboard side of the canoe causing gravity to take hold and barrel-rolling the whole boat and flipping us both into the water.

Later we spread out our soaked clothes on the Snows' isolated deck and lay in the sun naked.

"I've never been dunked by a woman before," I said into the sky and then immediately wondered where the words had come from. Sherry cut a look at me, a slight wrinkle in her brow. She too was caught by the oddity of the revelation.

"Dumped but not dunked," I said, trying to recover.

"You would have stayed with your ex if she hadn't been moving up?" she finally said. Sherry knew my ex-wife was a former police sniper who was now a captain running the internal affairs division for the Philadelphia Police Department. We had met while working on the same SWAT team.

"Not once I realized she was just collecting the pelts of men on her way up the ranks."

Sherry laughed out loud.

"Bitterness does not become you, Max," she said, reaching over to run her fingertips over my brow. "Honestly, she was a better shot than you, right?"

"That's probably true," I said.

She had no comeback and instead went quiet again, to gather a recollection.

"Jimmy was a terrible marksman," she said and I could tell from her eyes she was seeing her dead husband. "He was always asking for pointers, ways to pass the next qualifier without practicing. I don't think he ever drew his weapon out on the streets in his entire career."

I let her think her own thoughts for a second, knowing there was another beat just behind her lips.

"But?" I finally said.

"I always knew he would protect me," she said, her eyes coming back to mine. "You know what I mean? Not just back-to-the-wall, guns drawn protection. But protect me. Then he died and I think I actually felt betrayed by that, like it was his fault. So I hardened up, Max. I decided I could take care of myself and say to hell with the rest of the world."

She rolled over onto her back, her naked body completely exposed to the sky and the sun. I rolled to one elbow and stared at her, the bridge of her nose, the new sun freckles on her shoulder, and I found something missing. The necklace from her husband that she never took off was gone. I could have been presumptuous, could have hoped for the meaning of its absence. Instead I asked.

"Do you know your necklace is missing?"

Her eyes remained closed. She did not reach to her throat, or show surprise.

"Yes."

I reached over to lace my fingers through hers and rolled to my back.

"You want me to protect you, Sherry?" I said.

"Yes."

"Then I will."

"And love me?"

"That," I said, squeezing her fingers between mine, "goes without saying."

I saw her smile from the corner of my eye.

"No, Max, it doesn't go without saying. Not with me."

I turned my head to look at her profile. Her smile stayed, like she'd caught me at something.

"I love you, Sherry," I said.

This time she turned her head and looked into my face.

Again there were those brow lines like she wasn't sure where the unusual words had come from. Then she smiled.

"You know something, Max?" she said. "I believe you do."

For another couple of hours we lay there, she on her back, and I finally rolled over onto a towel and watched the western sky, studying the cloud pattern that was building out there on the horizon. It was not a typical Everglades weather construction. During the summer months the heat of the day causes millions of gallons of water from the surface of the exposed Glades to evaporate and rise and start to build a wall of towering cloud in the sky above it. But I could tell from the lessons of Billy Manchester—my attorney friend and his sometimes annoying habit of knowing everything—that the cloud I was watching in the distance was blowing in much too high for that weather pattern. These were the kind that came from elsewhere, pushed by forces that were not homegrown. But I was watching passively, assessing nothing. I was also listening to nothing, literally. Our surroundings had gone silent. No chirruping of the midday insects that fed in the heat. No bird call. In fact, the owl that had made it a practice to come out of its roof hole and had afforded us such viewing pleasure for the past two days seemed to be absent. I rolled onto my side again and looked out to the east where Wally the gator would normally have been sunning himself on the low mound of flattened saw-grass. He too was missing. I also made a mental note that I had not heard a distant engine of an airboat during the entire morning. But I only contemplated the absence of sound for a short few moments and then reminded myself how odd and luxurious such an occurrence was for people like us to enjoy. Sherry seemed to be asleep. We seemed totally alone.

CHAPTER 8

Buck was sitting sideways on a bar stool at the Miccosukee Resort and Gaming casino, intermittently watching the storm coverage on television, his boys over near the blackjack tables having their fist-tapping jive finger-twisting bullshit conversation with their so-called contact, and the bright flicker-flash of the chrome bottle opener riding tight and warm in the slick leather back pocket of the bartender. The girl was most pleasing to him, but he couldn't say for sure which one of his focal points might bring him the most trouble.

Even with the television sound off Buck could tell what was going on with the storm. Some guy at the other end of the bar had asked the girl to change the channel from some meaningless Marlins baseball game. Her manager would be pissed when and if he noticed. It probably wasn't good policy to bring reality into a casino, especially the kind that would tell some folks to go home and start buying plywood instead of gambling chips. The meteorologists had given the storm a name a few days ago and it was some sort of rule this year that it had to be female so they dubbed her Simone. The weather guys had been tossing around a bunch of "Sloppy Simone" jokes until she formed up in strength and purpose and killed three people on Grand Cayman Island coming through the passage south of Cuba. Now she was turning into a real bitch. She was a category three with a hundred-twenty-mile-an-hour winds and they had one of those electronic tracking maps up on the screen now and the weather girl with the tight sweater and bleached blond hair was waving her delicate fingers like she was on some kind of game show. She was pointing at the red spots where the storm had been at midnight, six this morning, and now close to three in the afternoon. Simone had wiggled around off the Yucatán coast but then took a sudden right turn to the north and started huffing. They put one of those "cone of probability" graphics up there that put the landfall possibilities anywhere from Galveston to the Big Bend of central Florida, and Buck whispered to himself: "Shit, them guys over on the roulette table got better odds than that, eh?" The screen flashed a huge banner—"Storm Alert, Tracking Simone"—and then went to some commercial selling gas-powered generators. Buck got the bartender's attention and then stared at her breasts while he ordered a double bourbon with a beer chaser.

"Looks like weather comin'," he said to the girl's eyes this time when she came back with his drinks, see if he could get her to stay down here. She was cute in a pale, thin kinda way.

"Can't be any worse than last year, uh, Mr. Hall," she said.

Buck tensed up, just a notch. The bartender had used the name on the credit card Buck had passed to her for the first round and he was caught by surprise that she'd memorized it. Maybe that was company policy too. It had only been twenty minutes since he'd scrummed up against some older guy in a bar upstairs and lifted his wallet out of his polyester sport coat pocket. Buck had gone straight to the men's room and locked himself inside a stall and lifted out fifty-three dollars in cash and two credit cards. The American Express card had the name Richard Hall stamped on it. Member since 1982. He'd dumped the wallet in the chrome trash receptacle and come downstairs.

"We'll worry about her when she gets to Naples, sweetheart," he said to the bartender, recovering. She gave him a nondescript tip of her chin and turned away. Fucking snowbird, he thought.

Buck's parents and their parents before them had watched such storms approach for a century. Like most people born and raised in southwest Florida, they didn't need some long-range predictions. Hell, these national weather forecast guys could track a fart coming off the African coast and watch it meander for three weeks across the Atlantic. Buck's father had taught him to watch the weather on the horizon, note the slope of the Gulf water swells, pay attention to the birds and the lack of feeding fish.

"The animals know what the world is doing long before we do, son."

Like most native Gladesmen, his daddy knew how to button down, tie off his boat, and strap down anything else that might fly off in a hundred-mile-an-hour gust or float away on an eight-foot storm tide and then just see what came. They'd dig out after. It was the way it was. Shit, look at New Orleans. Doppler weather my ass. If you could run, you ran. If you stayed, for whatever reason, you did the best you could and started again with whatever the storm left you. Survivors survived. The dead didn't.

It had been the same way in prison. You fought if you could, scammed if you could, joined up if you could, took what you could. Buck had taken the fight route just because he could. He'd chosen brass knuckles instead of becoming someone's hump. A broken eye socket, a few busted ribs, a couple of teeth in his bloody spit. He'd suffer the same any day. They ought to make a commercial: "Prison love—a beating only hurts for a while, being someone's bitch lasts forever."

Buck looked back over at the boys who were now feeding off each other's enthusiasm for posturing and starting to look like some video off MTV. Marcus was doing his hand thing, fingers splayed out like they were unnaturally twisted or spastic and then turning his wrists and elbows to point with his index and little digits—at what? Who knew. He was dressed in that equally perplexing style with the oversized jeans that billowed out and hung down, but mysteriously only came to his mid-calf. He had on a Hawaiian shirt that actually didn't look too bad to Buck even though it was too big and flying open to expose a T-shirt underneath with some bullshit rap message about "gettin' drizzed, yo."

Wayne was similarly outfitted but his shirt was some impossibly long T-shirt thing that came past his knees and nearly met the low cuffs of his goofy pants. Their friend who had joined them, and was supposedly a contact for the real dude with the information and locations of the Glades camps, was in the same getup except his long shirt was a Miami Heat jersey that Shaquille O'Neal himself could have worn, but it looked like a drape on this kid. All three of them were wearing stiff-brimmed baseball hats that had never been touched by the fingertips of baseball players. The contact had his lopped over to one side like he was hiding a deformed ear. The three of them were flicking their fingers and bopping around on the balls of their feet and blatantly staring at any female who walked past them and probably doing that *ppssst, ppsst* sound that caused some of the younger girls to turn their heads to them but made at least one woman flip them the finger. Buck figured the costuming was just another version of kids trying to belong, cliquing up with one another in an effort to be in with something instead of having to realize we're really out here all alone in the world. He'd seen the same thing in prison, mostly split along racial lines. Buck had learned quickly that the world inside was no different than the world outside. No one else was going to jump in to save you when your ship went down. You die alone, boys.

Buck downed the rest of his drink and was about to go over to his misfits and find out what the deal was. He was fronting this operation with two hundred dollars and all he was getting was some punk floor show. He slid off the stool but froze when a guy in a casino uniform approached the group. It made him nervous and he eased back onto the bar stool and turned his face half away but kept his peripheral vision honed on them. It took him a second to notice the dustpan in the uniformed guy's hand, a broom in the other. Minimum-wage sweeper boy. He tapped fists all around and then motioned the group back under an overhang. Smart, Buck thought. Kid probably knows where all the cameras are and knows that most of them are focused on the gaming tables and you don't want to end up on some videotape upstairs. The uniform took something from his pocket and passed it to Wayne, who gave him a small roll of bills in return. A tap of the fists again and they went their separate ways. Wayne, who had been so instructed, looked over at Buck, put one finger to the side of his nose and flicked it. Jesus, Buck thought. Was that the kid's idea of a high sign? Fucking scene from *The Sting*. Hell, that film was older than the kid was. Buck signaled the bartender for his check, signed it with Mr. Hall's scribble, and headed for the parking lot.

*   *   *

"You cool?"

Wayne and Marcus looked at each other, shrugging their shoulders like they were afraid to offer up the wrong answer to Buck's simple question.

"Uh, yeah," Wayne finally said, and both of them nodded their heads as they climbed into the pickup truck. Marcus took the backseat of the club cab.

Buck got behind the wheel thinking: Jesus H. I know these two haven't been smoking pot for at least a couple of hours. How did two human minds get so dense? He let it go.

"He gave us six possibles," Wayne said, taking a sheet of paper from his pocket and unfolding it for Buck to see. "Here's the GPS coordinates for each one so we could use that handheld unit and he said you can get out to the first one in a couple of hours."

Buck started the truck engine and looked over at the paper. It was the lined type you used in school, the kind with the three-ring binder holes in it. The numbers made no sense to anyone unaware of global positioning systems, but most of the people in the Glades had been using the GPS to mark fishing grounds and crab trap placements for the last fifteen years. Out on the Gulf waters it had become almost essential, a quick and easy way to find your way on a sea of nothing but bare horizon once you were out beyond sight of land. Then they started miniaturizing the technology so everyone and their grandmother were using the thing now. They even started building them into high-priced

cars and even cell phones so you could be a halfwit
and still find your way around. It was the way of the
world now, Buck thought. Easier and softer. Same with
the people. That's what made them such simple prey.
They got fat and comfortable. Might as well have been
asking for it.

"So this sweeper guy knows these camps?"

"Yeah. His uncle is a kinda contractor and ferries the
building supplies and stuff out to these places when
they're building them or redoin' them all modern.
Sometimes this kid goes along with his uncle to load
and unload the wood and shingles and plumbing pipes
an' all. They've got a big ol' airboat that lugs it," Wayne
said, rushing on with as much detail as he could so
that Buck wouldn't think he was just stupid and they
wouldn't have just wasted two hundred dollars on the
locations and that would really piss Buck off.

Marcus sat in the back where he always did, watching the backs of the others' heads. Wayne was stealing
his idea, of course, and he'd never get any credit for it
if it worked out. But then he figured he also wouldn't
catch all the shit if it didn't. That was the trade-off.

Buck looked at the numbers again. He'd have to map
them out to have a clue where they were. All three sat
in silence for a couple of minutes until Wayne couldn't
take Buck's lack of response any longer.

"Toby said this here one, at the top, is only about a
half hour north off Alligator Alley on the airboat and
then the others are pretty close too."

He kept looking at the paper, like you could see

something there, like he was studying the numbers just like Buck appeared to be.

"OK, we'll see about that," Buck finally said. "I've got a surveyor's map back at the house. We can plot these out and see just what kind of access two hundred dollars just bought us." Buck knew the Glades could be a tricky place to navigate even in the best of times. And although the boys were oblivious to the weather Buck had been watching in the casino, he knew a coming storm could work for them as well as against them.

He looked back over his shoulder as he started the truck and said to Marcus, "This plan of yours might still have life."

CHAPTER 9

Harmon was in the back of his house in Coral Springs, a cordless electric drill in his hand, spinning tight the wing nuts that held his hurricane shutters over the rear sliding glass doors. The sun was out. He was already sweating profusely with the effort of carrying and mounting the steel panels from his garage and stacking them in front of every window and door to his home. Each one was marked with its designation: N SIDE BEDROOM. S SIDE DINING. He'd been through this many times during his years living down here and now it had become ritual. But he never went so far as to say he'd gotten used to it.

With the attachment on the drill he whizzed the nut on the W SIDE BATH and then took a break. Inside his house the lack of light created by the sealed windows was already giving him a mildly claustrophobic feel. He poured himself a glass of cold water from the refrigerator and sat at the kitchen bar, watching the local weather channel on the television. The station had not been changed for the last twenty-four hours. His wife called him obsessed but he just flitted her off with the back of his fingers, told her she was right, it was probably a waste of time and effort, go on with whatever you were doing and don't mind me. She shook her head and did just that. Harmon kept his face turned to the TV. He was scared and given who he was, the years that his wife had spent with him overseas on security details in the military, even the time he'd had to hand-strip down a couple of asshole muggers on the street in Miami in front of her when they'd tried to rob them and he'd left them both with snapped bones, mewling like broken kittens on the sidewalk, he'd never showed fear. Harmon was considered an expert with a handgun. He was also good at close-quarters hand fighting, techniques he'd learned long ago that had become so ingrained that despite his age he could regain them in an instant, not unlike riding a bike or crushing a man's windpipe before he could yell out an alarm. Harmon was not a man who panicked and his wife and family had depended on that. But today he was scared and would be until the threat of this new hurricane had passed. Harmon had seen the strength of such a storm. It was nothing you could fight, nothing you could kill, nothing you could stand up against if it decided to cross your path. It was bigger and stronger than man. And if it wanted you, all you could do was huddle down with your head between your knees and kiss your ass good-bye, as Squires would say.

He took another deep drink of the water and refocused on the news. Hurricane Simone had swung north from the Yucatán Peninsula and then stalled for a day in the Gulf of Mexico. There it sucked up energy from the heat rising off eighty-two-degree Gulf water and ate itself into a huge category four monster. Some people likened it to spilling millions of gallons of gasoline on a forest fire, fueling a force that already couldn't be stopped from eating everything in its path. But Harmon had been in the middle of a forest fire. He had also been in the center of a hurricane and the comparison was lost on him.

On the tube the muted commentator was incessantly moving his lips while pointing out the steering currents—a high pressure system moving down from the western states and a sucking low off the southeast Atlantic—that was now bringing the storm back to Florida. The red-shaded "cone of probability" graphic was now a thinner triangle whose narrow end was just off the coast of Naples on the west side of the state and then spreading out to cover everything from the big blob of blue representing Lake Okeechobee on the northern edge down to Miami on the south.

"Goddamn reversal of Andrew," Harmon said out loud.

"What, honey?" his wife called out from the laundry room. He ignored her.

They had been together in 1992 when Hurricane Andrew ripped like a freight train over their home just south of Miami on an opposite track, crossing the state from east to west. Harmon had been working security at Homestead Air Force Base as a consultant. The money had been good enough to buy a nice four-

bedroom house with a pool and an acre of land shaded
by two-hundred-year-old live oaks that towered like
green clouds over his yards. On the sunny side of
the acreage he'd planted a row of orange and grape-
fruit trees that never failed to blossom in spring and
give fruit in summer. Eden. Even now the memories
brought an interior smile.

Yeah, he'd known that one was coming. He'd been
called onto the base to make sure that the hangars were
secure where they'd moved the military jet fighters
and lighter stuff that might get blown around. He'd
tightened up a contingency plan just in case they lost
off-site civilian power and had to go to their own generators. At home he'd tossed the patio furniture into
the pool as a neighbor had suggested and parked his
pickup truck closer to the garage so it would be on the
leeward side and less likely to be pelted by loose tree
branches and debris. He'd seen that some folks had put
masking tape in crisscross fashion over their front windows. Christ, even he knew that old trick was bullshit.
If a wind-blown branch or a coconut or something like
that hit your window head on it was going to crack the
glass anyway. You were still going to have to sweep
up. Scraping that glue from the tape off the windows
after the storm was four times the work. He'd gone to
bed that night without even watching the news. The
wind woke him at two a.m.

Go ahead, Harmon would later tell friends from
other parts of the country or the world when he trav-
eled. Push your vehicle up to ninety or a hundred miles

an hour on the expressway if you dare and then note the sound. Not the engine sound, because that won't compare with the rush of air blasting over your car hood and roof. Just listen to the sound and then stick your head out the side window and let the air rip at your face. That's a category four hurricane. That's the strength of the wind, tearing at your world. For hours.

Harmon was staring at the television, but not seeing the weather woman with her graphics and maps and little spinning red pinwheel depicting the present location of Simone. He was instead seeing the Oakwood grain of his double front door during Andrew, his face pressed up against it, his then solid two hundred thirty pounds trying to keep it closed as the wind bowed the two-inch-thick planks into the entryway. His wife was in the hallway closet, crying, huddled with their two children. But he could not hear her or anything else but the wind blowing through the rubber seal of the doorway, the air under such pressure that the sound was like Arturo Sandoval hitting a high C note on his trumpet for what seemed an eternity. He had looked around behind him at the walls lined with his books, really the most important things to him other than his family, and cursed himself for not preparing better. And then, at that moment, as he watched, the ceiling at one corner of his living room began to rise like the devil himself was gripping the house with a giant hand and then peeled away the entire roof and sent it flipping away into the night.

The house had been a total loss. They were lucky to

salvage some important papers, some pictures, some heirlooms. Most of his books had been ruined by the rain that had washed unimpeded through every room. After Andrew his family relocated farther up the state. Everyone in the house had survived unscathed but for the memories that crept back.

Harmon refocused on the television, took another drink of cold water. Back to work, he thought. Only the south side shutters left. He thought about Squires, could see his partner on the beachfront somewhere, sitting out in the open, laughing into the face of the rising wind and downing yet another draft at the hurricane party thrown by the locals down at the infamous beachside tavern called the Elbo Room. He was probably toasting the fact that the company wouldn't be sending them out to the oil rigs since this one had turned east. He'd be buying shots and toasting hell itself. Some of us took precautions, some just said fuck it, let it come. If she hit them head on, it would be difficult to argue who was smarter.

"Damn, Chez! It's blowin' like a snarly bitch out there now," Wayne said as he came through the door, wind and rain swirling in behind him even though he'd only opened it far enough to squeeze through. "Old man Brown's coconut tree is bent over like to touch its head on the ground and the water's already up to the fourth step over to Smallwood Store."

He shook himself like a dog that had just come out of the lake, the water flying off his slicker onto the linoleum floor and the nearby refrigerator. Buck and Marcus were again sitting in the kitchen, each with a hand of cards spread out in their fingers; a small pile of quarters and crumpled bills lay in the middle of the table.

"Hey, bring us a beer there, Stumpy," Marcus said without looking up from his hand.

"Fuck you," Wayne answered, peeling off the yellow foul-weather jacket.

Buck raised his own eyes at the boy's answer and then looked at Wayne, and then at the fridge. Wayne got three cans of Budweiser out and set them on the table. One he put in front of the empty chair where he sat. He didn't distribute the others, the smallest of rebellions.

"Don't call me stumpy," he said. Marcus just grinned into his cards. Wayne had lost his left thumb two years ago, working the stone crab boats with one of his uncles. He'd bragged about being allowed to work the traplines at the beginning of the harvest season. It was a man's job. The stone crab traps, big as a large microwave oven and just as heavy, were strung out by the dozens on braided lines, sitting on the bottom of the Gulf and baited with fish heads and chicken parts. When harvest came a giant motor winch on the stern of the boat started pulling up the line at a steady speed. The boat captains timed the operation down to pure efficiency, the traps spaced just far enough so a line man could hook the first trap as it broke the surface, yank it up with a boat hook onto the gunwale, pop open its door, snag the crabs inside, and toss them into a bucket and then rebait the trap with half-frozen bait, and shove the whole thing back overboard just in time to grab the boat hook and snag the next trap hitting the surface. It was all a delicate dance. But there was nothing delicate if your gloved hand got caught in the line or even got stuck enough to yank you into the spinning winch. Wayne's left hand had gotten caught. The line, perhaps luckily, only looped around his thumb, and with the power to drag hundreds of pounds through the warm Gulf water, it popped the digit off clean, the sound like a rifle shot, a sound many of the crewmen had heard before. Wayne was fourteen.

"Ain't no girl gonna go for a four-finger thief," Marcus had kidded him later. The comment, like the nickname itself, was something only your best friend could say. The boys had been neighbors since their toddler years. You always abuse the ones you know best.

"Yeah, you're probably right," Wayne had answered. "So what's your excuse, dickhead?"

Shortly after the accident Wayne took to holding his beers with his left hand, out in front so anyone and everyone would notice his deformity. He never hid the hand, carried it like a badge or something, maybe a chip that should have been on his shoulder. Marcus might have even been envious. It was better'n any damn tattoo you could get in Miami.

Marcus let the lack-of-a-girlfriend insult bounce off him; old joke, he'd heard it before.

"So I'm in for three bucks and I raise you another dollar," Marcus said, peering up over his cards at Buck.

The man kept his eyes down, pinching the cards. The tips of his fingernails turned white when he did this, the rest of the nail shading a darker red with the press of blood against their backs. It was a tell that Buck had tried to get rid of playing cards in prison. He'd gotten his ass kicked in poker for the first nine months in prison until a new friend finally let on to the obvious sign he was flashing to the rest of the players whenever he had a good hand. But these boys weren't so tuned into the small details of gambling. He saw and raised the bet back to Marcus, who scowled. Out of the hand, Wayne was bored.

"So we gonna do these expensive-ass fishing camps after the storm, right?"

No one answered. They'd been over the plan already. Buck had been twisting the images around in his head, just like when he'd lain awake all night in prison, working the details, what it was going to look like when he got out, what he was going to do, how this time he was going to be so careful there was no way he'd make the same mistakes again and get caught. Every opportunity could be the big score that would set him up.

"But what if the damn hurricane busts stuff up? A nice fishing rig or a stereo or somethin' ain't gonna be worth much if it's busted up," Wayne said. "I mean, I know it'll be easier to get into the places like you said, Buck, make it look like nature done it and all. But suppose the good stuff gets damaged before we get there?"

Buck understood the boy was anxious; that always

happened once you had a plan set and you were young and giddy, wanting to get your feet moving and your fingers on something profitable. He'd probably been the same way when he was younger, not as bad, of course, but somewhat the same.

"Son," he said, still not looking up. "You hear that howl outside, boy? Ain't a thing you can do about that 'cane coming in now. She's gonna do what she gonna do, then we'll run on out on the airboat as soon as she moves on through just like we planned. We'll hit them places and see what we can see. Those owners are gonna be busy in their regular homes for days. Their fishing camps will be the last thing on their minds. We got all the time in the world to loot through. Might be some damage, but there won't be anybody figuring what's gone until we've already sold it and have the money in our pockets.

"You got that? Right, Wayne?"

"Yes, sir," Wayne said, like he'd been put down by some teacher at the front of the class again. "I got it."

Buck heard the twitch of humiliation, or was that anger, in the boy's voice. He knew he had to keep his merry little band together.

"You did good with getting those locations, Wayne. But this storm helps us, right? Hell, it's almost legal. Like a salvage operation. We could find something that'll make our day out there and simply walk away."

"I'll call you," Marcus suddenly said, like he hadn't heard a word of what the others had been talking about. He laid down three queens and looked up at Buck, grinning.

Buck took a long draft off the beer, nearly half of it gone in one swallow and then, one at a time, lay down a ten high straight. Marcus shoved his chair back, disgusted, and went for another beer as Buck raked in the pile. A high-pitched gust of wind rattled the wooden shutters that had been nailed shut over the kitchen window.

"Mr. Brown all tightened down out there?" Buck asked Wayne.

"Tight like a tick," Wayne said. "Even got some sandbags piled up at the back of his boathouse. Old fart must be expecting a big one."

Buck snapped his eyes up. Both boys turned their heads at the silent change of pressure in the room. Even with their stunted powers of recollection, they'd realized the mistake that had been made.

"Old what?" Buck said, quiet like, almost a hiss, as if his voice was under pressure. Both boys were looking down into the pile of money on the table, neither willing to look up and meet Buck's gaze. The air stayed silent for a full minute.

"Sorry," Wayne finally said, no twitch of smartass in it, no possibility of even a flicker of grin at the corners of either boy's mouth.

"Goddamn right you're sorry."

Nate Brown was a second generation denizen of the Ten Thousand Islands. He was born on a feather-stuffed mattress in his parents' bed in their tar-paper shack in Chokoloskee somewhere between eighty and one hundred years ago. No one knew the exact year. In his time as the son of one of the original white families that moved to southwest Florida in the late 1800s, he had taken on a nearly mystical aura. He'd practically been born with a rifle in his hands. He knew every turn and twist and mangrove-covered trail from the middle keys to Lake Okeechobee. He was a gator hunter, a stone crabber, a net and hook fisherman beyond compare, a whiskey still operator, and a pot runner. He'd been to Germany in World War II, had worked behind the lines as a mountain soldier, and had a Medal of Honor to prove it. He'd gone to prison when he was sixty years old with the rest of the men in town rather than say a word about the infamous marijuana smuggling ring. Buck's father had told a thousand legendary stories of the old man and how he'd taught the younger generation of Gladesmen how to sear spit-fired curlew birds and hand-caught mullet, how to kill and skin a ten-foot gator in minutes under cover from the game warden's eye, how to outrun the high-powered Coast Guard patrols in a simple outboard flat-boat by using the sandbars and switchback water trails. How to survive in a place called the Everglades where few people chose to survive any longer.

The man was practically a god to the old-timers, and to Buck. And you don't call a man's god an "old fart" to his face. It wasn't until Buck finally raised his beer to his mouth and drained it that Wayne saw an opportunity to move without putting himself in danger and got up and fetched the man a new Budweiser. Outside, the wind kept up a low, steady bellow, like a fat man blowing across the mouth of a big clay jug. On occasion the tone would rise with the velocity of a gust. But mostly it hummed, still some distance away, out at sea, warming up to the task, preparing for its scream to come.

CHAPTER 10

"**S**he'll hold together," I said, like a mantra now, but I was wrong. The wind had increased fourfold in strength over the last hour. Sherry and I were now deep into the night. We'd lost the electricity from the generator long ago. In blackness the low hum had grown an octave higher, singing a song of nature pissed off. Then the east-side window of the room, behind where Sherry and I were huddled, suddenly blew out with an explosive sound of shattering glass. I covered both of our faces to shield us from the fragments, but when nothing came I turned a flashlight beam onto the back window and saw that every shred of glass and most of the window frame was simply gone, sucked out into the storm.

The change of pressure in the room and the instant exposure to the wind created a vortex of shredding papers and sailing books and dishes. Flapping fabric and smashing glass joined with the pitch of the wind to create a din that made me lose even my sense of direction. I thought of trying to somehow muscle one of the couch mattresses up to cover the exposed hole where the window had been and was still contemplating how I would manage it in the dark when the entire structure shuddered again and even the floor seemed to shift. I knew we were anchored into the substrata of the Glades on several foundation posts, but I still had the feeling of being on a ship floating on water and caught in a typhoon that would surely roll and sink us. The kitchen area window was the next to go, this one coming apart with a splitting sound, but the shards of glass this time seemed to follow a direct line through the room to the opening at the opposite side. The fractured glass was immediately followed by a rush of wind-driven water that now had a path into the building.

"Are we going to drown, Max? Damn, I'd hate to drown," Sherry said over the howl. Her voice was not panicky or defeated but marvelously cynical for our situation. I didn't want to repeat my lie that the building would hold together, but we were in the middle of the swamp, not on the coast. Since the depth of the water below us was barely three feet I figured as long as we could stay behind something to give us leeward shelter and keep the wind-born water out of our throats we certainly wouldn't drown.

"We're not going to drown," I yelled, but not with full conviction. I had botched this situation so badly I wouldn't blame her if she never trusted me again.

It had been late afternoon when the first bands of wind from the storm we'd watched forming in the west reached us. I misread it as a single passing front.

After it cleared we actually thought about cooking a dinner out on the deck. Then the second band washed through, much stronger and wetter than the first, and we retreated into the main building of the camp.

"A second front?" Sherry had chided me.

"Series of thunderstorms," I answered, smiling, but unconvinced myself.

"I think maybe I'll try to get some kind of weather report on the Snows' radio."

A shower of wind and rain quickly pelted the east side wall.

"I have a better idea, Max. Why don't I do the radio while you tie down that canoe since it's our only way out of here," Sherry said.

I had on my boat shoes and a T-shirt but the wood planking was slick with rain when I stepped outside and the drops themselves stung when they hit my legs at a hard, wind-driven angle. I moved the Adirondack chairs into the storage building, then, thinking ahead, filled the generator to the top with fuel so we'd have electricity through the night, and then latched down all of the doors. The wind kept growing, the rain more horizontal. I made a decision to not just lash the canoe down, but to actually wrestle it indoors. The main room could accommodate its length and I was losing confidence that this was just going to be a temporary blow. I propped open the side door and dragged the boat in, but Sherry did not turn to ask me what the hell I was doing or even look up from her study of the controls on the radio.

"I've been through the AM band twice and only got static and some kind of Spanish salsa music from a rogue station out of Miami," she said. "Maybe everyone has relinquished the airwaves to Howard Stern and Radio Martí."

I only half smiled and she kept turning the tuning dial. Three more times through the width of the band and she gave up.

"Maybe there's an antenna down someplace," I said.

I have sometimes been accused of being a proud man, but not to the point of stupidity. I went looking for my waterproof bag to retrieve my cell phone. I'd call Billy and find out what the deal was with the storm. He'd probably have a couple of his computer screens on and could pull up a radar scan in a few seconds.

"Sherry, have you seen my bag? The one with my knife and books and the cell phone?" I said, looking next to the couch and along the baseboard.

"Yeah. You had it in the canoe the other day when we rolled, remember? I put it in the bunkhouse bathroom because all the stuff inside was soaking wet. I laid everything out so the books would dry," she said and then caught herself. "But I didn't turn it on, Max. It was wet like everything else, but I didn't think about checking it."

If there was a flicker of worry in her voice I couldn't pick it up, but when I again started out the door into the rain I turned to wink at her, and she turned her chin just so and raised an eyebrow that somehow seemed to say: I hope the thing works.

Outside, I had to lean into the wind and could feel the rain stinging the side of my face. The twenty feet of deck to the bunkhouse door was slick and I felt like I skated across it. I had to push the door closed behind me with my shoulder and looked around to see my bag pulled inside out and hanging up on one of the bunkbed posts and the contents laid out on the top blanket. The Kooser poetry book was turned open at the middle, the pages still moist and stained black from where the water had caused the cover dye to run. The first aid kit and the knife, the reasons I took the bag out fishing to begin with, were fine. I picked up the cell phone and pressed the on button and waited for that ridiculous little tin jingle that tells you the network is on. I believe I stared at the small screen for too many seconds, hoping, before I pushed the on and off button three more times. No light. No jingle. We had our privacy now, I thought. No one but us out here.

Back in the main cabin, with the walls quivering and the wind humming, we made a cold dinner of sandwiches and beer. When the electricity went out, I considered going out to the generator building but probably made the first smart decision of the week and stayed put. In the Snows' cupboard Sherry found one of those big floatable flashlights that boaters use and we finished eating by battery light.

"I remember the first time I went to Girl Scout summer camp and was scared when they told ghost stories around the campfire and then I had to sleep in the dark with kids I didn't really know that well," Sherry said, and then she'd shown the flashlight up under her chin and went: "Boooooooo."

"I can't see you scared, deputy. Certainly you'd kick the boogeyman's ass and flex-cuff him."

"Yeah, well. You learn in the academy not to show fear if you remember right, Officer Freeman. It's only a tactic."

But this was different. There was no one to fight, no one to outwit, no one to strategize against. When your attacker is powerful enough to throw the ocean itself a mile inland, rip cinder blocks apart with its fingers, shred metal like tissue paper in its teeth, you simply cower before it and pray.

After the windows went I wrapped my arms around Sherry, my chest pressed into her back, the tops of my thighs against her hamstrings, and I could feel a vibration from deep inside of her. I turned once at a sound that screamed of metal and wrenching wood and I flipped on the flashlight and panned high. The light caught an opening between the roofline and the top of the opposite wall, beams lifting, an entire section of the roof flapping like a rug being shaken off the back porch, and then all holy hell broke loose as the section peeled away and the floor seemed to buckle and I felt my head take a shot from something heavy with a squared-off edge and there was a sudden coolness on my chest because I'd lost my grip on Sherry's warm body, and then blackness.

CHAPTER 11

Maybe it was fifteen minutes, maybe an hour. My sense of time was gone with the wind. But when my head finally started to clear it was still in the pewter haze of a washed-out sunrise. There was a dim grayness all around us and when I focused my eyes, I realized I was staring out onto an open horizon. The back and side walls of the room were gone, simply obliterated or just picked up by the wind and sailed far away. I panicked, jerked against what I was leaning into, and Sherry groaned deep in her throat. We were up against the remains of the kitchen sink cabinet, wedged partially between it and the still-standing refrigerator. I moved my legs, turned on one hip, and looked into Sherry's face. She was conscious, her breathing shallow but steady, her eyes at half-mast, almost like she was simply taking a lolling rest after one of her long-distance runs.

"You OK?" I asked stupidly. "I mean, shit, how long have I been out?"

She didn't respond at first and seemed to be looking out past me into the gray light.

"OK," she finally whispered and then focused on my eyes. "I'm OK, I didn't know what to do, Max. No place to go."

I moved my arm, aimed my hand, found the side of her temple with my fingertips and stroked the side of her face.

"Jesus, Sherry. You OK?"

Maybe she was smiling at my denseness, but the corners of her mouth turned up, just a fraction.

"Hell of a night," she said. "It's morning, but I can't get up."

She reached down with her left hand but only got to her hip and stopped. She had a rag tied around her thigh, tight from the look of it. The torn piece of sheet and the fabric of her sweatpants were stained a rust color. I sat up, felt a spin in my head like I was a kid on the tilt-a-whirl for a second, and then moved down without too much pain to Sherry's leg.

"Puncture?" I ask, probably hoping for something minor.

"No. It's broken."

"Compound?"

"Yeah," she said. "Thigh bone came right through the skin on the interior side. I thought my muscles were stronger than that, that they would've kept it in."

She was a cop. We'd both spent a lot of time at accident scenes gabbing with paramedics, picking up their medical cant.

"I was trying to drag you over here after the side wall ripped away," she said. "My foot must have gone right through a split in the flooring. I fell over and the bone just snapped."

I was staring at her face, trying to comprehend what she was telling me.

"When I felt for the pain I found the bone with my fingers. But I had to move, get us over. When I pulled my leg back out of the hole, I must have pulled the bone back in because it's not exposed anymore."

"Christ, Sherry." It was the only thing that came to my lips.

"When I got us a little out of the wind I was going to use your shirt to tie it off but a bedsheet came whipping by like I'd ordered the thing from room service."

Levity, I thought. She could have been crying; instead she was cracking jokes. Her blond hair looked almost brown, drenched and stringy with shards of windblown sawgrass stuck in it. Her face was smeared with dirt and streaks of her own blood wiped there from her hands. I was looking in her eyes for some sign of trauma or shock that just wasn't there.

"I'm OK, Max. I passed out a couple of times but it feels kind of dead right now. I'm not sure that's going to last if I try to move, though."

Sherry's brave suggestion motivated me to roll over to my own knees and then, slowly, gain my feet. There was an uneasy shift in my brainpan, like a load of water in a tub tipped from one side to the other, but I maintained my balance and the feeling passed.

In the dim light, I took in the shredded remains of the Snows' fishing camp. The western wall that we used for shelter and a quarter of the south wall were still standing. The two others were completely gone, like they'd been ground to mulch or simply sailed away. Glops of wet stuffing from the couch and the bed had been whirled and splattered onto anything that was still vertical: the refrigerator, the cabinet fronts bolted into the standing wall, the now pristinely empty bookcase that was equally nailed to the quarter wall. I took a couple of steps on the floorboards and heard glass crunching under my feet. Past the bookcase, into now free space, I could see the outbuildings, which appeared to have been de-roofed and then simply folded over like wet cardboard boxes. The large water tank, easily four or five hundred pounds when filled, was tossed thirty yards out onto Wally's now bald island. Several planks from the extensive deck had been peeled up with no discernible pattern and the walkway looked like a broken, haphazard piano keyboard. The air smelled of dank, sopping detritus, like the earth itself had been turned by some monstrous tiller and flopped back down on top of us. Looking out toward the south I could only see fifty or sixty yards in the grayness; the plain of sawgrass was flattened, as if by a steam roller. A few thicker, hardier stalks were just beginning to rise up like stubble after a mean harvest. There was civilization out there, the edges of the suburbs less than fifteen miles away. Speculating on what the hurricane might have done there was useless. But there would at least be medical response, even if they'd been hard hit. We didn't

have that luxury and, despite her bravery, Sherry was
going to need that sooner than later.

The thought turned me to searching the wreckage
around me. My pack. My first aid kit. The canoe.

Pulled in against the remaining wall last night, the
canoe was only partially intact. The ribbing and gunwales were unbroken but there was a gaping wound
in the middle of the hull. The paddles were long gone.
So too the small metal first aid kit. No clean bandages.
No astringent or antibiotic cream. Not even a fucking
aspirin.

I searched for water. The cooler we'd brought was
gone and with it the water and whatever food was
left. The upright refrigerator mocked me. The Snows
always emptied it of perishables and shut it down
when they left the place. We had not even bothered
to open it. Inside I found four small bottles of store-
bought water along with two jars of pickles, squeeze
bottles of both mustard and ketchup, and three cans
of beer. In the freezer compartment there were several
empty ice cube trays and a mushy warm Ace reusable
cold compress. I brought out the water, twisted open
one bottle and then bent to Sherry, offering it to her
lips.

"Ah, room service," she said, but could not smile at
the joke this time. "Anything up there from your vantage point that looks hopeful, Max? The view looks
pretty dismal from down here." She turned at the hip
to take in the crushed outbuildings but winced at the
effort. "At one point I thought of a signal fire but fig-

ured we could burn down everything we've got left to sit on and still not raise anybody's attention."

She wasn't just being cute. If the hurricane had done any significant damage on the coast there would be plenty of emergencies for the authorities to handle in their own backyards, never mind some idiot who went frontiering out in the Glades without so much as leaving any word behind concerning a destination. Who would miss them? And where would they look? Maybe if the river ranger at the park went out to my cabin to check on me. Maybe if he realizes my canoe is missing. Maybe if Sherry's supervisor couldn't contact her to come in for post-hurricane duty. Lots of maybes that could take days. I looked down at the stained bandage around Sherry's leg and didn't think we had days. From what little I knew about compound fractures, the sharp edges of the broken bone could be doing even more damage on the inside with every movement. Since the bone had once been exposed, infection was not just a possibility but a certainty. I sat back down next to her.

"I don't think we can afford to stay here, Sherry."

"Yeah, I figured," she said. "No communications link. Not much in the way of passing traffic." This time she found a way to tighten those laugh lines of hers but then turned her head to the bleak horizon.

"We walkin' or ridin'?"

"I'm going to search what's left of the utility room. There might be something we can use to patch the canoe. If we can get her floating, we're riding," I said, trying to at least match her formidable gumption.

"You're thinking maybe that last camp we passed? That one in the trees? Might have been sheltered at least a little bit?"

"You're way ahead of me, as usual," I said and meant it.

"No, Max," she said, turning back to find my eyes. "Not ahead. Just right with you."

This time I did lean down and kiss her lightly, on the mouth.

"OK then," I said and untied the flashlight from her belt. "I'll be right back."

The bunkhouse was completely gone, as if it had been swatted off the deck by a giant hand, only a few iron post anchors left bolted to the flooring where the corners of the building used to be. The utility building was flattened but there were still gaps of space under the collapsed walls, the largest made where an interior wall was still propped up off the deck by the generator. The heavy piece of machinery was bolted to the plank flooring and was close to one of the foundation posts. It had stayed put. I lifted a sheet of wood siding and shoved it aside, then sent a beam of light into the gap and start rooting around. After coming up with busted cans of paint, shattered jars of roofing nails, a completely intact box of "hurricane candles" and a single hammer, I found something useful: a silver roll of three-inch-wide duct tape. No home owner could live without it. My light also caught something chrome and shining on the floor and I was able to reach through a space behind the generator and get a hand on it. With

some twisting and yanking and considerable working
of angles, I came up with the sheared-off shaft of what
was once a Big Bertha driving wood. In memory I recalled a scene of Jeff Snow standing out on this deck,
the morning sun just coming up in the east, while he
wedged a tee in between the planks and took practice
driving old golf balls out into the distance. The envi-
ronmentalists would have frowned at his depositing
dozens of nonbiodegradable orbs of plastic and rubber into the pristine waters. But I had simply smiled
at his morning constitutional. The fat head of the golf
club was now gone, but the wet leather-wrapped grip
and a sharp, wicked metallic point at the end remained.
I told myself it might be useful, maybe as a splint for
Sherry's broken leg. But I knew there was something
about its resemblance to a weapon that made me take
it along with the roll of tape. If I ended up dragging a
half-submerged canoe through the Everglades I didn't
want to face a disoriented Wally or the rest of his ilk
with just a six-inch fillet knife.

When I got back to Sherry with my meager loot she
had already shifted herself on the floor and had gone
through the cabinet under the sink.

There she had found a clean dishrag and an intact
bottle of isopropyl alcohol.

"Maybe your friend kept it under there for cuts from
cleaning fish," she said. "Whatever, it's got to help."

First things first, I used my knife to cut loose the
blood-soaked sheet Sherry had used to tie off her
wound and then the sweatpants fabric from around

her thigh. The gash seemed less than ominous, like a half-moon slice from a pipe the diameter of a baseball bat handle. It was crusted shut with dried blood, but when I pinched the flesh on either side to open it a bit in order to pour in the alcohol, the hole opened and I could see how deep the cut went. Sherry twitched as I sloshed in the disinfectant and when I looked up at her there was a thin bright red line of blood on her lip where she was biting against the pain.

"Sorry," I muttered stupidly.

She closed her eyes and bobbed her head, excusing me.

I then lay the clean dish towel over the wound and ripped off long pieces of the sheet and tied the bandage in place.

"We should try to keep your leg straight and immobilized. You don't know what that bone end is doing inside," I said.

"Yeah, I do," she said, her teeth now clenched together. "It's cutting, Max. I can feel it. We just gotta hope it isn't near an artery."

"You're right. But we can splint it," I said. "God knows there are enough pieces of slat wood here to do that. Maybe strap it in place with the duct tape. That'll keep it straight when we load you into the canoe."

Now she was looking more skeptical than pained.

"Got to, Sherry. Time isn't helping us any here."

"I know," she answered. "But I was just getting comfortable, you know?"

"That'a girl," I answered, again complimenting her

guts and hopefully encouraging her spirit for what was going to be one hell of an ordeal we both knew was coming.

I used the rest of the roll of tape on the hull of the canoe, first folding a piece of a Rubbermaid dish drainer from under the sink to cover the hole and then strapping it in place with the duct tape. While working on the patch I'd found three other punctures and a cracked rib toward the bow, but was sure the boat would still float. My next task was to find a replacement for the missing paddles and I discovered a long curved piece of mahogany under some debris that I recognized as once being the plaque backing for a bonefish trophy that Jeff Snow had mounted and displayed on one of the camp walls. The edges were smooth for grasping and pulling strokes. It would do.

I salvaged a plastic container that once held coffee and stuffed the last of the water bottles in. We could use it to bail water if we had to. I put it in the canoe under the stern seat along with the flashlight and then stored the headless shaft of the golf club along the boat's spine. Though I knew there had once been several flotation cushions and some lifejackets for the Snows' children here, I couldn't find a sign of one. A damp, fabric-covered couch pillow was the best we had left. I propped it in the bow. With everything set I dragged the canoe over to the west side of the remaining deck and slid it onto the water. Sherry was next and I flexed my jaw and moved over to her, clearing a trail of any sharp debris or nail heads, anything that might catch her clothes. I knew how much it was going to hurt to move her and she knew it too.

"I'm going to get you under the arms and kind of drag you to the canoe," I said. "I figure it's the best way to keep the leg from bending."

"Oooh, big cave man. How about just grabbing a hunk of hair," she said, again with the forced grin. I shook my head.

"Then I can lower you into the bow. You use that pillow for your head and prop the leg up on the seat. That'll keep it elevated and maybe reduce some of the blood flow," I said.

She nodded her head, steeled herself as I got a grip under her arms and lifted her. Only then did she begin to cry.

CHAPTER 12

Harmon and his wife had stayed all night in the den that he'd built, at considerable expense, just for this. But he did not gloat over his foresight. He held his wife's hand while they watched the breathless weather reporters correct themselves every thirty minutes and then unabashedly make yet another bold prediction of the hurricane's path and speed and level of ferocity. The storm had gained in strength in the Gulf and then had taken a completely unforeseen loop and then charged due east into the South Florida peninsula. The red-dotted depiction of her path looked like a comical ampersand on the television screen, but Harmon was too scared for levity. Simone came ashore just south of Sanibel Island as a category three, and according to the supposed "hurricane hunter" aircraft, she maintained her bitchiness and speed right up until the Harmons' power went out and left them sitting in the dark, nothing but the familiar touch of their hands and the sound of the wind bringing its terrifying memories. Harmon assured his wife for yet another of the uncountable times of their safety. He'd designed this room himself. Placed it in the middle of their new home, no exterior walls, no windows. Those interior walls had been made with thickened steel studs and fiberglass-covered wallboard. Then the ceiling of this room was sealed with a single, watertight sheet of fiberglass. He'd inspected the entire roof of the house while it was being built for them, counting the double hurricane straps as they were nailed to each roof joist, not just every other joist as was the code. This was their bunker. Harmon took a lot of shit from the few neighbors he knew, just nodded when they called him paranoid. But he would never experience another Andrew. Never. He had seen how Andrew's winds had torn down the steel structure of the flight tower on the Homestead Air Force Base. Her winds had ripped away the corner bricks to expose four floors of rooms at the nearby Holiday Inn, sending the bedsheets and lampshades and luggage flying. Out in the Redlands' open fields, Harmon had personally seen a one-by-one-quarter-inch piece of wood lath the length of a child's yardstick that had been driven through the trunk of a coconut palm that was the thickness of a man's skull. When he told his friends those stories, they went quiet and stopped ribbing him. Even Squires stopped calling him a pussy and stayed away from talk of his partner's storm room.

Inside his bunker Harmon had gathered his books, most of them replacements, but a few from his collection that had been salvaged and restored after that 1992 storm. He'd begun his reading habit when he was in the military hospital in the Philippines and then later in Hawaii. He had been one of those early into the country of Vietnam, his group unnamed and barely accounted for. They were young, wire-strong Americans, most of them from the wilderness states with a talent for survival and abilities with firearms and blades that were used to killing large, warm-blooded animals. Tactical surveillance and assassination were their orders. Go in undetected, come out the same way. It was there that Harmon learned to fear no man. But they'd been sent into Cambodia, early. Made a designated kill. On the way out, maybe misled by a guide-turned-traitor, they found themselves in a dead-end gorge. The climb out was straight up. The Cambodian rebels, bent on revenge for the killing shot to one of their commanders, had seen the talent level of Harmon's group up close and needed an agent of death less vulnerable than themselves. So instead of confronting the Americans they set the narrow gorge on fire and let a strong and natural wind carry the consuming flame to the enemy. At one point the small six-man group, backed against the wall, had to decide to rush into the flame and kill what men they could or take a chance of climbing the wall with the flames following their track, stealing their air, a natural killing force unafraid and consuming. Against his judgment, Harmon was overruled and they climbed. The smell of his own burning flesh and those of his mates around him would never leave him. Only two, Harmon and an eighteen-year-old private, made it to the top. The private got them to their rendezvous spot. Both were flown by chopper to safety and Harmon, later, to the offshore hospital.

There he'd tried to escape into the fictional worlds of Vonnegut, Hammett, Spillane. But each time the nurses came to do the debriding, to scrub away yet another layer of his burned skin, reality opened its throat of raw pain and brought him back to the real world. The bunker in his South Florida home now held a hundred tomes of the history of the Vietnam War on one wall, all with their own perspectives, inclusions, conclusions. He had three first editions of *The Things They Carried* by Tim O'Brien, which he had practically, or as he often thought, impractically, memorized. What good did it do him to be able to quote the line on page one hundred thirty-two? Other walls in the room held other wars, for comparison or maybe even reassurance. The enemy is us, human beings, Harmon often said. We are all so much alike, so bent on superiority, all willing to kill or die for dominance or money or retribution or vengeance or some other reason. But nature cared nothing of such piddling motivations. Nature trampled anything in its path without choice or conscience, not like men. Harmon wasn't afraid of men. He was scared to hell of nature.

It was an hour before dawn when the worst of Simone hit and Harmon lay on the leather couch with his wife in their bunker, front to back, like trembling spoons in a darkened drawer.

"I'm glad the kids are at school."

Harmon only nodded a response to the first words his wife had said in an hour. They'd sent both of their kids to Notre Dame in Indiana. Landlocked. No hurricanes. No earthquakes. And God's own prejudicial eye watching out.

They waited for the wind scream to stop. Then they waited longer, until the rumble went away, until silence. Harmon checked his watch: ten a.m. When he finally opened the bunker door, his house was intact. He used the big flashlight to move through the living room and kitchen, spraying the beam up into the high corners, looking for gaps, for water stain. When he got to the back door he opened it carefully, waiting for something to fall, a tree limb, a piece of roof tile, the sky itself.

Out on the patio he heard the stiff ruffle of leaves, mostly from the giant ficus tree that he could see had blown down and now straddled his fence. In the pale light he did a quick assessment: there were two additional sheets of screen ripped away from the pool enclosure. The turquoise blue water had turned dusty, the surface layered with dirt and leaves and twigs that had blown in through the openings and settled. But all the ironwork still stood. He looked up and off to the south and saw the raw hide of his neighbors' roof where it was missing a quarter of its half-barrel tiles, leaving the black shred of tar paper exposed. To the east there was an unfamiliar gap in the horizon and Harmon had to think for a moment. What was gone?

What was missing? Then he realized the Martins' huge gumbo limbo tree, one hundred years old and seventy feet tall, had been pulled up and toppled, removed from sight.

"Is it safe?"

Harmon turned to see his wife, her shadowed figure just inside the doorway, her toes at the threshold, feet unwilling to move. After Andrew she had moved around the destruction of her home like a zombie, eyes wide and dry and uncomprehending. After three days she found their family scrapbook, clippings of the kids' ball games, pictures of first days at school, birth announcements, all soaked and ripped and ruined. That's when she started to cry and Harmon talked her into going to her sister's in Michigan. He stayed to clean up and clean out a lifetime.

But this storm was not the heavyweight Andrew had been. When Harmon walked around his property to the front there were plenty of trees down. The streets were cluttered with debris: broken roof tiles, branches as thick as a man's wrists, and the crumpled metal and plastic framework of the solar panels that had once been mounted on the Connellys' rooftop. Across the street Donna Harper's van had been pushed off her driveway and it now sat at an angle in her side yard. Harmon looked down the street. The new neighbors with the tape on their windows were unscathed. They'd gained another degree of false confidence.

He was still standing in the street, watching folks venture out to do their own survey just as he was doing, when his wife came to the front door.

"Ed. It's the satellite phone," she called out.

Christ, he thought. What the hell could they possibly want now?

CHAPTER 13

When he woke up, it had to be from the smell. Wet, turgid, soaked earth odor like a compost pit in the rain that had just been forked and turned. That dead fish smell of someone's catch that had lain in the bottom of the boat for three days while the fishermen went on a bender and then woke to a day when they were penniless again and had to get back to the job they both loved and despised. Buck had been there. And the morning after Hurricane Simone it smelled like he was back.

He'd slept through the storm. Not because he was drunk and not that he hadn't tried to get drunk. His ability to sleep through anything had come from prison. The constant night sound of men snoring, coughing, spitting, and jerking off. The antiseptic flavors of Pine-Sol and industrial-strength cleanser wafting up your nose. Buck had spent years in a place so foreign from his home that his only escape had been in dreamless sleep and it was as if he'd trained himself to do it, to fall into a slumber where he heard nothing, felt nothing.

He had also lost his ability to get drunk in prison. He had tried the homemade shit that the inmates put together with sugar and fruit from the kitchen crews and then cooked up in some secret ceiling hidey hole where the heat could get to it and ferment the hell out of it. But the taste wasn't worth the ugly high and he'd simply gone dry while he was inside. After his release he'd tried to drink himself into oblivion but no matter how much he consumed he couldn't get drunk. Nothing like a sober drinker. If you were into getting women drunk and willing, it was a breeze. You could match 'em drink for drink all night and still have a focus. You could play cards all night, get into bar fights, and still have the advantage of full reflexes and a clear, mean head.

The other thing he'd lost in prison was his tolerance for darkness. When he was young he'd hunted and gigged frogs and fished in the dark with the eyes of a cat. But there was no darkness in prison. No sunrise or sunset. Just the unnatural light of electricity, glowing 24/7 and never breaking. Now he would never admit it, but he was afraid of the dark, refused to sleep without some light source nearby. The jobs they'd pulled in the suburbs at night made him clammy and nervous and he'd had to push himself through the fear. Hell, the boys thought he was crazy when he started doing the jobs in daylight, opening the garage doors and looting the places and driving away. But it turned out to be the slickest job they'd done and Buck had not had to deal with the dark.

Last night the boys had gone home to their mommas late, before the brunt of Hurricane Simone hit. Buck had dumped all the empty beer bottles and cleared the table. He hated to wake up to that reminder in the morning. So while the storm had rolled through Chokoloskee, his stilt home swaying and creaking and threatening to come apart or simply topple over, he pulled his blanket up under his chin, put the battery-powered lamp on the table beside him, and did not come awake until morning when he believed he was roused by the smell.

He started a fire in the woodstove and put on a pot of coffee first. Then he dressed in a pair of dungarees and his boots. Outside the light was soft, like the sun filtered through dirty gauze, and it made everything dull as if the world had been turned into an old black-and-white photo from the 1930s. Then something he saw caused him to tuck a map under his arm, pour two cups of coffee, and step outside. Trees were down, the mangroves on the eastern side flattened, but even after only a handful of hours they had already started to rise ever so slightly, like they always did after an assault. Several varieties of shingles from rooftops and wood splinters from crab traps had caught the wind and tumbled through town. Now they all lay on the ground with a sheen of wet mud over them. Buck checked the watermark at the base of his steps. The tide and storm surge had come up to the second riser, about two feet, then receded back into the Gulf. There were a few dead mullet under his house, caught up in some rolled bales of chicken wire he'd stored there, like they'd been trapped on purpose. Part of the stink, he thought.

He walked lightly, picking his way, stepping over boards with the nail points exposed and around the low spots where coffee-colored mud hid their depth. He headed directly to old man Brown's one-hundred-year-old home and was relieved first to see that the ancient Dade County pine structure seemed untouched by the night's wind. Around the corner he heard the sound of someone coughing up a substantial quantity of phlegm and then spitting.

Nate Brown was in his side yard wearing a pair of dull yellow, knee-high rubber boots, a boatman's foul-weather gear, and a flopping rain hat. He had the heads of three dead chickens in between the fingers of his right fist, their necks stretched with the weight of their wet feathered bodies. The old man was bending at the edge of his wire fence and plunged his other hand into the mud and came up with yet another. He did not turn to look at Buck but had sensed his presence.

"Goddamned birds. Don't never learn they cain't run from no hurrican'," Brown said; his southern drawl gave any listener a sense he was pulling each word slowly and reluctantly from the past. "If'n they'd just stay inside the henhouse, they'd a been safe."

Buck watched the old man wedge the newly found head into his hand with the others.

"Pretty good blow last night," Buck finally said toward conversation, knowing he would get little in return. Brown looked up into the western sky like he was smelling the air in the aftermath as if to measure it.

"Seen worst," he finally said, and nothing more.

"Looks like you came through all right," Buck tried again, nodding back at Brown's house. This time there wasn't even a word in response. An answer would have been rhetorical and Nate Brown did not dabble in the rhetorical, especially with Buck. Brown had known Buck's father and his grandfather. They might have even been friends back in the day if such a thing had been admitted among the old early settlers of the southwest. But they were connected not so much by something as ephemeral as friendship as by blood and guts and a reliance on one another to stay alive in such a place at the turn of the century. Buck knew that while Brown had respected his father for keeping his mouth shut and going to prison for his part of the smuggling, the old man had no time for him. Even Buck knew he was not the man his father was. It did not stop him from trying to ingratiate himself.

"Sir, if I can interrupt. Could I offer you a coffee and get your advice on somethin'?"

Brown looked down at the dead fowl in his hand, the fist full of chicken heads as if asking their opinion, and then tilted his head toward the porch on his house. Neither man bothered knocking the mud off his boots as the storm had already deposited as much debris and wet dirt on the interior floor as it could hold. Buck thought they were heading into the old man's home, but Brown dropped the dead chickens at the doorway and then walked to the corner of the porch. With a few simple yanks of marine line to release the knots, he let loose the tie-downs to a small hand-hewn wooden table and a couple of straight-backed chairs he'd secured before the hurricane. He scraped the legs across the floorboards and settled in one of the chairs. Buck swallowed a rising humiliation at not being allowed into the house, but he knew it was the old man's way. He recalled the time when he was a boy and watched his father go into Nate Brown's home for late night meetings with other men. Once he had even crawled quietly to a corner window to listen, rewarded only by the slow, deep rumble of Nate Brown's voice but unintelligible words. There had been no way to see past the yellowish glow of a pulled paper window sash that night, and Buck could only imagine the men standing or sitting, circled around Brown like he was some Indian chieftain or voodoo shaman. It was only later he'd learned of the marijuana smuggling activities of his father and the others and tied them in with the strategy meetings. After Brown had done his time in the federal pen, he'd come back home and had made a visit to Buck's mother, to offer his condolences on the death of her husband. Buck remembered the quaking of his mother's entire body and the anger of her response: "You was supposed to be the one looked after them men, Nate Brown. You and your goddamn old Glades wisdom," she spat, and Buck remembered the old man's gray, unflinching eye going, for the first time he'd ever witnessed, to the floor.

"I'm sorry, Ms. Morris," he'd said. "But each man makes his own decisions dependin' on his nature, ma'am. That's just God's way."

"Fissst," Buck's mother hissed and he still recalled the recrimination in the unspoken expletive and how seeing it fly from his mother's mouth had scared him enough to step back.

"Don't you bring God into it none, Mr. Brown," she'd said. "If you was such a believer you'd remember that you was not supposed to lead them men into temptation."

Brown had continued to stare at the floor that day, and for a long time Buck thought the old man had been struck to stone by his mother's call on the Almighty. But Brown finally looked up and spoke: "I'm not a kingdom nor a power, Ms. Morris. I am just a man my ownself."

Despite his mother's recrimination at Brown and her admonishment to him to stay away, Buck not only continued to be obliging to the old man, but also took it upon himself to ask for his advice and guidance on things pertinent to the Glades and fishing and hunting. And Brown was willing to give it in those instances. It was the line into what he called thievery that the old man would not cross and would turn his shoulder to Buck if he smelled it coming into a discussion.

But if Buck had even one of his father's traits it was his careful ways. He did not rush headlong into things. He did not like to react emotionally to threat or doubt or even opportunity. He was no knee-jerker. So he'd given thought to this newly hatched plan. He heard the same stories the boys had of the new generation of Glades camps filled with the things that others' money can buy. It could mean a big haul. It could mean enough cash from Bobby the Fence to get him off this rail to nowhere. Maybe he'd find a way to clear out of this place, find a better way up in central or north Florida. Some guy in prison had told stories of cattle ranges up in Hendry County. Maybe this was his ticket to another century.

But Buck also knew that any job had its dangers and a careful man tried to plan, and no one in this world knew more about the Glades than Nate. So he'd brought the map he'd made to get the old man's sense of the spots they'd marked, the areas they planned to visit.

Buck set the coffee down on the damp tabletop and pushed a cup to Mr. Brown's side and then unfolded the map.

"I've got a bit of an airboat trip planned here, sir, and thought I might get your take on some of these here spots you might recognize," he explained, sliding the chart to edge up against the mug he'd given Brown.

The old man raised the thick china cup to his lips, took a long draft even though the heat of the coffee still sent steam up and around his prominent nose, and then leaned out over the map. Despite his unknown age, Buck had never seen the man wear a pair of glasses. Brown set the mug down and then reached out and placed his fingertips on each X-crossed spot on the map like he was feeling the place, conjuring a memory.

"This 'un here is too far north for any good fishin'," he said. "It'll be wet now after this blow, but in dry times they ain't but a foot or two of water.

"Now this 'un might could get you a few smaller tarpon, maybe some snook. This other is 'bout the same."

Buck just nodded his head, watching the old man's brow, the deep furrows made by a lifetime of squinting into the reflected sun rays bouncing off open water.

"This 'un here is in an awful pretty spot up in Palm Beach County. Ain't much to fish 'cause the river over this way draws 'em all, but there's some gators in a old hole we used to take ever season near there. Big, nasty sumbitches too, pardon the cussin', son."

"I've heard worse, sir," Buck said, like he was back in his teenage years and his father was alive and Brown was back in his seventies.

"Yep, I know," Brown said without looking up. "Prison'll learn you that."

They both sat in silence for a moment. Buck knew what the old man thought of him and his arrests. Even though prison was familiar to them both, Brown's and Buck's father's incarcerations had been considered a different breed.

"But you ain't goin' to these places to do no huntin' or fishin', are you, boy?"

It was an accusation, not a question and Buck hesitated in his response. He could try to make up a story,

something with a taste of civilization that the old man
might not be familiar with.

"No, sir," he finally said, eschewing a lie in the face
of a man he begrudgingly revered. "It's a salvage
operation."

Brown did not look up but Buck could see the lines
of a sneer start at the bridge of his nose like he was
beginning to smell something foul.

"You mean like when them boys found that there
Caddy Escalade out of gas on the highway up to Naples and *salvaged* the wheels and electronics?" Brown
said, this time looking up at Buck with a single eye.
Buck was mildly surprised that the old man had heard
of that incident with Wayne and Marcus. The fancy
wheel rims had sold for a nice price. He avoided the
old man's look, shifting his own back to the map.

"You know them boys is headin' for trouble.
Don'tcha, son?"

Buck was not going to get into a philosophical debate with the old man.

For some men in Florida, trouble had been a natural way for a long time. He thought of the stories his
own father had told of citizens in the early 1800s who
often "salvaged" the broken holds of ships carrying
goods from New Orleans around the tip of the Florida
Keys and up the east coast to New York on the tide of
the Gulf Stream. When those ships ran aground on the
sharp-edged coral reefs, it was considered a Floridian
holiday and pillaging was nearly a civic duty. Near the
turn of the twentieth century, land owners selling use-

less deeds to Florida swampland created millionaires overnight who fled with the cash and left the losers behind. Nate Brown himself had poached gators out of his favorite hunting holes even though they were considered off limits after the federal government created the Everglades National Park in the 1940s and the practice was deemed illegal. Those men all used the excuse that what they did, they did to survive. Buck had heard that rationalization a thousand times coming in late-night conversation from the darkened bunks of men up in Avon Park Correctional.

"Maybe it's just trouble of a different nature," Buck finally said, but he was still not willing to meet the old man's eyes.

"No, son," Nate Brown replied, his voice holding a weak resignation that Buck had never heard before. "The nature's the same. Sometimes that's the part of people that don't never change."

Buck pushed his chair back, knowing the old man was finished. He stood and started to roll the chart, but Nate Brown's finger was still pressed down on one last X.

"Let me give you some advice, Buck. If that's what you come for," he said, using the young man's name for maybe the first time since his childhood. "Stay clear of this one here."

He was indicating the X farthest south on the map.

"They's stories on this one. One told is that an old-timer built here and must have died over the years because no one seen him for years. Word was someone in his family took it over but they somehow got spooked and left the place empty. Then new owners that put out the word of no trespassin' and meant it. I been out there myself and heard awful strange music comin' from the place when there wasn't a shred of light on the property.

"Steer clear, son." And with that the old man removed his finger and sat alone at the table while Buck gathered the map, and said his thanks.

"Yes, sir," he said and then turned back to retrace his steps to his own place.

"We're gonna hit those places now."

The boys just looked at each other with a mirror expression that said surprise, but what the hell. They'd shown up midmorning after wandering around town in their boat boots, checking out the damage from the night. Buck was in one of those suspiciously dark moods of his. Wayne figured this was the way he must have been in prison and it was not a good idea to argue with him. Besides, when Buck wanted to roll, it usually turned out to be a hell of a lot more interesting than sitting around this place. They could easily tell their mothers that they'd been hired to do some kind of rescue or salvage work and with the promise of money on their lips they'd be off the hook for any cleanup at their own homes.

"I already been over at Owen Chadwick's tour business shed and his airboat is intact and I have the key," Buck said while he turned his back on them and stuffed something into his black, zippered duffel. They were both in that sort of uncomprehending dumb-assed mode he'd seen a dozen times in their teenage faces when he grabbed up the bag and turned back to them.

"What? You two suddenly lost your comprehension of English overnight?"

Again the boys stood quiet. They had learned that if they looked at each other for some kind of shared intelligence they'd get another dose of Buck's shit. So they stood mute.

"We got opportunity here, fellas. Those camps are either out there with their doors blown out for easy access to what's inside. Or they're in pristine shape while their owners are scurryin' around at their big-assed mansions in the city worryin' about how to get their air conditioning back on," Buck said.

"Nobody's thinking about them camps after a hurricane, boys. We got a window of opportunity here and, fellas, we're gonna climb right on through."

He ordered them to grab up some bottled water and some food and "whatever tools you think you might need" and meet him over at Chadwick's boat shed. Then he slung the duffel over his shoulder and started down the outside staircase.

"And hurry your asses up," he called out to them as they went in opposite directions. "We're burnin' daylight."

Buck liked to quote from John Wayne movies and with these two he often dredged up lines from that one called *The Cowboys* about Wayne taking a bunch of young kids on a cattle drive because the Duke couldn't find any men to help him with the job. In the Old West Buck would have been a leader, a man admired. He figured that might have been why he never objected to the nickname that got stuck on him in high school. Buck. Just like in the 1800s. Now there was a century he knew he would have fit into. Maybe driving cattle up in Hendry County wasn't that different today. Maybe he hadn't been born too late.

The boys must have heard the chug of the airboat engine turn over twice, three times while they were walking across the mud that used to be Marshall's Circle because when it finally caught and burst into a roar, they started running.

"Son of a bitch will leave without us for sure," said Marcus, toting his quickly packed duffel and a Lil' Oscar cooler filled with water bottles.

"Yeah? Where's he gonna go without us to do his lifting and totin'," said Wayne, who sounded cocky, but didn't stop running either.

When they jogged up to Chadwick's place, Buck had the big airboat out on a new mud slick near the old mechanic's nearly submerged dock. It was there that he usually loaded in the tourists who had been lured by his AIRBOAT TOURS OF THE ANCIENT EVERGLADES sign posted out on the Tamiami Trail. Anybody who'd lived here for any of the last three or four decades could still pick up some business from folks passing by from Naples on the west or Miami to the east who wanted a peek at the gators or bird flocks or just the open sawgrass range of still-wild land. The boys could never see the attraction. Buck thought it was as bad as running carnival rides, catering to gawkers and thrill seekers who had little respect or appreciation for what they were seeing. But he'd still served as a substitute driver for Chadwick as long as he got paid in cash.

The boys stepped up onto the flat boat deck, built like a pontoon skiff in light aluminum but with an angled bow so it could slide up over a small bank or plow right over tall grasses and thin-stalked trees. Buck had loaded the big open deck with a line of red five-gallon gas cans, a cooler, and his duffel. The boys tossed their bags behind the raised seats and then climbed up behind Buck's pilot chair. The huge, wire-caged propeller was right behind them and the airplane engine roared when Buck pushed the throttle forward to keep the rpms high. He reached back to them to offer a plastic bottle of little yellow chunks of spongy material you could stuff into your ears to cut down the thrum of noise. He didn't say a word, even if they could have heard him. They both waved him off. This was nothing they hadn't dealt with in Cory Marshall's Honda Civic with the Bose CrossQuarter speakers that thumped out Da Trill and vibrated the whole car on a Saturday night roll over to Naples. When Buck's head turned forward, Wayne pointed his finger forward and mouthed the words: "Let's flow, dude." Marcus read his lips and they both giggled like little kids.

CHAPTER 14

I knew that without my partner it was going to be a much harder pull, but I missed her more than I could calculate.

We were two hours into the trip back, twice the amount of time it had taken to make this leg to the Snows' camp from the thick hammock of pigeon plum and strangler fig trees where the hidden camp may have survived the blow better than ours. I was hoping that the place had been sheltered by the trees and might be a serviceable resting spot. Now, after plowing through miles of water that had become a cluttered soup of floating, rootless vegetation, hope had turned into a prayer. I was envisioning beyond logical expectation a dry room, potable water, canned food of some sort, maybe even a battery-powered radio-phone. In the last hour my fear had grown that the latter was going to be a necessity if Sherry was going to survive with her leg intact.

In the still, flat light, I was watching her eyes while I stroked with the makeshift paddle I'd fashioned from the wall plaque. At first she'd been hyperalert, her eyes dancing from left to right, checking, assessing, nervous like a kid riding in the jump seat and watching the landscape go by when she really wanted to be facing the destination instead of having her back to it. She would grimace with pain each time the canoe slid up with a jerk onto some flotsam that stopped us with its thickness. More than a dozen times already I'd had to climb out into waist-deep water and pull us through shallows, fearful of steering us around them too far and taking the chance of getting off the direct line of GPS coordinates. Each time I pulled from the front, my handhold next to Sherry's shoulder, my eye checking the pulse in her neck. Once refloated, I would get her to drink more water from the bottles, even when she argued, correctly, that we needed to conserve.

"You're the engine, Max," she said. "I'm just the passenger. If you run dry we're both sunk." I caught her repeating the same line an hour later, and Sherry rarely repeated herself. I started watching her eyes for signs of delirium. When they closed, for rest or out of exhaustion, I watched her lips to see if she was mumbling to herself. I kept talking to her, nothing complicated or even specific, just ramblings to keep her the slightest bit focused. Maybe to keep me focused too.

Now I was talking about springtime in Philadelphia, telling her about the blossoms on trees along East River Drive in Fairmont Park and how you could smell the aroma, even out in the middle of the Schuylkill River when you were rowing. While I talked I kept my eye on a marker, a clump of unusually high sawgrass, that I'd set using the GPS. One leg at a time, I thought to myself. I talked about high school, the guys in the neighborhood and some of the girls, piling onto the Broad Street subway at the Snyder Avenue station and riding down to the Vet on a Saturday night to see the Phillies play. We'd get Mitchey Cleary, whose older brother was a beer vendor, to slip us soda cups half full of Schmidts and then sit up in the cheap, seven-dollar seats and yell all night for Von Hayes to rap one out of the park to us in center field. I saw Sherry smile at that one, just a slight rise at the corners of her dry, cracked lips, maybe thinking about the beer. When I started going on about stopping off at Pat's at Wharton and Passyunk for cheesesteaks I realized I was punishing even myself by bringing up food and drink and I stopped.

"We're gonna be there in a little bit, Sherry. How's the leg feel? Can you still move your toes?"

I was hoping for circulation and secretly worrying about infection, maybe even gangrene. The Glades is notorious for the waterborne bacteria and microbes that break down the vegetation and could have easily made it into her bloodstream through the open slash in her thigh and even onto the exposed bone before she was able to pull it back in.

"I'm OK," she said softly, her first words in over an hour though she still did not open her eyes when she said them.

"Tell me more about the spring, Max. Tell me about trees. The shade. Tell me you love me, Max."

I thought again of delirium. What was the treatment? Shit. Had she answered my question?

"I love you, Sherry," I said. "We're going to be there in just a little bit."

It was raining again by the time I looked up from a more determined pace. I was stroking as deeply as I could, feathering out the rhythmic repetitions, trying to block out everything but the reach, pull-through, kick out with as little interruption of momentum. I'd been repeating this motion for years paddling out on my river, even in darkness with only the light of the moon to guide me, up to the dyke flow and back, working the edges off whatever new rock was in my head. I could do it now, through exhaustion.

The drops of rain on my head mixed with the sweat and ran into my eyes and the sting finally made me look up. I wasn't sure how long I'd been cranking but in the distance I could finally see what might be the remains of the hammock. From half a mile out, the dark rise of trees made the little island look like it had been sheared in half. A couple of taller spikes formed odd-looking inverted Vs against the background of pale sky. I took a break, fed Sherry the last of the bottled water we had, and then drank myself from the bailing scoop I'd fashioned from the Snows' coffee can. I'd convinced myself that the rainwater would be pure enough to keep me hydrated and whatever else got mixed in with it from the bottom of the canoe would just have to be ignored. The bands of rain from the back end of the hurricane had followed us along the path but now the bottom of the boat was filling too fast for that to be the only source. My jury-rigged job with the duct tape was failing. The canoe was leaking. Glades soup was seeping in and trying to swamp us, but there wouldn't be a fix now. If the darkening mound out there in front of us wasn't the one we were looking for, or if the camp inside its sheltering trees was blown away, we were in deep trouble. I bailed while I rested and then reached out to touch Sherry's foot. No reaction. I got to my feet and with my hands on either side rail of the canoe I leaned forward. I could still see the pulse in her neck so I sat back in my seat, began paddling again, head down, the pace a step faster than before.

I checked the GPS twice, three times, as we approached the island. The electronics were the only thing that could convince me. This was the place, but it looked nothing like the thick green, idyllic hammock we'd passed four days ago. The lushness was stripped away. Simone's winds had brought down the long graceful limbs of cypress and dumped them onto a mud-covered web of mangrove and what at one time might have been a fern bed. The taller trees now showed the splintered white wounds from where their branches had been ripped away and I was immediately reminded of Sherry's once-exposed thigh bone, and then pushed our way into the hammock's interior, looking for the structure of the camp, hoping.

It was easily midafternoon by now and the light was already failing. I finally had to get out and pull the canoe through a nest of tangled grass. I stumbled and jerked the boat to one side and Sherry gasped in such a high, keening tone I went to her side and couldn't stop repeating, "Sorry, babe, sorry, sorry, sorry."

She was grimacing, probably a good sign. And she reached down to put a hand on the injured thigh, another indication that she knew her pain and was still cognizant of where it was coming from. While I'd still been paddling I'd set the open cooler out in the space between us trying to catch whatever rainwater would accumulate inside. I now poured it carefully into one of the empty bottles and held it to her lips. She drank, almost greedily, until it was done.

"We're here, babe. I'm going to go find the camp," I said to her closed eyes. She tightened her lids and weakly whispered, "OK."

"I'll be right back."

I picked up the flashlight we'd brought and stepped easily but with a purpose, worried about the sharp branch points and possible sink holes that could end up leaving two injured on the island. I had to climb over a couple of downed tree trunks to get to higher ground and then started looking for a leaning tree trunk that I might climb to get a higher view. I was looking for the edge of a structure, an unnatural right angle, a glint of metal or a flat plane of painted wood. About a hundred yards from the canoe I found the thick secondary limb of a tree that was partially down but still attached to the higher main trunk. I climbed it on all fours until I gained some height. From here I could see edges of

water to the southeast and then picked up the shape
of bent metal directly to the west. The color was dusty
copper but there was also a patina of green at its edges,
an old-time sheet metal roof, popular out here and similar to the one on my own river shack. It wasn't more
than fifty yards away and probably would have been
invisible under the cover of the tree canopy but stood
out now through the stripped branches. I traced a path
through the vegetation that would offer the least resis-
tance and then jumped down to follow it.

The angles became clearer within minutes. After
wading through a couple of low mud bogs and climbing over several downed trees I began to make out the
body of the structure, wood paneling that had turned
ash gray from the weather, but was standing straight,
an optimistic sign. By the time I reached the raised platform of the camp, my hope was rising. The building,
simple and square, was intact but for the metal roof
at the northwest corner that had been peeled back by
the wind, the angle I'd seen from my tree stand. There
was some splintered damage below it in the wall, but
the deck planks seemed untouched though the film of
mud told me that water had risen over them at one
point. The windows were all shuttered with the old-
style, wood-slat covers, but when I bent to look up
through the spacing of those slats, there appeared to be
some other kind of barrier besides glass behind them. I
walked around to the south side, found the only door,
and tried the handle. Locked. And locked tight. The
lock set was made of stainless steel but had oddly been

painted some kind of faux iron. I shook it hard and then gave the middle of the door a substantial butt with my shoulder, half of my weight behind it. Not a budge or even the slightest give. The builder had been very careful.

I circled back to the northwest corner to see what the storm damage might offer and found a possibility. The west side was more exposed than the southeast where we'd approached. There were the remnants of a canal that was now choked with branches but navigable. I could row Sherry around and get her very close. Under the bent roof corner the siding was peeled away by the fingers of the wind and there was a black, open space in the top three feet of the wall, an opening big enough for a man to climb through. I dragged a downed tree limb across the deck and propped one end against the wall and used it as a step up and then took a good jump, high enough to get a grip on the bottom slat of ruined paneling, and pulled myself up. Hanging with one arm I got the flashlight and shone a beam inside. There was space and something gray-white below, possibly a bed, straight down the inside wall. Two wall studs were still in place but I could probably squeeze my chest between them and drop, headfirst, inside. I felt like some amateur cat burglar in a half-assed break-in, but figured if I could get inside I could unlock the door and search the place. I put the flashlight back in my pocket—I hate that thing where Tom Cruise puts the flashlight in his mouth while he's being lowered into some dark fortress. He's going to fall and gag himself with that thing someday. Then I got a good grip on an exposed ceiling joist and pulled myself halfway up and through the wall opening. After much shimmying and tearing of clothing and clunking of boot soles, I managed to drop to the inside, hands extended out, and found my first bit of luck by half-falling onto the edge of a bed before landing on the floor. It was noisy and graceless, but there wasn't anyone within miles to hear or even care.

Only the dull streaks of light seeping through the hole I'd created gave the room any illumination. And I must have been thinking of some kind of cop thing from my past because I rolled first, staying low, and then stayed silent. Finally I slipped the flashlight out and scanned the place: Table and two chairs. Kitchen cupboards and sink against one wall. Two beds, bare mattresses, lined up foot to foot against my wall. There was something like a desk against the third wall, next to the outside door. All the windows were darkened and I used the flashlight beam to help me move to the door but still banged the corner of the table with my thigh and the scraping noise it made as its legs dragged across the floorboards made me shiver. Not a scared shiver, but unsettling, like I'd moved something that had not moved in years. I found the doorknob, stainless and substantial and locked. I twisted out the button, tried it, and when the door still didn't move I scanned higher and found another heavy-duty deadbolt and snapped it unlocked. It took a couple of yanks to get the door open; the frame was probably warped out here in the humidity and heat. I swung it wide to let the natural light stream in, and the outside air actually smelled fresh compared with what spilled out of the old place. I took a useless look around the deck and then stepped back inside.

The light did little for the place. There were no pictures, hanging fish trophies, or even a calendar on the walls. There were no magazines on the table, no coffee cups filled with pens on the bare desktop, no dishes in the sink drainer. But mounted on the wall above the kitchenette counter was a blue and white metal box labeled FIRST AID KIT. I slid it off its hooks and went through the contents: rolled bandages, tape, antibiotic cream and a bottle of antiseptic, some sterile gauze pads, and a thermometer. There was even some insect repellent and aspirin. I could probably wait to re-dress Sherry's wound here, but the aspirin and bug dope I would take back to the canoe. I set them aside and then moved down to what appeared to be a half-size refrigerator at the end of the counter. Inside there were three half-gallon plastic jugs of water, at which I smiled. I took one out, noted that the top was still sealed, and then twisted it off. I still took a precautionary whiff of the contents and then drank in long gulps. I had not realized how dehydrated I'd become from the rowing and the heat that, despite the cloud cover, had drained me. I even contemplated pouring some of the water over my head in the sink but then thought better of the conservation of the gift. Who knew how long we might have to stay here? After another drink I looked again inside the refrigerator and found two old cans of Del Monte sliced peaches and a single wrapped package. Inside the plastic package, surrounded by tinfoil, was a bar of solid chocolate about the size of a man's wallet. Since the refrigerator was without power, the chocolate was the consistency of warm butter, but I still pulled off a piece from the end and devoured it. The energy is what I needed, sugar to snap some of my dulled synapses back into shape. I took another gulp of water and with a clearer eye looked around the room again. The door to the second room was off-center and to the right. I stepped over to it but my eye picked up the flash of a metal box against the frame at chest level. I used the flashlight again and found myself looking at a digital locking device. I'd seen them many times before. But why the hell does someone have one on a room out in the middle of the Everglades?

I punched at the top row of buttons, numbered for a combination. No response, though without power I wasn't expecting it. I examined the door more closely, then gave it a shoulder. Nothing. I put some weight behind the next one. Thing was solid. I knocked at the flat surface with the butt end of my flashlight. The sound was distinctly metal, and then I banged on it a few more times at an angle. By scraping off some paint I could see that someone had taken pains to paint a faux wood design on what was a substantial metal door. My only thought was that something valuable was inside. You don't build an extra-heavy-duty safe room without something to keep safe inside of it. But the guesses were endless out here: Food? Hunting weapons? I swept the flashlight through the room again. Not a clue. This side of the place was sparse. Too sparse, in fact.

"Hell with it," I said out loud and the sound of my own voice went dead in the thick air. I snatched up a water bottle, left the front door open, and stepped out onto the porch and checked my handheld GPS. I figured to go through the brush again and then row the canoe around. I could pull Sherry out next to the deck and then get her inside on the bed. Maybe I'd overlooked some blankets, something to keep her covered. I'd tackle the locked room later. Maybe it was the sugar hitting the back of my head, maybe the sharper image now of Sherry's leg, still propped and bound in the bow of the canoe without me there to watch her. But suddenly I wanted her inside, somewhere safe. The light was seeping out of the late afternoon sky now and even though the coming darkness would be no more intense than any other time out here, I did not want to be exposed again.

When I had climbed and slogged and ducked through the beaten hammock to the canoe and spotted Sherry's head through branches in the distance, I called out her name but the dark blondness of her hair did not move, and it scared me.

"Sherry!"

No answer. No movement. I started crashing through some downed poisonwood.

"Sherry!"

Her hand came up, palm facing away from me, fingers straight up and stiff, not a sign but a signal and I stopped. I tried to see beyond her, into the bush and the twig mass that I'd dragged the canoe through to its resting spot. I kept my vision low, water height, and then tried to move slowly.

Ten yards closer and I spotted the nostrils, like moss-covered walnuts resting on an equally dark log. But these were too symmetrical and behind them, maybe a foot, two hooded black marbles shone. It was hard to tell how big he was from where I stood, or whether he was on a solid mass of vegetation or still floating. I have seen gators get up on all fours and charge with amazing speed. But under most circumstances they like to lie quietly, like a spring trap, and snap their prey with a speed and strength that seemingly comes from nowhere. This one might have been stalking Sherry, or her scent, moving at incremental inches until it was at striking distance. My rustlings in the hammock seemed not to have distracted it in the least. Usually, man-made noise, a passing airboat or even shouting and the whacking of boat paddles, caused the animals to whiplash their tails and dive down and away into any nearby water. Usually. What the passing hurricane had done to the flow of nature was unpredictable and I was not going to guess the mood of this monster. Last year a woman jogger who had simply stopped along the edge of the lake in a Broward County park to dip her feet in the water was snatched by a fourteen-footer, pulled into the lake, and dismembered. With gators there was no such thing as predictable.

I was thinking strategies and to go along with them I picked up a good sturdy limb that had been sheared from an old-growth mahogany above. I set down my supplies and pulled my knife from its scabbard and started hacking strips off one end of the limb, half a dozen downward strokes, the blade so sharp it slid through the two-inch-diameter stake like it was putty, and left a glistening, bone-colored point. You could poke 'em. I'd seen the wildlife resource officers for the state maneuver even the nasty ones by poking them with long-handled nooses and then roping them. But I had no such interest. Just a poke in the snout if the thing came forward. Maybe a jab in the throat if he opened that mouth of his. I took hold of the stick like a foolish caveman and moved toward Sherry. When I got next to her she cut her eyes to me and whispered in a raspy voice: "Jesus, Max. What the hell are you going to do with that?"

Adrenaline had perked her up. She was fully conscious.

"Hell if I know," I answered as truthfully as I could and handed her my knife.

"And what the hell am I going to do with this?"

The gator snuffled, I swear, and let out a whoof of air that rippled the water in front of him but he did not move.

My insane reaction was to yell at the top of my lungs and then lunge out at the animal, bringing the broom-length staff of mahogany down with a sharp swat on the surface of the water. The spray erupted in front of the beast's face and in response it snapped out with amazing quickness and bit the end of the stick and pulled it from my grasp.

"Shit," I said, and reached back into the canoe, fingers searching, and found the long metal staff of Big Bertha that I'd tossed in the boat at the cabin. I whipped the headless golf club out and it whistled past the gator's nose, and he seemed momentarily awed by the sound. He froze but I did not. I reloaded for a second shot and this time I lunged and stabbed at the thing's face, jabbing at the nose but missing and unintentionally sticking the end of the metal shaft a good three inches into its eye socket.

The gator did not roar, did not make any sound at all but spun his huge body away and the slew of his huge tail sent a wave at us, catching me up in the chest as if a ski boat had just peeled by, and when I shook the water from my vision I saw the ass-end of the gator slipping through the greenness headed in the opposite direction.

We were frozen in silence for a few beats, listening to the rustle in the brush echo away, listening to me breathe in gradually slowing gulps, listening, each of us, to our own heartbeats trip down.

I finally turned to Sherry and it appeared as if she had not moved since I left her. Her face was sallow; either sweat or water from the gator splash had covered her face. But at the corner of her mouth was a tickle of a grin.

"I would have just shot the bastard," she said, and the tickle went to both sides.

I retrieved the fresh water for her, which she drank carefully and also with one of the aspirin. I then gave her the package of chocolate, which she started to gobble, but thought better and licked more than bit at the mushy bar. I told her about the cabin, that it was intact and that there were some medical supplies but nothing that was going to help much with the pain.

"Just get me inside, Max. The pain I can deal with."

I backed the canoe out and climbed in. There was now a good four to six inches of water in the bottom but I didn't bother bailing. I could remember the route I'd figured from the treetop and we paddled around to the water entrance of the cabin in less than twenty minutes.

"How long was that thing lying there watching you?" I finally asked as we got underway. I was still cutting my eyes in either direction, watching for unnatural ripples.

"Seemed like forever," Sherry said from the bow. "Probably as long as we were watching him over the past few days."

The water and no doubt the chocolate had raised her energy and her humor.

"Wally?" I said.

"Same beady eyes," she said and again the smile had partially returned.

She whimpered only once when I lifted her out of the canoe and set her on the deck. The splint was holding up. But when I carried her through the entrance of the cabin and lay her down on one of the beds, I came away with a dark bloodstain on my shirt sleeve and right hip. I got out the first aid kit, ignored the scissors and used my own sharp knife to cut away the duct tape and then the old sheet bandages, and finally more of the leg of her sweatpants.

Her thigh was swollen, maybe from infection, maybe in combination with the tightness of the wrapping. The skin around the wound was puckered and white and I guessed that it was from the constant moisture. Keeping anything dry out here was a struggle. Under these conditions, impossible. I laid the knife next to her and then poured the alcohol onto the wound and used the sterile gauze to clean it. Sherry watched but didn't make a sound even when I picked up the flap of skin and poured more into the gash. I slathered on the antibacterial cream and then used the other sterile pads to cover and then wrap the thigh with another gauze roll, not as tight as before. She needed antibiotics, probably a straight IV drip, probably a drip with all kinds of fluid to hydrate, fight the sure infection, stop the possibility of gangrene.

"OK," I said. "Let's get your shoes off, make you comfortable."

She was already looking around the room.

"Anything in the back room? Radio? Keys to the helicopter?"

I pulled off her mud-covered shoes, those funky red Keds with the yellow laces.

"Haven't gained entry yet to check it," I said, and used the alcohol-soaked gauze to clean her toes and get a take on their color. I was looking for pinkness, hoping for circulation.

"Yeah, gained entry," she said in a mocking tone. "I see the digital lock, Max. What's up with that?"

I was concentrating, very carefully poking the pads of her toes with the sharp tip of a corner of the aluminum medicine tube, hoping for reaction, but getting none.

"You saw the digital lock, right, Max?"

She couldn't feel her toes. I needed to get her out of here to a hospital.

"Yeah," I said, standing up. "I gotta check that out. Who the hell does that out here, right?"

CHAPTER 15

Harmon was in his bedroom, going through the closet, his closet, the one he didn't share with his wife, the one that he in fact forbade her to use. He knew she probably had gone through it in years past, just looking. You don't keep secrets from your wife for thirty years. She would have looked at his gun collection, the electronics that the company had him keep there for emergency use, maybe even the multiple passports he tucked away in a drawer. But if she had questions about those things, she didn't bring them up. She knew that he had been in the military and left unsaid any doubts she had now of the legality of his work. It was yet another reason he was always trying to find leverage against the men who employed him. He'd seen colleagues killed and wives left behind without a clue or a safety net. He knew the company would disavow any knowledge of him and see no obligation to take care of his family if something befell him. Harmon was not the kind of man to say, "That just comes with the business." If that were the case, he wouldn't still be in this dangerous business, no matter how well it paid. If he went down, his instructions for his wife and all the money he had hidden over the years and the evidence against the oil company would be at her disposal. He took care of his own.

"Arlene," he called out to his wife, who was in the kitchen and still pissed at the news that the boss had called. "Where's that other jacket I had?"

He checked off his travel list in his head as he touched each item and stuffed it into his bag: the satellite phone, fully charged. The helicopter pilot would have the same model and they would be able to stay in touch regardless of the lack of power or cell towers in the area. His Nikon digital camera, which he'd been instructed to carry in and take detailed photos of any damage and the general disposition of the property, including any lack of foliage coverage, from the air. A couple of two-liter bottles of water because even if this was an easy hour-long drop-in, document, and get back out, he knew the danger of the humidity and the heat of the Everglades from experience. A radio frequency transmitter, routinely used to electronically unlock abandoned or sealed oil rigs and restart their power systems. His Colt revolver with the snub nose, the last one in his collection and an item he never went to work without.

"I've no idea. I thought you wore one on that last trip you guys took," his wife answered, her voice growing as she approached down the hall.

"I lost that one," Harmon said, thinking about the bullet hole in the fabric. He continued sorting through clothes hanging on a rod in the back of the closet.

"Well, I thought you said this was going to be a quick mission. You can hardly be going somewhere cold if it's going to be quick," his wife said, her head looking around the corner of the bedroom door but not entering when his closet was open. Yeah, he thought, she's been in here.

"Doesn't matter if it's cold, honey," he said. "You know when I'm on a job I like to have pockets to put things in." His wife walked away.

They had done this dance a hundred times. Vietnam, Granada, Nicaragua, Kosovo. When he'd retired and gone private he watched her breathe a sigh of relief but still felt her eye on him as he began to spend more time in his library and running the streets in an old pair of combat boots and generally driving himself and her crazy from inaction. When he started going on week-long "security" trips for the company, missing the kids' games or some special ceremony, he knew she was unhappy with the shift once again in his priorities. He was not a domestic man. She knew that. "For you and the kids" was always his response when she gained the guts to outright ask why he did what he did. It pays very well, Arlene. I'm a pro. I'm not going to do something stupid and leave you guys hanging, you know that.

Harmon did not say those words just to mollify. He was a confident man, knew his abilities, even with age. Once set on course he did not believe he could fail. That was his life's playing card, the source of respect from others, the mind-set that had kept him alive through a dozen missions. He did what he did because his soul needed it. But he was not so dumb as to not provide, just in case. He'd left instructions for his wife, just in case. He covered his ass.

"Here's your other jacket," Arlene said, returning to the door with the short spring coat with the big seamed pockets that gave him easy access and room to maneuver whatever was in them.

"Thanks, honey," he said.

"Bring that one back with you. OK?"

"Yeah, sure. You can bet on it."

CHAPTER 16

"**W**hoa, check it out," Marcus said from across the room, and Wayne seemed to be able to tell by the sound of his friend's voice that he wasn't just shittin' him. Wayne was staring, really staring, down into what looked to be a pile of oddly angled polished wood. Marcus stepped over some pots and pans and crossed the bare carpet that sat square and clean and seemingly untouched in the middle of the room.

"What?" Wayne said, watching Marcus kneel and stick his hands into the pile of wood. Marcus came up with a half a dozen CDs, spread in his fingers like a poker hand.

"Dude's got some music, man. Good stuff, too. Twista, Jay-Z, Tha Marksmen," Wayne said, reading off the labels.

"And check out the machine, man," he said, pointing at the stereo player still sitting in a slot in the wall cabinetry. "That's worth some cash right there, unless we wanna keep it, you know."

Wayne looked up to give his pal a wink that seemed

to assure him they would do whatever they wanted on this little heist safari of theirs. It was a pact they'd come to after their first stop this morning, a moderately damaged fishing camp just on the southern edge of Broward County and the closest GPS coordinate on the list. That camp had been nice enough in its time, a two-bedroom deal with a great room that had one of those big round metal fireplaces in the middle to warm the night in winter. But one wall was now completely gone, ripped away like a leaf of notebook paper, leaving some curtains blowing in the wind, off-white lace curtains that Marcus could tell were better quality than the ones his own mom had in their regular home, not their vacation getaway. They'd found some music there too. But it was mostly old-style R & B stuff, John Lee Hooker, Wilson Pickett, stuff his old man used to listen to before he left. He and Wayne had attacked the place like scavengers, picking up fishing reels, an intact kitchen blender, and half bottles of Chivas and Van Gogh vodka all strewn around in the aftermath of the storm. That's when Buck stepped in and said he was laying down "ground rules." We only take shit we can sell: jewelry, real nice pieces of electronics like handheld GPS or shortwave radio stuff, or maybe portable TVs. Only take the sealed booze. Check the drawers and stuff for real money and don't ever pass on some tin container that might have a stash in it. "These city assholes come out here to party like there's no rules. There's a lot of pot and coke and stuff they keep out in these places, so use your eyes, boys."

Yeah, they'd use their eyes. And if they found any drugs, they were going straight into their pockets and he wasn't going to know any different. Wayne winked at his bud. After about an hour of sorting through the place, Buck called them in.

"Can't spend too much time in one place, boys," he said. "Not that we're worried about anybody coming by that we won't hear ahead of time, but if it ain't a rich site, we're gonna move on. There's bound to be a mother lode out here someplace."

It was the flicker of excitement in his eyes that got the boys motivated. It wasn't often Buck got jazzed by anything. Even when they did the jobs in the suburbs when shit would get hinky or that time they found that coin collection that they'd sold for eight grand, Buck was still level, moving ahead, but never jumping, never showing emotion. But there was something different in the guy's eyes this time. He was liking this shit. They loaded up the airboat with a few things and got her started again. Buck had decided they'd go well north and east to one of the high spots on the map and then work their way down toward home "just in case we find something heavy."

This new place had some definite possibilities. But it was weird. Marcus again went to the middle of the big room and did a three-sixty, scanning the walls, where some of the shelves and cabinetry appeared absolutely untouched. But like the kitchen pots and pans that were jumbled on the floor about fifteen feet away from where they should have been, so too were some couch throw pillows and a lamp and a DVD player about fifteen feet from the den area where they matched. A bookcase on the eastern wall was empty, the books fifteen feet away, piled up against the refrigerator and kitchen island. And in the middle Marcus was standing on a pristine, pearl gray carpet. His eyes moved up the walls to the second floor, to the sheared-away beams that had once supported a cathedral ceiling, until he was staring straight up into the clouds passing high above. It was like a tiny tornado, spinning within the chaos of the hurricane, had peeled away the entire roof and then dipped its finger straight down into the building and did a little twirl and then left.

It was disconcerting to Marcus, and he stood there thinking of the time when he was very young, maybe about the time his father had left. His mom had decided to make changes in their lives to forget the past and she'd completely redone his room; moved his bed to another wall; the dresser, the bedside lamp, even the posters, all shifted. He remembered now how it had confused and scared him when he would awake in the middle of the night and have that overwhelming feeling that he didn't know where he was. That fear came over him now, that he was someplace so foreign and unsafe that there was nothing familiar to hold on to.

"Marcus!"

Buck was leaning over a spiral, wrought-iron staircase that gave access to the bedroom upstairs.

"Marcus? What the fuck, son. You gonna help or just

watch, boy? Get your ass up here and go through this other bedroom."

"I got it, Buck," Wayne said, then turned to Marcus. "Why don't you see if you can pack up that player with something waterproof, man."

He nudged Marcus with the satchel he'd filled with CDs and had slung over his shoulder and on the way past whispered, "Got us some booty here, brother."

Wayne was sounding giddy too. "Both you guys are fucking lost," Marcus said.

Buck was filling the gas tank of the airboat when a hot, dangerous urge came into his head, and he stopped to wonder where the hell it came from. He could suddenly see himself: the red five-gallon can in hand, sloshing the contents in a careful path along the first floor baseboards of the entire place they'd just looted. Make sure you get it on all sides and in the corners so that every remaining wall would go up in flames. Fuck 'em. Asshole city boys and their seaside mansions out here, he thought. He could especially see the now broken photos curling up and going black in the flames. He'd picked one up in the den area: four guys no older than him, big-ass grins on their faces, the two on the ends holding trophy-size mangrove snapper, the two on the inside holding half-full bottles of piss yellow Corona beer. One actually had on a polo shirt, probably with his country club logo on it but Buck couldn't tell. One had a ring on his right hand with a rock as big as the eye of the fish he held hooked in the gills. Buck was not normally a jealous sort. He didn't look at fancy sports cars at the casino or on trips into Naples and lust after them. The big plasma television sets he saw when he was creeping one of those suburban homes did not have any allure to him. He'd go down to the bar at the Rod & Hunt Club and watch their big screen game for the price of a few beers.

But for some reason this monstrous, yellow-painted structure built like an ass pimple out here in the middle of the Glades and filled with all the comforts of those homes had put him in a pissy mood. Hell, he ought to be thanking the owners. He'd found their stash of booze, a case of some kind of imported rum, back in the corner of a pantry closet. He'd picked up a fine pair of binoculars upstairs in one of the bedrooms; six hundred bucks retail, probably unload them for two hundred to Bobby the Fence. Then he'd pulled out the drawer that he almost missed in what was probably the master suite. The thing was actually built into the bed frame. He'd stubbed his toes on it, expecting his foot to slide under the mattress when he'd stepped up close to the bed and instead kicking the solid frame below.

He'd gone to his knees and saw the handles and the lock. The pry bar he carried took care of the latter. When he pulled out the sliding drawer he was not exactly surprised, considering the boys he'd seen in the photos, to be met by the odor of gun oil and the sight of carefully wrapped firearms. But the five weapons he took out and arranged on the bed mattress were exceptional.

A 30-30 Winchester rifle, old style as far as he could tell, but in such pristine shape it had to be a collector's item. He couldn't help but pick it up, throw the lever action, and sight down the barrel, dreaming scenes of the Old West. Yee ha. He smiled. Born in the wrong century.

Then there was the Mauser, a German-made World War II classic, heavy, built to last, knock down a fucking mule with one shot. As he had already figured, these guys weren't real hunters, they were playboys, out here to make noise with their expensive toys. There was a twelve-gauge over-and-under shotgun there as well, the most utilitarian of the group and no doubt used to knock a few curlew out of the evening sky just for the hell of it.

Then there were two handguns: an old 9mm Glock, the one law enforcement gave up on after a couple of heavy-fingered cops said they fired prematurely, and a .45-caliber revolver of the style Clint Eastwood's Dirty Harry might have carried but too fucking big for anyone to lug around these days except for some asshole drive-by gangbangers who thought the sound of it was cool because it was louder than their car stereos when it touched off.

Buck had stared at the collection for a few seconds. In his excitement over the total haul in the house, his natural wariness of the weapons was lost. No, he didn't like guns. He'd heard too many stories of their violence and how it inevitably came back on you. But there was something about this day that was feeling too easy, everything working out the way he'd envisioned it, the way he boasted on it to the boys. It was all going smoothly and Buck had spent nearly thirty-three years on this earth and nothing had ever gone completely smoothly for him. The guns were now stashed under the pile of other things they'd decided to take. Buck had slipped them there himself, not bothering to tell the boys what he'd found. He'd taken three boxes of ammunition from the secret drawer and wrapped them and the rifles and the big .45 in a blanket and covered that with some raingear he'd found to keep them as dry as possible.

Now he shook off the urge to torch the place and emptied the gas can into the tank and then tossed it onto the dock of the house. Fuck it, he thought. Don't overdo it just to get back at the assholes for trespassing on your life. This mission ain't about them. If you set the place on fire, you're sending up a smoke signal that anybody could respond to. Do the job, Buck. What you gotta do. Be smart.

"OK, boys. Let's move on. We're burnin' daylight," he said. Buck and the Duke. He reached into the seat trap and took out the GPS.

"Next on the list ain't but an hour south. If she's still standing we might be able to spend the night there."

Wayne and Marcus put a final knot in the line holding their newfound booty and climbed up into the backseats.

"You say so, captain," Wayne said, and when Buck hit the ignition and the big engine caught and the noise ripped into the heavy air, the boys looked at each other and grinned and passed the bottle between them. They'd already opened the Van Gogh vodka that they'd lifted from the kitchen and found they liked the espresso flavor.

CHAPTER 17

I was in the water, waist deep, sloshing around at the edges of the raised cabin deck, one eye peeking up under the two-by-eight stringers for some sign of a trap door, the other watching for Wally.

I had climbed back up on top of the structure when it became apparent that there was no way I was getting into the mysterious room from the inside. I'd already dismantled part of the metal frame of the other bed next to Sherry, an old prison trick inmates pulled to salvage strong enough chunks of metal to shave sharp and make killer shivs out of. I used one of the unsharpened chunks as a pry tool but it had been useless against the frame of the security door and after I worked for an hour to peel back a piece of baseboard and then chopped at the low corner of the wall, I gave up.

Outside, I even climbed back up on the roof where I'd found access before and scoured the panels for a ceiling entry to the other room. I found a vent that might have been for recirculated air. And a damaged edge I was able to peek into, only to find a secondary sheath over the room, some kind of fiberboard or waterproof polymer that was too tough to gouge through.

"You look too frustrated, Max," Sherry had said when I gave up and rejoined her. The aspirin from the medical kit had brought her fever down some. Her eyes were more alert. I'd opened a can of sliced peaches I'd found warm in the small refrigerator and used my fingers to fish out individual pieces and feed them into her mouth. The sugar and solid food had helped.

"Those are just my normal age lines," I said, tightening my face to make the look more severe. "You certainly know that by now."

Again the light grin came to her face, accented by the glistening smear of peach juice on her lips.

"No. That look is you grinding on something. The other is frustration at something that's beating you."

"OK," I admitted. "There's got to be a way into that fucking room."

I told her what I'd found through the roof, the change in materials that seemed only to surround that half of the building.

"Why would someone build one part of the cabin one way and the other so much more fortified?"

"Fortified or waterproof?" Sherry said.

"Both," I said. I had traced the electrical lines from the small refrigerator and a waterline from the sink. Both went through the floorboards in the direction of the other room. I'd taken another trip outside in search of a generator room I might have missed. Nothing. The electrical supply was in the other room as well.

"High-tech lock, waterproofed and fortified. There's something valuable inside," she said.

"Out here, in the middle of nowhere?" I tossed it back to her.

"Drug drop. Distribution point?"

"Cop thinking," I said, with a cynical twinge.

"Duh, yeah."

I might have thought of it myself. But it had been a while since I'd worked narcotics and only in the streets of South Philadelphia, never in the swamp.

"OK. It's isolated enough for drop-offs, but the only way you distribute from here is by airboat," I said. "Only way quick enough."

"Too piecemeal and too expensive," she said and ate more of the peaches.

I stared off toward the end of the bed, like I was thinking, but really looking at her toes, for discoloration. Though her mind was sharper and her mood higher with the food and rest, we were going to have to get her out of here soon. The chances of someone coming by or looking for us were minimal. Even if Billy started looking for me, which he would, or if Sherry's supervisors got anxious, would there be anyone dispatched to my river shack? And when they found it, if it were still standing, would they make a jump in reasoning that I'd been stupid enough to take us somewhere by boat? It could be days and we sure as hell didn't have days. I didn't see a way to patch my canoe with the materials we had. Whatever was in that room might be our savior if we were to have one.

"The Fisher Body plant in Lansing, Michigan," Sherry said. Her tone turned my head because she did not seem to be directing the odd and disconnected words to me but to the wall. She was looking off to a memory.

"I must have still been a teenager. It was one of those stories in the news that for the first time took my attention away from that bullshit in high school."

I knew Sherry had grown up in Michigan, the daughter of blue-collar parents, working class in an area and in a time where working class was a prideful title.

"I remember it because I was scared to death back then of being stuck somewhere without air. Maybe I'd been swimming somewhere in the lake and lost my breath or maybe my brothers had locked me in the closet or something when I was little. But I was always scared back then that I would be trapped somewhere without air."

I looked closely into her face, then straight into her eyes, checking for the dilation of her pupils. If she was going into some kind of hallucination from the trauma, I might have to just patch the canoe as best I could and make a run for it. I took her hand in mine.

"There's plenty of air, Sherry. We're OK. All right? You can breathe here, baby."

Her eyes reacted and she shifted them to me.

"Oh, shit. No, I'm sorry, Max," she said. "I'm not flipping out on you. No. I was thinking of an old story, back in my hometown.

"There was this accident at the auto factory. There were these three workers, guys in the paint department on the line at Fisher Body where all the cars for GM were assembled. These guys were doing cleanup in one of these deep pits where they dipped the cars for rust-proofing or something. They were pits that were sealed and waterproof. Maybe it was some kind of maintenance that they had to go down in these things and clean up excess paint or something.

"But whatever they were using, maybe some new solvent or something to break down the paint, they got themselves surrounded in a cloud of the stuff. They couldn't breathe and started choking and collapsed and when the supervisor realized what was happening, he went down the ladder to help them and he was overcome by the stuff too. By the time someone got an oxygen mask on to go down for them, they were all dead."

She was staring at the wall again, remembering. I gave her time. Sherry is not someone you ask too early what the hell her point is.

"After that, the company installed trapdoors in all the sealed pits, a way to get out if something happened, a quick-release porthole in the floor that someone could get out of if they fell in or got caught down there."

Again, I got caught looking at her eyes, like I had many times since I'd met her, amazed.

"I'll go down under the room and check it out," I said.

"Good idea," Sherry said and smiled, a real smile this time, and not just a grin.

*   *   *

I was in the water, waist deep, watching for Wally, looking for a seam, a handle, any indication of a trapdoor. I knew the stringers below were probably creosote-soaked timber. Out here the wood would rot in no time in the constant moisture even if it was up above water level. I found the timbers green and slick with algae. The odor was ripe in the way a compost pit would be if you stuck your nose into it. The fingers of my left hand were curled up over the edge of the deck and I was using the flashlight in my right to beam the spaces between the stringers. My feet were squishing in muck and it took effort to pull each one up out of the suction and take a step down the line. My ears were tuned to any stirring in the nearby grasses, any grunt from a large predator with a bad eye. I worked my way all the way around three sides before the light caught a raised anomaly in the otherwise black-green underbelly of the cabin. Spotting down parallel stringers there was an edge, barely an inch difference, protruding from the flat board surface. It was about eight feet in from where I stood.

I had to let go of the deck and it felt peculiar to me to hesitate doing so. I also had to dip deeper into the water, to my chest, to get my head down under the first stringer, and I thought twice about that movement also. There was something spooking me about being deeper in the dark murk that had not been there before. I shook it off and, keeping the flashlight above water, reached for the next handhold while pulling my boot out of another sucking hole. From close up, the edge I'd spotted became a square, positioned between two stringers. I scraped at it with the edge of the flashlight. Metal. Again of the stainless variety to resist erosion or rust. In the shadow of the wood beam I found the handle, a lever really, of the kind you see in submarine movies or on oven kilns. There was no key entrance on the rounded end, an indication that it did not lock from this side. I twisted and it moved, slightly. I put some muscle into it and heard the internal cylinder slide. It would make sense of course that an escape hatch would not be locked to keep rescuers at bay, if that was indeed what it was for. When I heard the click of metal snapping loose of metal, I pressed up on the door. Stuck. I had to reposition my feet so I could get some leverage and tried again, this time with my forearm, and I heard the sucking noise of a seal being broken and the door finally gave way. Once open, the smell of sweet musty air poured down over my head and face, air that had not mingled with its outside brother in a very long time.

CHAPTER 18

Harmon was thinking about some half-baked Hollywood movie scene of the dedicated hero searching for his drunkard partner when he parked behind the beachfront just west of A1A and started up the sidewalk to the infamous Elbo Room. He knew Squires would be there. He was always there when the weather got rough. The hurricane had left a feel of some dusty Mexican town in its wake. The cyclical wind had come off the ocean in the second half of the storm and sand from the beach was drifted up against the curbs and around the doorways and sheets of it were still swirling in the streets. Later the maintenance guys for the city would be shoveling it back up over the low retaining wall but now they were too busy shoving splintered trees off the roadways and assisting emergency power crews with downed utility poles. It had been a bit of an adventure driving through his neighborhood and then making the circuitous route all the way to Las Olas Boulevard and east to the ocean. He'd been redirected by roadblocks three times and twice had to use side streets to get there.

Luckily, they'd closed the bridges over the Intracoastal Waterway in the down position, not that anyone was fool enough to move their boats, though you always heard of some idiot who was racing for the dock or had been torn off his anchorage during the blow.

At the corner of A1A and Las Olas there were only a handful of people on this, one of the most historic gathering spots in South Florida. The ocean breeze was still kicking. A long piece of ripped canvas awning was flapping from its frame on the second floor somewhere. The neon that normally illuminated the bikini mannequins and beer sales posters and displays of cheap sunglasses in the storefronts had gone dark. But as Harmon rounded the corner he could hear the strains of Stevie Ray Vaughan playing "Boot Hill" on the juke and he knew finding Squires was going to be a snap.

Unlike in the movie version, he did not expect the big man to be passed out on some small table in the corner and have to pick up his head by a clutch of hair à la some Clint Eastwood spaghetti western. He was not disappointed. Squires was sitting at the bar, his back against the countertop, his feet propped up on a second stool, and a bottle of Arrogant Bastard Ale in his hand. From this familiar perch Squires could see the ocean and the sidewalks. On good days he could watch the sun dollop on the surf and the girls pass by. On bad ones he could spot the hustlers and bill collectors and trouble coming. He cut his eyes immediately to the south when Harmon stepped inside. He grunted and took another sip of beer, knowing what kind of day this was going to be.

"Shit," Squires said.

"Yeah," Harmon said, hitching his hip up onto the empty stool beside his partner. "You got that right."

"Nothing good brings you out on a beautiful day like this. Where the hell we goin' now, boss, and don't tell me out into the Gulf, man."

"Would have called but all of the cell towers are down," Harmon said. "And I won't tell you the Gulf."

"Have a beer then," Squires said and raised two fingers to the bartender who had not made a move toward their end even though there was only one other patron in the place.

"Elma!" Squires said. "From my private stock, please."

The bartender, an elderly mainstay of the place named Elma Mclamb, put her crossword puzzle down and reached down under the counter to open the door of a small cooler and came out with two bottles of Arrogant Bastard. The beer came from a brewery in San Diego and was only distributed in a few of the western states but Squires had acquired a taste for its dark flavors while doing some work for the Marines and now had it shipped to the Elbo Room at his expense. If Harmon hadn't known the man better, he might have thought it was some kind of show-off status thing, but Squires was not a poseur. And he rarely shared the stuff.

The two men sipped from the bottles and looked out over the gray waters of the Atlantic to the horizon where the colors of sky and ocean were so close one could hardly find the line that separated them. Harmon understood why his friend chose both this place and the view: neither changed. The Elbo Room had remained pretty much the same worn and welcoming place it had been since the 1960s when they filmed *Where the Boys Are* on this stretch of Fort Lauderdale beach. The two street-front walls of the tavern opened full to the sidewalks; the shutters that covered them were raised every morning at nine. Inside, the oval bar held the scars and chipped initials of three generations of teenagers emboldened with skittering hormones and the freedom of spring break. The city put a big damper on the annual craziness back in the 1990s when the yearly bacchanal got too big and rowdy for the changing times, but even the high-priced restaurants and the faux mall that sprouted up to replace the wet T-shirt bars and seaside novelty shops couldn't destroy the tradition. College kids still came. Locals looking to show off their cars and tans and energy still moved up and down the strand. The city couldn't change that any more than they could stop the tide from sliding up and down the beach.

Squires liked the constancy, in fact got surly when things changed.

"You ride out the storm here?" Harmon finally asked.

"Upstairs," said Squires. "They closed the shutters down here so we went up on the balcony. Better view anyway."

"You guys are nuts."

"Yeah. But it was cool. The only time these days when you can look out to the east and not see any freighter or container ship lights out there waiting to get into the port," Squires said. "And when the power went out, man, it was blackness all up and down the coast. Reminded me of jumping out the back of a C-one-thirty at twenty thousand feet over the desert. Very cool."

"If you say so, big man," Harmon said.

Squires took another long pull on his beer.

"So where we goin'?"

"Local job," Harmon answered. "Boss wants us to catch a helicopter ride out over the Everglades. Says they've got some kind of a research facility out there that needs a storm assessment done. In his words: 'Make sure it's not exposed.' "

Squires gave him a questioning eye.

"Didn't know we had a *facility* out in the Glades."

"Me neither. But the man seemed pretty concerned, you know, that tick in his voice that means somebody higher up the ladder is the one asking."

"Yeah. Everybody's got someone up the line," Squires said, finishing the beer. "So when we going?"

"The pilot says he's got to get his ship back out of the hangar after they broke it down and secured it for the storm. We're looking at tomorrow morning, earliest," Harmon said. "It's out at the regular site at Executive Airport. You can get out there all right?"

Squires nodded.

"We taking anything special?"

"This place is supposed to be empty. So just pack your standard inspection gear. Shouldn't take us more than a few hours. You'll be back for happy hour."

"Sounds like a good day to me," Squires said, and again raised his hand. "Elma!"

CHAPTER 19

By the time they got to their next target, the boys were drunk.

They'd been sitting up behind Buck in the wind and noise of the airboat passing the Van Gogh vodka back and forth and giggling. Buck had his earplugs in and never bothered looking around. He was focused on the GPS coordinates and planning out in his head how he was going to unload the guns they'd stolen from the last place. It was a nice haul overall, but instead of maybe calling it a day and figuring they'd done well for themselves, Buck just kept pushing on, a little giddy himself over how well this idea was all coming out. They hadn't seen another boater or even an airplane since they'd left the docks. It was like one of those neutron bombs had gone off, killing everything and leaving the world just for their picking. Hell, they had two or three thousand dollars worth of stuff on board already. The guns themselves should go for two if that greaser Bobby didn't try to rip him off. Buck knew that the middleman had the advantage of knowing how much he hated dealing with firearms.

Fucker would lowball him and Buck would end up taking less than he should just to get rid of the stuff. The guns made him nervous just thinking about them stacked below. But the tenseness wasn't strong enough to throw him off his euphoria. Christ, if they picked up another score like the last one, maybe he'd be on his way to Hendry County in a couple of weeks.

When they'd gotten within a mile of the next fishing camp, Buck spotted the hard edges of a building out on the gray horizon and pointed to it with one hand, not knowing that his crew behind him was more interested in the vodka and its effect on their fuddled equilibrium than on his navigation. He wove his way through some low sawgrass and stayed out on the gaps of open water as best he could while maintaining a fairly straight trajectory toward the camp. As before, he started running a scenario through his head just in case they pulled up to some owner or even a local checking out the damages. Rescuers, he'd decided. We're just out here looking to see if anyone needed help, was possibly stranded or hurt. Good Samaritans was what they were.

But as he steered closer, coming in now from the northwest, Buck could see that no cover story was going to be necessary. The hard angles he'd seen from a distance were now forming up to be one single wall, the only one that remained standing. The rest of the place was trashed. The neutron bomb. No survivors.

Buck pulled back the throttle and turned around, catching his assistants playing some kind of preteen thumb-wrestling game and smiling like a couple of idiots out at the forensics unit for the criminally insane at Raiford. I got a real criminal enterprise going here, Buck thought, my own crew of Luca Brasi. "Don Corleone, I come to you on this da day of your daughter's wedding . . ."

He thought about the Godfather's leg man, his eyes popping out of his head with a garrote around his neck. He could squeeze these punks. But then who's gonna do the heavy lifting? He swung the airboat up to the partial dock and cut the engines, and the cessation of movement gained the attention of the boys, who, it was now obvious, were drunk as skunks. Buck reached between them and snagged the near-empty vodka bottle and flipped it over his shoulder into the water.

"Find what you can find and let's get out of here," he said and the boys turned their faces away like eight-year-olds who got caught jerking off. Buck jumped down onto the deck and headed for the smashed outbuildings, leaving the useless pantry and kitchen wall to the boys.

"Fuck him," said Marcus, only loud enough for Wayne to hear. "Guy could ruin a good wet dream, know what I mean?"

Wayne looked at him with a blank stare.

"No, I guess you wouldn't, Stumpy," Marcus said and stepped away quickly, laughing, but also avoiding Wayne's reach.

"Ain't nothing worth a shit in this mess anyway, 'less you're looking for a nice fish trophy," he said, bending to pick up a fiberglass bonefish that lay crippled with a broken tail on the floor, its long wooden mantel missing.

Wayne poked around in the stuffing and swirl of ripped curtains and cracked debris, kicking at the piles with little interest and stumbling a bit from both the effect of the alcohol and the odd sense of still being on a boat. The missing walls caused the edges of the plank foundation to meld with the water and the open horizon and he was caught by the feeling he might step off the edge of the world if he wasn't careful. He tried to focus on something close and thought it was way weird that the refrigerator and the kitchen wall were still standing. It was like old lady Morrison's house when the wrecking crew came to scrape it off the plot where they built the new marina in Chokoloskee. They were kids and watched in fascination as the big-clawed backhoe chewed through the roof and pulled down the walls of a place they'd passed on their bikes a thousand times. No one their age had ever lived there, only the old woman whose husband had died years before. Then one day the ambulance came and they carted Ms. Morrison out on a stretcher and the place stood dark and empty for years. They might have gotten a glimpse inside when they went trick-or-treating or something as children, but when the place was laid bare by the machinery, they watched in fascination as the pink-papered walls and the porcelain sinks and even an old four-poster bed got scraped into a pile and then loaded into a dump truck. When the claw scooped up the toilet all the kids laughed but only for a second, then they rode on, down to the docks where they could fish and skip stones out onto the bay and do the dumb-ass things you did when you were young without a thought about your own house being scraped off the face of the earth by a storm or by a fucking backhoe.

"Hey, dude! Check this out."

Wayne stepped over a window frame of shattered glass and then nearly stepped into a hole that had been busted through the floorboards. He joined Marcus and looked down into a pile of rags.

"Blood, man," Marcus said, pointing down at a crumpled sheet. They'd done enough hunting to recognize the dark, red-brown stain. Wayne picked up a corner, sniffed the copper smell of blood and dropped it.

"Damn, dude. Don't have to be some bloodhound," Marcus said, pinching his face in disgust at first and then raising his eyebrows in that stupid grin. "Dawg."

"Somebody was here, man. And it wasn't that long ago neither," Wayne said. "Look at the empty water bottles and stuff." He pointed at the trash around the sheet and then opened the refrigerator door, found it empty. He bent down, sat on his heels, and with a slat of broken siding began poking at the pile. "You better go tell Buck to come look at this."

After Marcus turned away Wayne reached down and hooked the corner of a Velcro strap he'd spotted and pulled out a blue fanny pack, the kind runners and maybe a few fishermen might use on a flats boat. He'd waited for Marcus to go so he'd have a chance to scope

it out for himself. He zipped open the pouch and inside
rummaged through a wad of soggy tissue paper, a tube
of lip balm, and a pair of slim sunglasses. He raised the
open pack to his nose and drew in its odor. A woman's.
He liked the smell, and even the faintest aroma of perfume or body lotion, the thought of where it had been,
aroused him. He breathed it again and opened his eyes
and saw the glimmer of gold deep in the corner of the
pouch. He reached in with his left hand and pinched
it between his fingers and came out with the necklace.
Even the dull sunlight picked up a facet in the stones
and his eye picked up the spark. He untangled the
gold chain and then draped the jewelry over his other
hand, like he'd once seen a clerk in a store in Miami
do. The two jewels, an opal and a diamond, lay against
his palm, one reflecting, the other glowing, next to the
folded skin flap where his thumb used to be. Wayne
did not notice the juxtaposition of beauty and scar.
He was caught instead by the thought of where those
stones had last been lying, against white, smooth skin,
perhaps nestled in a perfect cleavage. When he heard
the steps of the others, he quickly palmed the necklace
and shoved the fanny pack back under some debris.

"We were just going through stuff and found it laying there and figured, you know, you ought to see it,"
Marcus was saying.

Buck leaned down and took up the bloodied sheet
in his hand, unfolded it and held it by two corners, ex-
amining one rough edge. He too brought it to his nose
and breathed.

"You're right," he said to Marcus, who nodded as if it was a foregone conclusion. "Somebody probably out here in the storm and got injured. Looks like they sopped up some blood and then went and tore some strips off this, maybe for a bandage." He looked out on the site with a new eye.

"I found some gas cans under some other shit in the outbuilding. It's high-test, which means airboat fuel."

"How do you know it ain't just regular boat motor gas?" Marcus said. "Or generator fuel."

Buck gave him that "you ain't been there" eye and said: "There's a difference in the smell, boy."

Wayne didn't say anything, thinking only about the scent of a woman that was now in his hand.

"They must have packed up and took off for the city as soon as the 'cane stopped blowin'. They sure as hell ain't comin' back this way soon," Buck said, again looking out on the horizon.

"Well, there isn't anything worth a damn here any-way," Marcus said. "Let's go."

It was supposed to come across as a confident, half-in-charge kind of statement but Wayne looked at his friend when he caught that uncertain quiver in his voice. They'd been on dozens of these escapades and Wayne could always tell when Marcus was getting nervous.

Buck had them help dig out the gas cans he found in what was once the generator shack of the camp. It took all three of them to lift the collapsed wall and kick away some broken studs to make enough room to remove them. Buck stepped into the space they'd made and passed out the cans to Marcus, who then ferried them over to Wayne in the boat. There were six cans in all and one had been punctured, half of its contents having leaked out onto the wood plank floor. Buck again thought of the lighter in his pocket but just whispered, "Fuck it."

Over at the airboat Marcus handed up the last can.

"We find any more gas we could stay out here for a week," Wayne said, digging at Marcus's show of being nervous and tired of their expedition.

"Yeah, well, the master criminal there has only one location left on the GPS list so unless *he can smell it*, there's only one camp left and we can go the hell home."

Wayne just bent to lash the final can in, a grin on his face. Marcus was missing the way Buck had identified the gas and Wayne was getting a tiny dash of joy out of it. Marcus may have been hefting the cans across the decking, but Wayne was the one handling them and tying them in place. He had seen the waterproof marker on the bottom edge of each red plastic can that labeled each one: AB. That had to stand for AirBoat. Buck didn't need a nose to tell that. But he sure as hell was good at puttin' Marcus in his place.

"Fuck you grinnin' at, Stumpy? You want to stay out here all week too?"

Wayne ignored him and when they were finally set, both of them climbed up into the seat behind Buck who was again checking the GPS and the list.

"OK, fellas, let's make this next one a jackpot," he said and turned the ignition, and the engine erupted with that sonic frapping sound. Wayne leaned forward to feel for another bottle under the seat, and when he straightened back up Marcus was staring at him with some kind of incredulous look on his face.

"What?" Wayne mouthed.

Marcus reached out toward Wayne's neck but got his hand slapped away in response.

"What the fuck is that?" Marcus mouthed, his words wiped out by the sound of the engine.

Wayne's hand went without hesitation to the opal and diamond necklace that he had affixed around his own throat. The chain was a little small for him so the stones hung high and exposed above his T-shirt collar when he'd bent over. He looked directly into Marcus's eyes with a seriousness that his friend recognized as a mood you did not cross with Wayne.

"It's mine."

Marcus didn't need to hear the words. He just showed his palms, rubbed them together and showed them again, just like the blackjack dealer does after shuffling the cards to prove to the players he has nothing up his sleeve.

"Whatever," he mouthed back into those eyes.

CHAPTER 20

With stale air tumbling down on me, I pushed the hatch door up and heard it clank on its hinges like a submarine portal. I aimed the flashlight up into blackness and could only see the white circle of my beam on a plain ceiling. I had to reach up and put the light over the edge and then do a pull-up on the hatchway until my face cleared the opening. The scene made me think of that famous World War II and Korean War cartoon with the eyes and big floppy nose just visible above a bullet-pocked wall. "Kilroy was here."

From this vantage point my flashlight was now drawing a circle around some kind of metal cabinet or panel with knobs showing in shadowed relief. I hoisted myself the rest of the way up, swung my hips onto the ledge, and sat there with my legs hanging through the porthole, pant legs and shoes dripping a patter of droplets into the glades below. I moved the light beam in a slow sweep, illuminating unblinking eyes of yellow and blue and red all around me. The single room was an electronic bat cave. Monitor lights, all dead from the lack of electricity, were in rows on the fronts of panels that had to house computers, sensors, calibrators of a kind I would not be familiar with. I thought of Billy, the lawyer and brains of our partnership, who would be able to make at least a knowledgeable guess at what I'd found. I could hear him saying: "My, my, Max. What do we have here out in the middle of godforsaken swampland and what the hell is it out here for?"

I had the same question, but more immediate problems. First I climbed up out of the hole and started working the walls. The stacks of electronics seemed to bunch on the western side, rising to just above eye level and shining in a metallic sheen like brushed steel. On the northern wall stood a low desk and countertop, two roll-away chairs, and room for spreading out paperwork or diagrams or something. In one corner was some kind of a printer but it was loaded with graph paper and had one of those wire styluses you'd see on old lie detectors. I was thinking seismic sensors, the kind that measure Richter scales. But earthquakes don't happen in Florida. I was thinking measurements in the earth under the Glades, but to what purpose? I was thinking too damn much. The eastern wall was empty but for the door that led to the rest of the cabin and a punch-code lock that matched the one on the other side.

On the south wall was what I took to be the generator, housed in a floor-to-ceiling booth with air vents at top and bottom and a power lever that was pulled

down in the OFF position. There was a keyed handle
to the cabinet door that gave access to the inside.
When I inspected the sides near the floor I could see
the cable—the same color as the one feeding the refrigerator in the other room—running from the generator
down into a hole in the floorboards. I was thinking of
the crowbar, if it might be sufficient to pry the cabinet
open, get some electricity flowing, toss a wet towel in
the fridge, chill it and then wrap Sherry's head, bring
down the fever, do something to help her.

I swept next along a table on the wall. Three-plug
jacks for some kind of electronics and three corre-
sponding connectors for phones or Internet. And near
the end, an empty power recharge plug for three handheld mobile phones. On the end of the table was a Bose
five-disc CD changer with the speakers built in. A real
home-away-from-home for some trio of computer nerd
hackers or pirate radio stoners or who the hell knows
what, and I realized I was getting increasingly pissed
at the uselessness of it all until my light caught the red
cross of another first aid kit on the wall and the twin of
the other refrigerator in the corner.

First I checked the kit and saw that the plastic tie
that acted as a seal was unbroken, which meant it must
be full. Then I crouched to the refrigerator door and
as I went to pull the handle my hand was stopped by
the growing sound of an airboat engine. The noise was
coming up through the open hatch, the only way it
seemed to be able to penetrate the walls, and I scrambled over to listen and make sure I wasn't just deliri-

ous. No, the thrumming sound revved and then cut back, the throttle of the engine in someone's hand. Rescue. Civilization had arrived.

I scrambled over to the hole and plunged my legs through, landing waist-deep in the water. I yanked my boots out of the bottom mud and then, forgetting the hatch and leaving it wide open, I bumped my head three times before making it out from under the camp foundation. Out in the open I twisted around in the direction of the motor noise. Sherry, I thought. Got to let her know what's happening.

Her eyes were at half-mast when I got to her side. I put my palm on her brow, still hot, but hotter than before? I couldn't guess. She turned her head to me.

"Swimming, Max?"

She still had some strength.

"We've got company," I said. "An airboat just pulled up nearby. We're on our way out, girl."

She let out a sigh of relief, or maybe just loosening that built-in determination of hers, that reservoir of strength she was holding in abeyance for what was to come.

"Who, Max?"

"I don't know yet. I just heard the engine outside. They've got to be coming to check on the place." I put the half-filled bottle of water I'd recovered from the dead refrigerator to her lips. "Here. I'm going to go lead them in."

"OK."

Maybe she was thinking more clearly than I. Maybe

she was just more of a cynic, still being a working cop. Maybe she was just more intuitive. As I got up and started out the door she said, "Max. Be careful." And I did not give the warning a second thought until I got out on the deck and saw a kid standing on the trunk of a downed tree, staring at me from twenty yards away.

CHAPTER 21

he kid was skinny and awkward looking in a coltish way and his baseball cap was turned around backward on his head. His legs looked like sticks in a couple of denim bags and the long-sleeved shirt he was wearing draped on his shoulders as if on a hanger, the cuffs flapping down to his fingertips. He did not say a word. No "Howdy stranger." No "Yo, what up?" No "Wow, somebody survived." Nothing. Just a stare.

I stepped out toward the edge of the plank foundation and started to say something when a voice called out from my immediate left and the sound of another person's words caused an uncharacteristic startle that made my neck snap in the direction of the sound.

"Hey, mister. How you doin'?"

It was another young man, dressed the same as the other but missing the hat. He may have been older, his neck more filled out, shoulders carrying some meat. His hair was buzz cut and instantly reminded me of police trainee academy, or maybe one of those juvenile detention camps.

I started to say, "Hey, are we glad to see you," but I held my tongue, some taste of wariness stopping me. It did not take me more than a couple of seconds to realize that by their positions, I was being flanked.

"Well, guys, I could be better," I said instead and stopped my forward motion. In fact, I took a step back, not an obvious retreat, but at a slightly angled step so that it was not as difficult to see both of them at the same time with my peripheral vision. I wanted the move to come off as polite, not tactical.

"That was your airboat I heard," I said, not a question, a statement. A question can put you in a subservient position, like you want something, like you don't know as much as they know, like you're not in charge. A street cop does not ever want to be in a subservient position to people he does not know. I learned this years ago, dealing with pimps and pushers and just plain assholes on my beat sector of South Philly. They are lessons best not forgotten and suddenly they were boiling up in the back of my head like the prickly sensation on my neck.

"No. That would be my airboat you heard, friend."

The voice came from my right and behind, more disconcerting because I was more vulnerable and because the deep sound of it was older, more mature, more confident. I hid my startle this time and turned with, I hope, a normal, easygoing attitude.

This visitor was not wary. He planted his big palms on the deck, swung a leg up, and mounted the platform like a rodeo cowboy mounting a horse. He was athletic.

His forearms were cabled with muscle. He was not as tall as my own six-foot-three, but he was easily fifteen years younger, and even more disconcerting than his boys, he was smiling. A smiling stranger in the middle of the Glades after a major hurricane trashed the area. I did not trust any inch of him.

I turned my head to check any movement by the others and noted that they'd held their positions. The smiling man took one step closer and offered his hand, reaching out as though respecting my space. He was acting friendly. He was being careful.

"Bob Morris," he said in introduction and I reached out, holding my own spot, and took his hand.

"Max Freeman."

"Pleasure, Mr. Freeman," the man said, then looked out past me. "Come on in, boys, don't be rude. This here is Mr. Freeman."

I was checking the man's eyes. They were a gray so pale that they were almost colorless, and unflinching. His shirt was canvas and washed too many times. When he took my hand I noted that his own was soiled in cracks and under the fingernails and now I saw the smudges of dirt along the hard muscle of his neck tendons. He had been out for some time in this swamp, handling dirty things. The other two scrambled up onto the deck with less grace but still the kind of lithe comfort that you see in farm boys, or in this part of the country, young boat hands.

"We was kinda surprised when you came out, Mr. Freeman. Didn't expect to find nobody out here after that 'cane blew through," the man who called himself Morris said.

I offered nothing. Let him tell it. Let me get a sense of it. Sometimes silence encouraged them.

"We, uh, own our own camp just up the way to the northwest there toward Immokolee and were just out to see the damage and, you know, she was hit pretty bad," he continued.

I nodded knowingly. "It was one hell of a storm."

"Yep, she was."

Morris looked at the boys and they all nodded their heads in agreement that a hurricane that ripped down walls and sailed roofs away and flattened hundreds of acres of tough sawgrass was indeed a hell of a storm.

"So how'd you make out?" I said, matching the simplicity of their language, maybe leveling some playing ground here, trying to come off as nonthreatening. The boys cut their eyes to Morris.

"Oh, well, we got hit pretty good up there," he said. "Most we could do was a bit of salvaging, you know, a few things we probably shouldn't have left out there in the first place.

"So, you know. We figured since we was out, maybe we should stop on our way back south and see if any of our neighbors needed help. You're the first person we run in to. So, you OK, Mr. Freeman? Is there anything we can do?"

I thought of Sherry on the cot in the room behind me. Yeah, these guys seemed a little hinky. Their approach, seemingly surreptitious and planned, put me on edge. Their appearance, like a band of salvagers at sea, was not altogether unrealistic out here in the Glades. I'd spent time with some far-flung Gladesmen and to call them a rough bunch could be considered a kindness. When the Morris guy had turned to point where they'd left their airboat, I had studied the swing of his loose shirt and seen no lump or catch to indicate he was hiding a weapon in his waistband. And out here those willing to use a firearm were more proud to show them than to be sneaky about it. I checked each of their eyes one more time, not that I had a choice.

"Yeah, you could," I finally said to Morris. "I've got a friend inside who is badly hurt. She's got to get medical help as soon as possible."

They filed into the room behind me and I wasn't sure what look was on my face when Sherry watched me lead them in. She had forced herself up onto one elbow. Maybe she had been listening. Maybe she'd heard my reticent voice. She was faking alertness, I knew, because the glossiness in her eyes did not match the relative strength of her posture.

"This is Sherry Richards," I said. "We got knocked around quite a bit by the storm and she's broken her leg. It's a bad fracture and I'm not sure how much blood she's lost but we're going to have to get her to a hospital.

"Do you guys have a way to call in a rescue helicopter? They could probably get out here before it gets too dark."

Morris touched the bill of his baseball cap and stepped forward. "I am really sorry to see your pain, ma'am. We will surely do whatever we can do."

Morris could see behind Sherry's front of strained focus. He could tell she was hurting and stepped forward again, not enough to be pushy or in a way that could be taken as impolite, but seemingly out of concern. He let his eyes move from her face down to the heavily bandaged leg.

"Y'all think you'd be able to move, ma'am? If we could get to the boat, I mean. She's a bit of distance through the hardwood yonder."

Sherry was watching the man's eyes, just like I had, just like any cop, assessing, with whatever lucidity she had left.

"I'll do whatever I need to do, Mr., uh, Morris, was it?"

"Yes, ma'am," he said and then turned to me. "You see, Mr. Freeman, we done lost a lot of equipment over to our place. All our radio stuff was dunked wet and lost. And the only cell phone we got, we ain't had much luck with. Figure that the towers and all were probably knocked down by the storm."

He was looking past me at the boys when he said this, as if for confirmation. When I turned to see their reaction I caught one of them, the thicker one, looking at the metal door to the other half of the cabin. He could not have missed the electronic locking mechanism next to the frame and was perhaps puzzled by it.

"Well, sir. We do have some fresh water on board we

could bring in and we can take a look for anything we might use for some kind of a stretcher or something," Morris said. "Is there anything inside the other room there that you figure might help us on that account, Mr. Freeman?"

I hesitated, and then lied, not knowing for sure whether a guy like Morris was perceptive enough to recognize the hesitation.

"The door is locked up," I said, nodding to the obvious mechanism that none of them had missed by now. "So I'm not sure what's in there. And to be honest, with your boat we could probably be to the state park ramp in just over an hour so I'm not sure we're going to need anything more, Mr. Morris."

The man looked again straight into my eyes, a practice that by now was a little unnerving, and when he smiled that little faux-friendly, backwoods smile again I felt my fingers start to flex. The testosterone of fight or flight was leaking down into my fist from somewhere back in my brain.

"OK, then. Why don't we just go see what we can get from the airboat to see how we might get the missus out of here," Morris said pleasantly.

When all three of them moved toward the door, my first thought was that they would leave us. In a few minutes we would hear the engine start and they would pull out to continue on their way. They don't need us, we need them.

"How about if one of you stays to help me break down this other bed," I said. "You know, maybe we can use the frame as a gurney and all four of us could lift her through the trees."

They all stopped, the boys looking at Morris.

"Now there's some thinking, Mr. Freeman. Sure. Wayne, stay here and help with that idea. We'll go get some tools and whatnot from the boat and plan out a path. That just might work."

Again the smile, which also stopped the beginning of a protest from the one called Wayne.

"We'll be back directly," Morris said and then he and the other boy walked out. I heard them splash as they jumped down from the deck and all I could do was hope that they wouldn't look carefully under the foundation and notice the opening left by the trapdoor that I'd forgotten to close under the next room. As the sounds of their movement faded, I watched the sullen look on the kid's face deepen. He might have been wondering if he too was being left behind.

"So, Wayne," I said, reminding him that the older guy had already let his name out, a betrayal to some degree. "Let's see about using this bed as a trauma cot."

He looked over as I pulled the other bed frame out away from the wall.

"I tried to break it down some already," I said, pointing to the metal strapping where I'd removed my impromptu pry bar. "Maybe you can figure a better way. You look like you might be the mechanical one of your brothers."

"They ain't my brothers," Wayne said, bending to pull at one corner of the frame with his left hand.

"So, your name isn't Morris?"

"No. It ain't."

"You kind of look alike," I said, interviewing, and hoping it was not too obvious.

"No, we don't," the kid said.

I was guessing that he might be fifteen or sixteen, but on closer inspection, the barely discernible mustache he was trying to grow made me think he was possibly older, just a little behind in maturity. A follower? A simple ride-along? When I was still a cop in Philadelphia, I'd shot and killed a twelve-year-old tag-along who had joined one of his buddies for a late-night convenience store robbery. I'd been responding to an alarm and when the first guy out of the store took a shot at me, splitting the muscle and tendon in my neck, I returned fire and hit the second person out, a child who took the 9mm slug in the middle of the back. Just a boy, dead at the scene. It was the event that led to my resignation for medical reasons. It was the reason I'd come to South Florida to escape my inner-city dreams. Maybe it was part of the reason I was standing here, stuck to some natural destiny.

"Let's flip it over," I instructed. "It might be easier to disassemble these legs. It will be a lot easier to move that way." I started to turn my end and the movement forced the kid to expose his left hand for the first time. I'd noted his reluctance from the moment I'd seen him standing in the open, his shirtsleeves hanging down past his fingertips, his hand held slightly behind his hip. At first I'd thought—weapon. A handgun or even a knife. Now as he reached to twist the metal frame of the bed, I saw that he was missing his thumb. The scar told me it wasn't something that happened at birth. It was a definite injury and one he was careful about showing. I thought of the round, quarter-size scar of white tissue on my own neck where the bullet on the street had burrowed through. I had not caught myself reaching for it in quite some time. I'd lost the habit, if not the memory of killing a child.

Wayne got down on his knees to inspect the bolt system on the legs of the cot and then looked around.

"Y'all got any tools?"

I was right about his mechanical inclination.

"I had to bend the metal of that strap to get it off, just worked it until it broke," I said.

"Yeah, I seen that," Wayne said, like I'd pulled some third-grader stunt on the thing. He got up and I watched as he walked to the sink, now disregarding me. He went through a drawer and came out with some silverware—a spoon, a couple of butter knives with blades so dull they'd have a time cutting butter. I'd passed them all over on my earlier inspection.

"So none of you guys seem to be injured from the hurricane," I said, continuing my interview. "Your place must have held up pretty well."

"Yeah," he said, giving up nothing more. Not a storyteller.

I watched the kid set to the bolts, using the straight lengths of the two knife handles to pinch the metal nuts in parallel and then turn them. The fingers of his left hand worked in an odd but efficient manner, making up for the loss of his thumb. He'd adapted. Maybe this kid had never heard of the evolution of the opposable thumb that let man crawl out of swamps like this one a million years ago. Right now I was hoping for a little less sophistication in his perceptiveness.

"Mr. Morris said your camp was up to the northwest, so are you all from Belle Glade or Clewiston or what?" I said.

"Hell, no," the kid reacted, like I'd put him in some rival high school. He started to go on but thought better of it.

"How 'bout I loosen these up and you can finger twist 'em off, sir," he said instead, looking over at me before moving on to the next leg.

"Yeah, sure."

I changed positions with him and we worked together. The kid was either naturally closed-mouthed or savvy enough not to let loose any more information about himself and his buddies than he was forced to. His could be an attitude from too many times in the backseat of a police cruiser or in the local juvenile lockup, or a simple backwoods avoidance of people unlike himself. A perceptive kid would have noticed the difference in our clothing, my speech, even in the way I moved. I'd already done the same with this trio. I was leaning toward the supposition that they were Gladesmen, or closely descended from. Easy in the water. None of them carried a sweat in the humidity, meaning their bodies were used to the climate. Their boots were old leather, the kind that was oiled and waterproofed the old-fashioned way. They were all lean, the leader with a cabled musculature that meant tough manual labor and a diet that was more local and natural than the empty calorie, fat-filled urban or suburban fare. But my eye had been a lazy one too. I'd searched the kid over, looking for clues, and missed the biggest one.

Wayne took a few steps back after he loosened all the nuts and stood while I finished the job. I looked up a couple of times, continuing to ask questions that might give me more information to size his crew up, give me some clue why they were rattling my internal cop alarms. A couple of times I caught him looking down at Sherry, who had gone quiet. It was hard to read her pain now or tell how much her head was in the moment or moving deep into survival mode, concentrating only on the internal, on keeping her core together. From where I was I couldn't even see if her eyes were open. Not for a moment did I think of the kid's eyes roving over her body, the fabric of her sweats cut away almost up to her crotch when I'd cleaned and bandaged the leg wound. Her blouse, soaking wet and transparent, stretched across her breasts. Then she said something—"water"—in a rough whisper.

The kid jumped, and then started looking around.

"Over there. The bottle by the end of her cot," I said, directing him.

He stepped over and picked up the bottle and moved to Sherry's side. She turned her hand slightly, opened her palm and he had to bend over to get the bottle to her. But instead of taking it, she motioned to her mouth with her fingers and the kid bent lower, nervous about pouring the water into this woman's open lips. I stayed on one knee, watching, but still working the other bed's legs. All I could see were the tops of both of their heads from behind and then the sudden, violent movement of Sherry's hand, clawing at the boy's throat.

"You thieving little bastard," she suddenly shrieked in a voice I had never heard before.

The kid's head started to snap back, but inexplicably stopped for a fraction of a moment, and then, suddenly loosed, reeled up away from her.

"You fucking little thief," Sherry screamed again, the rough dryness of her throat making the words come out like a shovel blade stabbing gravel. "You picked the wrong cop to fuck with this time, you little shit."

The kid's eyes were wide as saucers, eyebrows dented by fear, like he'd seen a witch come alive in his face, and I jumped up wondering if he actually had.

"Jesus, Sherry!" I shouted, and stepped over the bed frame I was working on. "What the hell?"

She was up on her elbows now, her face turned a crimson color that was such a stark contrast to the paleness it replaced that it looked devilish. She was staring at the kid, her eyes focused and hateful. Without saying a word she opened the hand that I'd seen her go at the kid's throat with. Two stones, one a diamond and the other an opal, tumbled from her palm on the end of a broken gold chain.

It didn't take a second for me to recognize the necklace Sherry's husband had given her, the one that she had finally removed before the last time we'd made love on a soft Everglades night that seemed impossibly far in the past now.

I stepped toward the kid, not even realizing that I'd stood up from our dismantling job with one of the wooden bed frame legs in my fist.

"Where the hell did you get that!" I started. But the words had barely left my lips when the cabin door burst open and Morris stepped in with a big .45 in his right hand, its big black nosehole pointed at me.

"Whoa now, folks," the man said. "How about we just settle down some, OK?"

"They're cops, Buck," Wayne started shouting. "God-damnitall, they are cops."

Morris, whose name had now turned into Buck, moved his eyes from me, to the boy, to the bed frame on the floor and finally to Sherry, who was still on one elbow, but otherwise prone on the cot.

"Now just calm it down there, boy," he said and the kid seemed to snap his mouth shut like it was a command he was familiar with.

"Uh, Mr. Freeman, sir. Would you kindly lay that

there chunk of lumber down, please, and move over that way?" Buck said to me, using the muzzle of the gun to indicate the direction. He stepped farther into the room and the other boy, whose eyes were now only slightly smaller than his friend's, followed him, dropping a canvas sack holding something that clunked heavily onto the floorboards.

The fact that I now had two names, Wayne and Buck, wasn't much of a trade-off for having a handgun pointed at my chest and a band of thieves as Sherry's only chance of survival out of this hellhole. I laid the bedpost down.

"Now if you don't mind, sir," Buck said, "could you tell me just what the hell is goin' on?"

I gathered myself. I now knew I was looking at a crew of looters. I have seen it before as a cop in Philadelphia and everyone with a television has seen it on the tube following major rioting or disaster in American cities coast to coast. In some instances it's an "I'm gonna get mine" attitude. The storefront window is blown out, cops are busy helping others, I'll go in and take what I can take. In the aftermath of Katrina it was sometimes people just taking something that floated, something to eat, something to live. In places like Miami and L.A., it was just brazen, crowd-incited criminality and greed. I knew the only way Wayne had gotten Sherry's necklace was by rummaging through the ruins of the Snows' cabin where she must have lost it. This group had been there and this place was their next target.

I wasn't going to guess the motivation. Right now

I was going to be the greedy one and try to make the best of the situation for Sherry and myself.

"I don't know," I lied. "I think my friend just woke up and freaked or something. Your buddy here was giving her something to drink and she just woke up and started clawing at him. He got scared and jumped back when she started screaming and it surprised the hell out of me too."

Buck looked down at Sherry, who now collapsed off her elbow and was lying flat again with her eyes closed. I stepped over to her and went down on one knee and he let me. Wayne started to whine: "She said she was a cop, Buck. She ripped that necklace off me and said I stole it and she was a fucking cop."

I tipped the water bottle to Sherry's mouth and had to pour it through her parted lips just to get any of it in.

"That true, Mr. Freeman?" Buck said behind me. "She's a law enforcement officer?"

"She used to be," I said. "Long time ago up north somewhere. Some little town in Michigan but she re-tired down here years ago.

"Look, Morris," I said. "She's delirious. She's dehy-drated, lost blood, is in some deep pain and isn't mak-ing a whole lot of sense. I just need to get her some help, get her in to land, the state park boat ramp where we can get her to an ambulance.

"And," I added, "could you not point that gun at me? That's really uncalled for and it makes me nervous."

The guy looked out at the end of his arm, like he'd

forgotten he even had the .45 in his hand even though I knew from experience that particular weapon is heavy as hell. He lowered the gun and crooked his finger in a "come here" command to Wayne, and then bobbed his head to the other one.

"We're gonna step outside if you don't mind, Mr. Freeman," he said like he was asking permission. "So I can sort this out."

I nodded and all three of them stepped outside, but they left the door halfway open, the boys on the other side, and Buck with his gun hand still on my side, his head tipping back to check my movements every few seconds. I heard him say, "Goddamnit, boy," but the rest of the conversation was low and unintelligible with the heavy door in between. I checked Sherry again and she half opened her eyes, cutting them to the right like she was trying to locate the others. She wasn't as out of it as she'd appeared, but the color had run back out of her face and I had never seen her look so weak.

"He stole my necklace, Max," she whispered. "*My* necklace. Jimmy's necklace."

"Hush, hush, hush, baby. I know," I said quietly. "I know. But we have to get you out of here, Sherry. We need these guys now. We can worry about everything else later. Right now, we need them."

I was trying to keep my voice soft, understanding, appeasing because I was not sure how much she understood. I needed to calm her and I knew I was working against her nature. She was not the kind of woman who stands by when she feels violated, when someone has pissed her off. Even her subconscious was going to fall back on natural reaction if you push her.

"Don't let him take Jimmy's necklace, Max," she whispered, and the words stung me as much as they bolstered my resolve not to let her die.

CHAPTER 22

"Goddamnit, boy," Buck said, his gray eyes turned to ice, as hard and cold as either of them had ever seen. He was staring at Wayne but Marcus could feel the anger roll out over him as well. "What the fuck was goin' on in there?"

Buck took a second to look back around the door at the man and the lady on the cot. It was a second Wayne needed to gather his voice, lower his fear, and swallow some of his embarrassment so he would not bring more of it onto himself.

"She said she was a cop, man. She said it right to my face, Buck, and she wasn't talkin' about no back in the day either," he said, his voice quiet but direct. Direct enough for Buck to listen.

"Why?" he said.

The boy looked at him.

"What made her decide to tell you she was a cop?"

He hesitated.

"She wanted her necklace back," he said, just as quiet, just as direct.

Marcus let a rush of disgust escape through his teeth

and Wayne cut his eyes at him. It was Buck's turn to hesitate.

"You gonna fill me in on that one?" he said, aiming the question at either one of them.

"I found a diamond necklace at the last place. It was in one of them fanny pack–like things in that trashed-out room where we found the blood and I took it, you know, found booty like we said."

"And he was fucking wearing it around his neck like some kinda punk or something," Marcus said, and the two exchanged a glance that was almost as cold as the one Buck held for the both of them.

"She went for the necklace?" Buck said.

"Like a goddamn piranha," Wayne said. "I seen it in her eyes at the last second, man. She saw it and was pissed. I thought she was gonna take one of my eye-balls next."

Buck again peered around the door, and Marcus might have smiled at that one about the eye but for the deep shit they were already in.

"And that's when she said she was a cop?" Buck said, getting back to it. "After she ripped her own necklace off your neck?"

"Yeah," Wayne said. "Then she said, 'you messed with the wrong cop this time,' and she fucking meant it, Buck."

All three of them were quiet then, Buck thinking, the others waiting. Anxiety finally won out and Marcus said: "Let's just fucking go, man. Let's just get in the airboat and go. That lady ain't gonna last long out here the way she's hurt and that guy doesn't even know who the hell we are, Buck. We take off, chances are they both fucking die out here and that's that."

Wayne started nodding. Run. It had always worked before. Just run.

Buck looked down and shook his head, back and forth, twice, slowly.

"And if they don't, Marcus?" Buck said without looking up. "If either one of them gets rescued by some camp owner in a couple days, you think they won't look for a couple of shit-kicker Glades boys and a two-time ex-con with only one strike to go that been lootin' houses and left someone to die out here? Especially if that someone really is a cop."

Both boys were dumb with silence.

"And if the lady dies and that big guy gets so pissed he swims the hell out of here, they'll bring felony murder charges against all three of us. The court will say she died during the commission of a felony. That'll be your felony, Wayne, robbery of a fucking necklace," he said, pointing at the face of that dumbness. "And our theft."

From their openmouthed look, the boys were losing their stupefaction and focusing on the term "felony murder."

Buck again checked the other side of the door. He already didn't like guns and the effort of holding the big .45 in his hand seemed to have drained his energy. I got six rounds here, he thought. Maybe I should kill all four of them and wash my own self of it all. Goddamn it. Your daddy didn't teach you nothin', did he, boy.

When they stepped back in I could see the change. The raised .45 was held a little tighter. Buck's knuckles were white as he squeezed the grip. No more bluffing.

"I am truly sorry, Mr. Freeman," he said, and I almost jumped then at the words; only the thought of what they might do to Sherry caused the muscles in my legs and back to hold. They were curtain-closing words coming from a man with eyes that now seemed to see nothing but survival, and the look was one I recognized. I now had no doubt he was an ex-con, learned from the inside.

"I'm gonna have to ask you to move over there by the door, sir, and sit," he said waving the handgun.

"Wayne, you go on and get that roll of tape out of the bag there and strap Mr. Freeman up by the ankles and the wrists. Behind his back, boy."

Buck had obviously grown tired of the younger one's miscues. The identifying necklace should have never seen the light of day until some buyer somewhere was ready to remove the stones so it would be unrecognizable.

"Now whoa, whoa, hold on a minute," I said, trying to slow things down. "What the hell, fellas. You guys got something going on out here where you're just salvaging after the storm, we don't give a damn. Hell, we're not even owners of any property. We just got caught in the wrong place at the wrong time. Whatever you guys are doing, it's none of our business and it can stay that way."

The kid crossed my ankles and started strapping with a roll of waterproof packaging tape, the kind with a nylon filament running through it. Tough to tear, tougher to break. He seemed pissed now, taking out the anger that he wanted to direct at someone else onto the job at hand. I'd be lucky to still feel my toes in an hour.

"Hands behind your back," he said, like he'd heard it on an old movie. But when I hesitated Buck cocked the big hammer on the pistol and I pressed my lips into a line and followed the order. The kid did the same angry trick on my hands, though I was ready and turned my knuckles in, forcing the tendons on the inside of my wrists to bulge as much as my strength could pop them. It would give me some room when I relaxed. I hoped it would be a voluntary relaxation and not because my brain matter was all over the wall behind me.

As much as the binding hurt it was nothing compared with having to watch the other little shithead do the same thing to Sherry.

Wayne finished with me and then started to toss the roll to his friend who was too busy staring down at Sherry's crotch to notice.

"Yo, Marcus," the kid said, fucking up again, using his buddy's name, not that it mattered anymore.

Marcus caught the tape roll and started wrapping Sherry's ankles to the posts of the cot. She whined once when he pulled her broken leg over to strap it and I felt angry tears come into my eyes. Retribution had not been part of me as a street cop. The only person I'd ever wished death on was my own alcoholic father who almost nightly dumped his badge and revolver on the kitchen table before he started smacking my mother around with an open hand. But as I watched this kid pull Sherry's arms up and bind them and then run his fingertips down her now unprotected chest and over her breasts, he became number two.

"Get the fuck over here," Buck snapped at the kid. He picked up the canvas bag by the bottom corner and let several metal tools spill out onto the floor: a stout iron crowbar, two different-sized screwdrivers, and a pair of vise grips, a claw hammer, and small axe.

"I seen by the markings on that door, you already tried to get into the other room there, Mr. Freeman," he said without looking at me. "But maybe you just didn't have the right tools with you, huh?"

He stepped over for a closer look at the door and the electronic locking device.

"But scootch on over out of the way there, sir. I have had some practical learning on how to get in and out of places folks don't want you to get in or out of."

I slid myself down the wall and didn't say a word about the hatchway under the room that I'd left wide open in my haste to meet these assholes. I was trying to decide if we were better off biding our time, hoping against hope that the two immature hicks would continue to fuck up somehow and give me an opening, or should I just tell Buck about the entry, let them loot whatever they wanted from the room and maybe he'd be satisfied and leave. The other possibility I was not yet ready to confront: that he'd simply kill us both and leave it to whomever stumbled onto our rotting bodies in a few days or weeks to piece it together. Hell, maybe he'd just kill us and haul our corpses onto his airboat deeper into the swamp to dump and let nature break us down. There are no small number of bodies dumped in the Everglades where all manner of forensic evidence is consumed by everything from alligators and wild boar right down to the billions of heat- and waterborne microbes. Sherry and I had both investigated some of those homicides. A chunk of dead biology doesn't last long in this soup. We'd be on a missing persons report. Lost in the storm. A couple years after Katrina there are still folks missing from New Orleans, and we weren't anywhere close to a city.

I was working on the scenarios, rolling them around in my head, when Buck took the crowbar to the door-jamb, gouging with a sharp edge at the outside of the frame, maybe figuring like a cheap thief he could bust a hole and then reach through and simply turn the lock button from the other side. The other two stood and watched, waiting like dutiful, anxious apprentices for the foreman to sic them to task.

"Know what the problem is with people like you, Mr. Freeman, who come out here in the Glades to take what you want whether it's the fish or the game or even the fresh water for yourselves and leave nothin' but garbage and trash behind?" Buck said while he pried at a corner.

I did not answer, sure that he would do so for me.

"Y'all think you're entitled, you know? You think that just because this is open country and it don't look like what you have in the cities on the coast, that it's free and clear to just take and do what you want with. Build what you want in it. Come out here and piss in it and then go on home.

"You know, my daddy and his daddy before him spent lifetimes living out here, taking what was natural and right and working their asses off and they didn't do it for riches, Mr. Freeman. They done it for survival and they done it for their families and really all they ever wanted was to be left alone and left to it."

The one called Wayne shifted his weight; the axe was now in his hand, hanging by his side like he was itching to do damage with it. The other one, Marcus, was still sneaking looks at Sherry, who was silent now but I kept watching her, the rise and fall of her chest, and it was slight but steady. Both of the boys looked bored, scratching at their dirty necks like they'd heard this speech before and had little interest in it. It was getting dimmer in the room, the light now slanting through the doorway that they'd left open, the window to the east gone dark in shadow.

I had held my tongue but decided to take a chance.

"I don't disagree with you, Buck," I said, purposely using his first name, and it caused a flicker in his eyes.

"I know a man, actually someone I would call a friend, who lived the same kind of life your own family did. I've heard him talk the same way many times. The name is Brown. Nate Brown. Maybe you've heard of him?"

The use of Brown's name caused all three to stop moving. They may have even stopped breathing for a second. The boys looked at each other. Buck stood stock-still, staring at the end of the crowbar.

"Go on outside," Buck finally barked. "Find a damn window to get through or somethin'." The boys picked up the tools from the floor and left.

Buck set the crowbar aside and bent down on his haunches to look me in the face, sitting on his heels in the way of farmers and country folks who work the dirt but refuse to sit in it. He adjusted the .45 in his belt, the grip exposed and handy.

"So, Mr. Freeman. You heard about the legend of Mr. Brown from some drunk fisherman or somethin' and now you say you know him and me? Is that it?"

I'd actually met Nate Brown during my first year in my shack. I had found the body of a child on my river who had been one of a string of abductions and murders of children from suburban homes. Brown had helped me to find the madman responsible and remove that stain from those he considered his people. I admired the old guy and his quiet ethics. But this man was nothing like him.

"I said I know Nate. I never said I know you, Mr. Morris. I said I'd heard Nate talk about the same things you just did but I'm pretty sure I wouldn't run into Nate Brown out here looting other people's properties after a storm just for leftovers."

Buck's eyes took on an internal look, glassed over like he was seeing something in his own head that needed to be studied. The anger I expected didn't come. Or the denial.

"If you know Nate Brown, Mr. Freeman, then you know he is a man who did what he had to do in his time. And it wasn't all legal then neither. The Gladesmen do what they have to do."

"Buck," I said, "I know Nate as a man who holds his own ethics in high esteem. I think he does the right thing, for the people he represents and their way of living out here. Maybe you've got some of that in you."

I was trying to work an angle, pry at whatever relationship this young man had with Brown and the generation of Gladesmen before him. He stayed silent.

"Maybe Nate would be salvaging. Maybe he'd be doing what he had to do to survive," I offered. "But he wouldn't be hurting innocent people. He wouldn't be turning his back on someone who needed his help."

Buck stood up and now he was looking down on me. He was still working it in his head. He was being careful. Thinking things out. But there was a tension now in the guy's eyes and I could see his hand flexing on the handle of the .45.

"Times change," he finally said, turning toward

the door. "You might do some ponderin' on time, sir. 'Cause you might not have a whole lot of it left."

When he walked out the door he closed it and then, with substantial force, jammed the blade end of the crowbar into the space between the bottom of the door and the flooring planks, effectively locking it.

CHAPTER 23

As soon as I heard Buck's footsteps leave the deck I started crawling up the wall, shoulder and head pressing hard against the panel, pushing hard off my heels to gain an angle, then working it like a big old inchworm, a foot at a time until I was able to get my feet under me, and then stand. I was breathing hard. There was no doubt a raw abrasion now on the side of my forehead and my ear burned from the scraping pressure. Tough shit. I stood in silence and now nearly in darkness. When Buck closed and locked the door the only sunlight that sneaked in was from the northside window. I listened for movement outside and was just about to move when I heard the *CHUNK!* sound of the axe blade against the south wall. The boys were probably trying to chop their way through a window and I knew that it would be a few minutes before they uncovered the fiberglass skin that wrapped the room next door. It would puzzle them for a bit, but I wasn't sure it would stop them. As the noise and the steady blows increased, I used the cover to jump on the ball of one foot to the refrigerator, steady myself and crouch. Twisting my wrists, I got my freed fingers around the handle and pulled the fridge door open at the same time as I rolled to the floor on one shoulder. I didn't give a damn how awkward I was. I had one goal in mind.

Scuffing back over on my hip I was able to position myself with my back to the opening and then flex my arms into it and use my fingers to search the low corner of the fridge. My trick with the tendons had given me a fraction of space under my taped wrists to work with and the effort to get over here alone had loosened it even more. It took some repositioning, some sweat running down into my eyes, but my fingers found the bottle of water and the rest of the wrapped chocolate I'd left there. The boys either missed it or didn't care enough even to check it out. Anything without value to them was considered useless. But Sherry needed water and she needed some form of energy to keep her brain synapses from shutting down further. I snagged the bottle and chocolate and cupped them in my fingers and then rolled, shoulder to shoulder, to reach her side.

"Sherry," I said. Trying to whisper, but in the empty room my voice still sounded loud. When the chopping began again I hissed hard.

"Sherry. Come on, baby. Wake up! You gotta drink, baby. You need the water."

I rolled to my knees and again, using a shoulder for leverage, I got a hip up onto the bedside and then straightened to a sitting position.

"Sherry!" This time I spoke in a full hard voice and luck was with me. At the same moment, the sound of a splitting piece of wood vibrated through the shack and then in the silence that followed whatever progress they'd made outside I heard my name next to me.

"Max," Sherry said, though I did not recognize the awful timbre of her wounded voice. "Max. Don't let him kill you too. Don't let that little bastard take you away from me."

I looked down from over my shoulder and her face was barely visible in the dark but what light there was caught the tear on her cheek. She was hallucinating, confusing one of the boys here with the teenager who killed her husband. But she'd somehow slipped me into the muddled equation.

"I won't, baby. No one's going to take me away, Sherry. But you have to eat, honey. You need to get strong."

While I talked, I used my free fingers behind me to unwrap the chocolate and then looked over my shoulder and moved it to her mouth. I rubbed it against her lips and then sighed when I felt her tug at it. The busyness outside continued but even if one of the crew came back in now I didn't care. When Sherry stopped nibbling I went down and retrieved the water bottle and tipped it onto her lips. Most of the water ran down over her chin and neck but I could hear swallows and just the sound of it made my own throat cooler. With my hands tied it took a few minutes, hell, maybe more than a few, before I heard her say, "More." Again I gave her the chocolate first, then the water, and the pull was stronger and the swallows more full.

"She dead?"

It was the first thing Buck said after someone kicked away the pry bar and all three walked in. His flashlight beam had swung first to the wall where I'd been and then to Sherry where I now crouched. I had to turn my face away from the brightness and I could tell through the open door that it had gone full dark outside. The boys were carrying a big cooler and an old Coleman lantern and set them down in front of the makeshift kitchen counter.

"No. Not yet," I said. "And if she does die, you boys move up the line from simple looters to murderers. That's going to look real nice on your résumé up at Raiford, Buck."

The young ones snickered. They'd gained some bravado since they'd been outside, hacking at the windows of the next room, maybe even gaining entrance. More likely, though, they'd realized how isolated we all were. If a tree falls in the woods with no one to hear it, does it make a sound? I heard one of them pumping the lantern and then the flash of a match. Wayne lit the mantle and turned up the gas and the throaty, hissing noise was accompanied by a brightening glow that nearly filled the small room.

Unexpectedly, Buck stepped over to me and grabbed a fistful of my shirt over the shoulders and with a strength that surprised me he used his leverage to yank me halfway up and then drag-toss me to the western wall. I rolled over once and tumbled into the electronically locked door. Without a word he then pulled Sherry's bed out away from the wall and positioned himself at the foot and shoved it across the plank floor until the head of it banged against the wall beside me.

"There you go, Freeman. Take care of your woman over there," he said. No more "mister," no more "sir." Buck had turned mean. The boys looked a bit shocked at the sudden outburst, but then those subtle, that's-what-I'm-talkin'-about grins came to their faces. Tough guys now. All three of them.

"All right," I said, wincing at the sting of the new abrasion where my face had met the floor. "Cut my hands loose and give me that first aid kit so I can change her bandages."

Buck stared at me for a moment. The light was behind him, his eyes in shadow and too obscured for me to see what was in them. Then he reached into his back pocket and came out with a knife in his hand. He flicked open the blade with his thumb and a snap of his wrist and then motioned to the one called Marcus to take it.

"Cut loose his hands," he said. When the boy hesitated, he turned on him. "I ain't repeatin' myself to you little fuckers again. That shit's done. You do what I say, when I say!"

The boy took the knife and stepped over to me, bent behind me and sawed through the tape between my wrists. At the same time Buck picked up the first aid kit off the counter and tossed it across the room at me.

"I ain't decided whether the two of you are gonna live or die tonight," he said and it was a statement of authority, not indecision. "So you keep her goin' if you can."

Then he turned his back on me and pulled one of the two chairs over and sat down. "Let's eat, boys."

I turned my attention to Sherry. She had not uttered a sound when Buck shoved the bed across the room and her eyes were closed now. I massaged my hands and fingers, getting the blood back into them, and bent so my lips were to her ear.

"I'm going to change your bandage, Sherry," I whispered. "I know it's going to hurt. But it's got to be done."

Out of the corner of my eye I saw her tighten her eyelids. She was conscious and at least partially alert. With my fingernails I went to work on the tape that held the splint and then started to unwrap the gauze. I had to pull her hip toward me to unroll the bandages. Under two layers it was stained with blood. The third time I rolled her hip toward me she opened her eyes and deliberately cut them down toward her side. I thought at first it was a gesture of pain but when she furrowed her brow and did it again I followed her sight line. Under her back I saw the wooden handle of my knife. I'd laid it next to her when I first changed her bandage and she'd been lying on top of it ever since. Buck and his crew had come in to this friendly, with no reason to search us for weapons or consider us a threat. Things had changed, but their mistakes hadn't. I glanced over at the trio but they were intent on their food from the cooler. I slipped my hand under Sherry and gripped the razor-sharp knife. Now I was armed.

I continued working on Sherry's wound. The last layer of gauze was sticking to her leg from the dried blood at the edges. I poured some of the isopropyl alcohol over it to loosen the catches, tugged at it again, and she winced with pain.

"Sorry."

She squeezed her eyes tight again in answer.

Exposed, the flap that had ripped out when the broken bone ruptured through her skin was red and there was a circle around it that was also starting to flame. Infection. But it was impossible to tell how deep. I washed my index finger and thumb with the alcohol and then pulled the flap up. Sherry sucked air through her teeth.

"Careful over there, doc," Marcus said and then sniggered.

Even the boys were growing bolder. That too would be to my advantage. I did not respond. I took the tube of Neosporin from the first aid kit and again squirted the antibiotic cream into the wound. I used the last roll of gauze to rewrap the wound and then taped it in place. Shuffling down to the end of the bed, I checked Sherry's foot. It was cold to the touch and even in the indirect light from the lantern I could see her toes had gone pale. Circulation was going bad. The rest of the leg seemed swollen. She'd never be able to stand on it. We weren't going to be running anywhere. By the time I finished I was drenched with sweat. A trickle ran down the space between my shoulder blades, no doubt leaving a path through the grime I could feel now like a second skin.

I checked over my shoulder and the crew was paying no attention to me. They'd started eating whatever they brought in the cooler and seemed confident that I was not much of a risk, though I could still see part of the handle of the .45 protruding out of Buck's waistband. While the suck and smack of their eating noises continued, I spun around into a sitting position and used what was left of the medical tape to strap my unsheathed knife to my calf. I pulled my pants leg over it and then shimmied back to the wall and pressed my back against the locked door. Logistics was now my problem and I rolled the new scenario around in my head like a rough stone, nicking at the bumps and fractures and fissures, trying to smooth it so I would have some kind of a plan that might give us a chance.

Would I be fast enough to cut the bindings on my ankles, make it across the room, get my knife into Buck's neck, and then handle the boys before they could react? How quick was the Gladesman? He'd already shown his physical ability by tossing me across the room when he'd caught me unaware. But this time I'd be the one with the surprise. Would the young ones freeze up? Or were they seasoned enough to not panic and use their own blades? I looked up from under my eyebrows. Buck was hunched over in the chair, licking his fingers, and cut a look over at me. He was not relaxing; he was doing the same thing I was, working at his next move. They were waiting for something and I was sure he was the only with an idea of what that would be.

"Take a can of those peaches we found over to Mr. Freeman," he said to the boys without designating which one. The idiots looked at each other.

Wayne finally rose from his position on the floor. He bent and picked up a can and then used the knife from his belt sheath to stab through the tin and cut open the top. He looked over at me and hesitated.

"Should I tie his hands up first?"

"Only if you want to feed him yourself," Buck said, a touch of condescension in his voice that made the other one smile.

Wayne brought the can over to me and set it down on the floor a foot or so from my bound ankles.

"Can you get me a fork?" I asked.

"Yeah, right," the kid said. "Somethin' nice and sharp." He turned and walked away.

I stretched out and took the can and then shuffled on my knees to Sherry's bedside and then with my fingers I gently fed a peach slice to her. At the taste of the sweet juice her lips parted like a weak fish and she suckled at it at first and then slightly opened her eyes and took the whole thing into her mouth. I waited for her to chew and swallow and then gave her another.

"You're a cop too, ain't you, Freeman?"

Buck was speaking, but I did not turn my eyes from Sherry's.

"You've got the look. That confidence thing like cops and prison guards got. I seen plenty of it over the years."

While Sherry ate I swallowed a couple of the peach slices myself. I had not eaten anything but a small piece of the chocolate in more than twenty-four hours and was thinking of my own strength.

"I think Wayne here was right about what he heard when the lady said she was a cop. And I think you're one too. You ain't called her your wife or your honey or your *fiancée*."

I fed another slice to Sherry and one to myself. I was listening, just as Buck had obviously been doing. I may have underestimated him and that was a bad sign.

"What I think, *Officer* Freeman, is that she's your partner," Buck said. "You all might have been stupid enough to be out here in the Glades during a hurricane, but I don't believe that it was for no reason."

He paused again, maybe letting his thoughts catch up with him. It reminded me of the long, southern drawl used by Nate Brown, who never hurried his speech, but never said much that was just filler either. I found myself wondering whether they lived in the same area of southwest Collier County.

"No, officer. I think you all know exactly what's in that fucking room next door and that's the reason you're out here," Buck said. "Nobody builds a bunker like that out in these parts without having something damn valuable to store inside. And the fact that we got two cops out here trying to get into it makes me believe that there are drugs involved. Bricks of cocaine? Bundles of pot? Stuff got air-dropped into the Glades and then pulled out by some group of dealers who are smart enough to store it out here until they got a buyer on the coast that can move it fast."

Again he took that pause, and when I looked up his face was in shadows but the light was on those of his young crew and they were more hang-mouth stunned than I was.

"No shit! Buck," Marcus said, a smile beginning to build in his eyes.

"Whoa," was all Wayne could say and if Buck's scenario hadn't included a couple of law enforcement officers, one near death and one tied up in the corner, the two of them would have high-fived each other.

Still I didn't react. I had to give Buck some credit. If I hadn't already been inside the computer room next door, seen the digital readouts and odd collection of cables and wiring, the tale he was spinning might have made perfect sense to me too.

"So whataya say, Officer Freeman? Am I right? You and your partner there doing a little recon work and got stuck in the storm?"

This time I kept my eyes focused on the dark circles where Buck's eyes could still not be seen in the shadow, but I knew he could see mine.

"No. You're one hundred percent wrong," I said. It

was an easy line to say convincingly because it was the truth.

That childish hissing noise came from one of the boys behind him.

"Yeah, right."

"Well, it don't matter what you say now, officer. I'm thinking we got a big payday coming and when daybreak comes so we can find a way into that room, that's what we're gonna do come hell or high water," he said and tossed Marcus the roll of tape.

"Tape his hands back up," he said to the boy.

Marcus came over, swaggering a little now, and gave me a little chin nod, and I reacted instantly by crossing my wrists and offering them up to him.

"So you ain't such big shit after all, Mr. Law," Marcus said, wrapping the tape around while I again flexed my tendons to keep the binding as loose as possible. But I had already won my battle. The kid had either been too cocky or was just plain stupid. Because I had submissively raised my hands to him, he'd taken the easy offer and bound them in front of me instead of making me roll over and taping them behind my back.

"An' Wayne!" Buck said, snapping orders to the other one and reaching down to pick up a package sheathed in oilskin that they'd brought in with the cooler. He unwrapped a gleaming over-and-under shotgun and tossed it three feet into Wayne's surprised hands. "You got first watch."

CHAPTER 24

When the traffic lights are lying on the ground, you consider the intersections as four-way stops, and then steer around the dented and broken yellow thing in the road, and then avoid the power lines still attached to it if possible. It's one of those rules you learn in South Florida if you've been here for a few hurricanes.

As Harmon made his way to the Fort Lauderdale Executive Airport at dawn, he wondered why folks couldn't figure that out. Do all transplanted New Yorkers just figure, "What the fuck, I'll just plow right on through and everybody else can look out for me because only the rude and pushy survive in this world"?

Electricity was still a memory two days after Simone rolled through. Even the concrete poles were leaning like a team of tug-of-war combatants, pulling lines that had yet to snap. Many of their wooden brothers had lost it at the waist, sheared off and splintered at their middle, broken marionettes tangled in their own string. City and county road crews had shoved most of the large branches and debris off to the side of the major highways, but any side street was a maze like those games the kids used to draw while they waited for food at Denny's: get the farmer to market without being stopped!

Harmon had already steered around a hundred broken roof tiles lying in the streets of his own neighborhood, had driven up into some guy's yard to get around a forty-foot ficus tree that completely spanned two-lane Royal Palm Drive, and slipped between the crossing arms at the FEC railroad tracks at Dixie Highway, which were halfway down, their ends sheared off but still waving in the wind.

He stopped again at the intersection of Commercial and Powerline Roads and watched the headlamps of six vehicles slide through, cutting him out of his turn until he was forced to inch out and physically stop cross traffic before they'd defer to him.

"Go back to Brooklyn," he whispered under his breath.

When he finally got to the airfield, the early sunrise was backlighting a dozen lumps of dark plane wreckage, twisted angles and barely discernible fin shapes. He shook his head at the number of tumbled aircraft that had been strapped down out on the tarmac for lack of an indoor hangar to park them. Some appeared to have simply folded in on themselves, fuselages crushed in the middle like broken spines. Others sat upright but their wings were missing, picked off and discarded like a mean kid might do to a giant dragonfly. There was little activity on the south side of the airfield so Harmon broke all normal driving rules and made a beeline across the tarmac to the Fleet Company hangar. He could see Squires's Jeep sitting next to the open bay doors, and before he got to park, his partner and another big man appeared, moving slowly out of the huge building and putting their backs into the task of wheeling a helicopter onto the airfield. Harmon pulled up next to the black Wrangler and sorted through his ops bag; let them do the heavy work, he wasn't in the mood for heavy work today.

Again he checked off the list in his head as he touched each item in his bag. He stopped at the frequency transmitter. He'd used them before to electronically restart the power systems on ocean oil rigs. You needed lights to land and the frequency could switch them on and unlock doors before you even touched down. And then his fingers settled on the slick skin of a brick of incendiary C-4 explosive.

This was not standard equipment in the states and the order to take it along was unnerving to Harmon. In domestic work he and Squires were a security team, not a demolition unit. Yeah, they might have had to muscle some rig workers in the past. And yeah, they did have to entice the manager of one gas operation to confess to his paper swindling with the help of a gun muzzle pressed to his forehead. But the idea of blowing up and melting infrastructure on home soil was a new twist for Harmon. He knew ATF guys. He knew how good their bomb investigators were. If they were put on the site after a suspicious explosion they were bound to find something.

But Crandall's instructions had been pretty clear. He was the boss. "If the place looks compromised, like anyone has been on the site and might expose its purpose or existence, fire it off the planet."

The orders had set Harmon's senses buzzing. There was something here unknown to him and that always got him going. What was going on inside the United States that the company would be willing to take a chance and incinerate a site? Won't know until I get there, he had finally determined. But you bet I'm not blowing anything until I know what I'm blowing. Harmon zipped up the bag and got out, locked the doors of his Crown Victoria, and crossed over to where the men were loading the aircraft.

"Morning, chief," Squires said to him. They shook hands as usual, and as usual Harmon visually checked his partner's eyes for broken blood vessels and dilated pupils or any other sign that might indicate he was not completely sober or was too hungover to perform his duty, which basically was to protect Harmon's ass. And as usual, Squires showed absolutely no sign of impairment. The man was a physical wonder work. He was dressed in his black cargo pants and a black T-shirt, a plain baseball cap on his head that only seemed odd because of the absence of a logo. He looked like a SWAT team member and you wouldn't be far off to describe him as such. Harmon on the other hand had refused to revert back to a time of what he sometimes called his ill-spent youth. He had dressed that morning in a pair of blue jeans and a knit polo shirt, same as always. The night before he had fueled the generator system of his home and started the emergency power system. His was the only house on his block that had shown light through its windows after dusk. He had kissed his wife this morning on the cheek when he left. He'd told her that he would be home before nightfall. She always knew that his promise was contingent on many factors, factors she never bothered to ask about. She had been with him for many years. She was his wife when he was still in the military and still bore his children. When he got out and started working clandestine missions she knew too what his nature was and that it would never change. There was a need inside him, maybe a pride in doing what he did and what he considered to be his only talent and calling. She knew. But they did not speak of it. It seemed as though both of them were more comfortable in the guise that he was a simple businessman off to work on unusual but routine projects. Her response that morning was the same as it had always been: come back safe.

"This here is Fred Rae. He'll be your captain today," Squires started with that singsong delivery every flight attendant has memorized. "Please stow all your carry-on luggage in the bins above or in the space provided under your seat. As we will have a full flight today . . ."

The chopper pilot took Harmon's hand but was looking past his shoulder at Squires with a quizzical look.

"Don't mind him," Harmon said. "He loves the smell of napalm in the morning."

An accepting smile crossed the guy's face. He shook his head slightly and turned to continue his preflight check. Harmon and Squires huddled.

"OK, sarge," Squires started, always pulling out the military speak when he was moving on an operation. "We got any objective here or you going to continue to keep that to yourself until we get dropped in on this mystery zone?"

Harmon looked at his partner. Always a hard guy to keep anything from.

"Dropped in?" he said.

"I saw the fast rope bags already loaded in the air frame."

"Yeah? Well, all we have is a quick turnaround. Crandall's orders are to fly out to these coordinates in the near Everglades, some kind of a research facility, zip down to the station because there's no place to land the chopper. Then we check out any damage the storm might have done, make sure it can be powered up by the remote, take some pictures, and then call back the chopper to lift us out. Few hours, tops."

Squires let the info roll around in his head, maybe comparing it with earlier assignments, maybe with the memories in his head of ops in his vast military background. He pursed his lips. Nodded his head.

"I fucking smell something, chief," he finally said. "And it ain't kosher."

Harmon looked away. His partner was already suspicious and he hadn't even mentioned the C-4.

"You don't even know what kosher means, Squires,"

Harmon finally replied, picking up his bag and hefting it into the helicopter.

"Means legal."

"Like we haven't done anything illegal?"

Squires fixed a nonjudgmental gaze on him.

"Not this close to home."

On the pilot's signal both men climbed up into the cockpit, Squires riding shotgun in the rear seat, and they clamped radio headsets over their ears as the whine of the single engine slowly increased and the blades began spinning to action. There were no other active aircraft on the field that Squires could see. When they started to rise in the gray sky they swung immediately to the west, the rising sun at their backs, and below the most obvious destruction of the now finished storm was in the dumped airplanes and scattered trash of trees and the patchy scabs of rooftops where orange barrel tiles had been stripped away. A hangar near the end of the runway was caved in, as if it had been chopped at the middle of its roof peak by the edge of a giant hand.

"Mr. Rae," Harmon said into the mouthpiece, his voice sounding with an electronic crackle, "can we travel at a higher altitude, please. I really don't need to see this all again."

CHAPTER 25

I had willed myself to stay awake, aided by the buzz of mosquitoes and the self-appointed task of keeping them from landing for a blood feast on Sherry's skin. On the other side of the room it was Marcus whose turn it was to sit watch. He was in the wooden, straight-back chair, the iPod wires flowing out of his ears and the shotgun lying across his thighs. On occasion he would start bobbing his head to a tune I couldn't hear and close his eyes but I had to hand it to both boys: whether it was fear of what Buck might do if he found them asleep or if they were simply used to a late-night existence, neither of them nodded out. Whenever the sound of animal movement, or of a scraping across the floor by me or their napping crew-mates, both sentries' reactions were swift and fully alert. So much for sneaking out the blade strapped on my ankle and easing over to cut someone's throat and gain control of that gun. It only happens in the movies that way. In real life I would have to wait for a mistake, a surprise that might come from an outside source, a prayer answered from someplace else.

Long ago I had dribbled the last of the canned peach juice into Sherry's mouth and with the back of my hand felt the heat coming off her forehead and neck. I conceded that my ability to gauge might be diminished, but I convinced myself that the fever had gone down with the liquids and the food. She had opened her eyes several times, though it was hard to read how reactive they were in the dim light of the Coleman lantern.

I was also trying to gauge what time it was, waiting for the sunrise. With the knife strapped to my calf I'd got more than I could have hoped for. I could cut the bindings on my ankles quickly enough. Then I'd hold the blade with my insteps and slice through the tape on my wrists with a single stroke. Then it would be hand-to-hand combat against three—at least two of them armed and who knows what the other kid brought back with him from the airboat. I'd spent most of the silent night flexing my fingers, keeping up the blood flow and working the scenes in my head, how I would move, the advantage of my height and length, the possibilities of when, but not where. I couldn't wait any longer. I'd have to take my chances here, in this small room where their movement would be confined. I'd need the shotgun first. It was a vicious thing at close range, but in this tight space the shot pattern wouldn't have time to spread out. Whatever it hit would be a shredded mess. The exact timing, though, was impossible to plan. I'd need to wait for sunrise because even if we were lucky, even if I neutralized all three, there was no way I could find the airboat in the dark. That was my reasoning, but I was still asking myself why they had waited this long. They could have blown a hole in a window of the other room with that shotgun alone and then torn their way through the internal skin. Even if Buck had convinced himself that the room was filled with narcotics, wouldn't he have taken a chance of unloading it at night with flashlights rather than wait until morning when they'd be operating in the open? Maybe they'd grown cocky, working out here where they knew the territory, where they knew the water routes and the range of boats and sounds of intruders. Maybe they thought they were invincible.

My own head work was draining my energy. It had to be close to sunup. I closed my eyes and might have even dozed off because when I woke, all my planning of the night before went down the tubes. Circumstances out of my control forced my hand, and like every good special op gone funky, you sometimes do best by saying "fuck it" and adapting on the fly.

From the reaction, all of us heard the sound of the chopper blades at the same time.

My eyes snapped open; my fingers, numb from the loss of blood and movement, had that tingling sensation in them that makes you want to yelp, then they almost involuntarily went down to my pant leg where the knife was hidden.

Across the room the kid, Marcus, stood up with the shotgun, the wooden legs of the chair scraping across the plank floor. When I focused, Buck had changed

positions from when I last checked him. He had been
sleeping, stretched out next to the lamp, but was now
sitting with his back against the wall, eyes fixed on the
light. Wayne just rolled over on one elbow and said:
"Huh?"

"It's a helicopter," Buck said. His voice not anxious
or even surprised. "Small one by the sound."

Marcus moved toward the door and his buddy
quickly got to one knee and, uneasily, still unsteady
from sleep, followed him. I was thinking, "Now! While
they're distracted," but when I glanced back to Buck he
was pointing the .45 directly at me.

"That's all right, officer," he said. "Don't bother getting up; we'll check it out."

The boys stopped at the door, Marcus now with his
hand on the knob.

"Cops, you think?" he said back at Buck, who was
now on his feet. He did not have to shake the stiffness
out of his joints. He was moving sleekly, like a cat that
had already stretched.

"Maybe a rescue chopper," Wayne tossed in. "You
know, hurricane relief stuff."

"And maybe the fucking dope dealers just swing-
ing by to see if their stash is still here or blown over
hell's half acre by the storm," Buck said, approaching
the door and causing Marcus to pull his hand back
away from the knob. He then turned to me, showing
the nose of the pistol. "Or maybe the boy is right, Officer Freeman. Maybe you got some friends out there
after all."

No one moved for a handful of seconds, listening to the woofing sound of the blades, the volume increasing and then slightly beginning to fade.

"Well, boys. That's his first pass," Buck said. "Let's wait while he goes out to bank a turn back around and then go eyeball 'em."

They waited ten more seconds and then Buck nudged Marcus, and the boy opened the door, letting the other two out first. His mistake.

"You watch Freeman," I heard Buck say. "And stay the hell under the overhang." I then heard the thumping of footsteps on the deck, maybe a splash of someone jumping into the water. Marcus stood just outside, his hand wrapped around the door keeping it half open as he peered out. I was thinking I'd lost my chance at the shotgun, but would I even need it? If it was a police chopper, Buck and his crew might run. If it was rescue, maybe they'd wave it off. I listened to the aircraft sounds start to build again, coming back. Marcus looked inside to check on me and his face was anxious but void of any new recognition. The chopper now sounded like it was hovering and the kid stepped out again, pulling the door nearly closed with him. I couldn't afford to hesitate again.

I pulled my pants leg up and secured the knife taped to my calf, and in a quick and silent slice I freed my ankles. Without hesitation I then squeezed the handle between my boot soles, looped my wrists over the blade, and pulled through once. The edge was so sharp it flowed through the tape like paper. I rolled to my knees, eyes on the door, and stood, but that tingle, that electric shock of muscles gone to sleep and suddenly called upon, zinged through my right leg and it buckled. I went down to one knee but the fall was not nearly as startling as the sound of blaring music that jumped alive from the next room and then the electronic beep and metal clack of the computerized door lock snapping open.

I was stunned for a second by the opening beat and chords of Bob Seger's "Feel Like a Number" but before the first stanza I was up out of the blocks like a sprinter toward the outside door.

Marcus too must have been frozen by the sounds and whatever the hell he was seeing outside because his hand did not start to move from the door. I was a step away and when the light between the jamb and the door started to widen I threw my body weight into it, trapping the four fingers I had watched in disgust as they trailed down Sherry's breasts. I heard the kid scream in pain and felt him push back at me, and instinctively I took one hard-lunging swipe downward with my knife.

The door closed flush with the jamb, my shoulder against it, and with my right foot I dragged over the crowbar that Buck had used to lock me in and kicked its edge under the door and pinned it. Only then did I rest my back against the panel and look down to see four fingers, sliced off at the second joint, lying like droppings on the floor next to me.

*   *   *

Now I wasn't flying on a plan but on adrenaline. I went first to Sherry and saw her twisting onto her side, struggling against her trapped hands. But just above her head on the wall I also saw the lights on the electronic door lock glowing green. Something had tripped the power, like a driver hitting the garage door opener with the remote halfway up the driveway. I figured someone from the chopper had the switch so I twisted the handle and shoved open the door with my hip and was met with a rush of the high volume music: *Dat! da dat! da dat!, da da daaaa. Dat! da dat! da dat!, da da daaaa.*

> *I take my card and I stand in line*
> *To make a buck I work overtime*

I put my bloodstained knife into my back pocket and grabbed the ends of Sherry's bed frame. I scraped the legs over and then with my back into it like a rower I pulled her through the door opening and into the computer room. Then I jumped back to the door and slammed it shut and punched a series of numbers I will never remember into the locking device, and like a miracle the lights on the lock went red.

In the closed room the music was twice as loud. Something about another drone, something about feeling like a number. I remembered the CD player on the southern wall and strode over to it but it took me one more stanza to find the OFF button, and the room went quiet.

I pulled my knife again and sat down on the edge

of Sherry's bed and cut loose her wrists and ankles. Then without hesitation I laid my head down on her chest. I was listening to her heart, yes, but it was not my only purpose and she responded by wrapping her freed arms around my shoulders and holding me with the little power she had left.

CHAPTER 26

Harmon looked at the GPS in his hand and then down at what seemed like a thousand acres of trampled backyard wallowing in standing water and said, "Take her down. I think we're here."

The helicopter pilot looked to his right to see if the look on Harmon's face meant he was serious and Harmon simply looked back and shrugged his shoulders. The pilot was told by whomever hired him to follow Harmon's instructions and don't ask questions. They were less than an hour northwest of the city and had left all civilization behind when they flew over U.S. 27, the demarcation line where South Florida changes from rows and rows of orange-tiled roofs to the gray-green world of the Everglades.

As the chopper descended, the landscape only became slightly more defined. Now they could see that those darker green blobs below were actually stands of trees. The slate-colored patches were open water, reflecting the color of the sky. And the brownish smears were acres of sawgrass beaten down at the moment by the path of the storm. Harmon pointed to a kidney-shaped island that looked more and more like a pile of pickup sticks as they got closer. Soon they could make out tall trees snapped off at their tops and vegetation and debris at their base so thick it was difficult to discern anything more. They came in lower and then from the backseat Squires called out: "Structure at eight o'clock." The pilot swung his head down and to the left. Harmon was on the blind side.

"Bank a turn and get as low as you can," Harmon said, climbing out of his seat and squeezing into the back with his partner. While they swung around, Harmon and Squires readied the fast ropes, tying them to U-bolts secured into the floor of the chopper. Harmon slid open a side door and looked out.

"Eleven o'clock," he said into the microphone. "See it?"

"Yeah, I got it," the pilot said. "I'll get you over that decking at the rear."

"Nice armpit they got for us to visit this time," Squires said. "I'm not picking up any movement but that don't mean a thing considering that ground cover. Shit, somebody coulda parked a fucking yacht in there and you wouldn't spot it." The big man took the Mk23 handgun out of his operations bag and strapped it to his thigh.

When they were thirty feet over the dark wooded deck both men slung their packs over their shoulders and put their feet out on the landing runners.

"I'll call on the satellite phone for a pickup," Harmon said to the pilot and by turn, Squires first, they rappelled like circus artists down the ropes.

"Fuck! They are cops," Buck said when he saw the first man slide down the rope and touch down on the deck. The guy unsnapped his line and had a nasty-looking handgun out faster than Buck had seen most men flick a switchblade. He was dressed all in black, like some goddamn SWAT dude who meant business. Then the second guy came down.

"What the hell?" he whispered to himself. This one was dressed like he was going to a baseball game: a pair of jeans and a golf shirt and some kinda loose jacket flapping in the wind. He landed just as softly as the other one but as far as Buck could tell he wasn't armed.

Buck was now waist-deep in the water and obscured by a clump of fern and downed tree branches. When they first slipped out of the cabin he eyeballed the helicopter, expecting to see a rescue decal on its belly or at least a Sheriff's Office logo. Instead it was unmarked. From his angle he couldn't even see the identification numbers and he had to assume it was a private chopper. Dope dealers? Owners?

Then he and the boy both slipped down into the water, using the deck as cover. When the chopper door opened and a couple of ropes came tumbling out, he'd ordered Wayne to take the shotgun around to the other side of the cabin so they could flank whoever came down, just as they'd done to Freeman. When the first man slid down he saw the SWAT getup and thought cops. Now he didn't know what the hell was going on, but the gun in the SWAT guy's hand jacked up the situation and he kept the stolen .45 up and ready. He just hoped Wayne could see that the dude in black was armed.

Buck stayed down, out of sight, and when the helicopter pulled up and the sound faded the place went silent again. Buck was quietly working the possibilities. If they go through the door and confront Marcus and find Freeman and his partner, what the hell happens? Maybe he should make a break for the airboat now, let the boys fend for themselves. Maybe he should wait, take a chance on these guys opening the other side of the place. He knew drugs were inside. A huge score. A once-in-a-lifetime score. A score just like his daddy couldn't resist. If he made this work he would ride off in the sunset to Hendry County where he belonged, workin' the open range, no more penny-ante burglaries and dodging the cops. How can you walk away? Buck watched the two men bending their heads together, talking softly, and then the one in black started moving east toward the door. No, thought Buck, this has been thought out. No turning back now.

Suddenly a scream ripped through the humid air that raised the hair on the back of Buck's neck and dropped his jaw at the same instant. The sound was filled with more surprise and pain than Buck had ever heard even in the concrete halls of Avon Park prison and his reaction was the same as when he was inside:

his legs started moving, as if you could run away from such terror even in an eight-by-ten cell.

He moved to his left, out away from his cover, his eyes focused on the men who both seemed to have been frozen by the shattering cry. Then he saw Wayne; he'd come up out of the swamp at the sound of his friend's scream and was up on the deck, running with the shotgun held foolishly at port arms. Water was dripping off his shirt and pants legs and there was a look of anguish on the kid's face as his mouth formed the word "Marcus!" and he slid around the corner into full view of the helicopter men.

The barrel of Wayne's shotgun never even made it to point when the SWAT man spun with his handgun at the ready and fired twice. A spray of blood instantly mixed with the droplets of water flying off the kid's chest and two blossoms of red bloomed on his upper chest as he went down. The shotgun clattered forward across the wooden planks and came to a sudden stop under the foot of the man with the jacket. The other one was still in a military firing position, both hands steadying his handgun and then, as if he'd seen him all along, the big man shifted the sights of the weapon onto Buck, who was thirty feet away in the swamp, his feet still, his eyes trying to decipher what had just happened.

"Don't move, asshole!" the SWAT guy said, and then started moving down the deck, stepping then sliding, shuffling his feet, keeping a stance and a balance as if he'd been trained and did this kind of thing every day: drop out of the sky, shoot a kid in the chest.

Buck had his hands up in response to the man's pointed gun. He still held the .45, now high and over his head, pointing at the still-lightening sky. The man was nearly even with him when, back behind all of them, Buck saw Marcus come out from around the east corner. The kid was bent half over, his right arm extended out in front of him, the end looking like a bloody stump. The boy's face, though, was up, and in his eyes were an odd look of shock and a plea for help.

"Jesus," the jacket man said and the tone of his voice and maybe the look on Buck's face caused the SWAT guy to turn his head. And that's when Buck shot the big man in the back, the .45 roaring.

The second shot hit SWAT man as he spun, entering his face just below the cheekbone and at an upward angle exiting at his sideburn, the big caliber round removing his ear at the same time. The third shot dropped him to his knees, where he melted in a heap.

Buck did not like guns, never had. But that did not mean he was inept at their use.

After the third recoil he swung the sights back down the deck to where jacket man was. This one had been unarmed when he arrived but now he had the over-and-under twelve-gauge shotgun in one hand and bloody Marcus in the other. He had the kid's neck in a hold and had positioned him as a shield. He seemed fixed that way, his knee down on one of the bags

they'd dropped, holding the kid, figuring he was protection of some kind. Buck held the .45 on them both
as he climbed out of the swamp and onto the deck. He
seemed incredibly calm as he stepped over Wayne's
crumpled body. The kid was whimpering and seemed
to be shrinking by the minute, gone fetal, folding up on
himself, like a balloon leaking air. Buck stopped short
of the SWAT man's body and did not look down at it.
Somewhere in the background he thought he heard
music. But his eyes were on jacket man's eyes.

"Well, sir," Buck said, reverting back to what he
thought of as southern charm even if it was now heavily bloodstained. Still, sometimes just the feel of the
words in his own mouth made him calm, calculating.
"I ain't sure who you are, mister. But it appears we are
in what they call a Mexican standoff."

Jacket man said nothing, his finger poised on the
trigger of the shotgun. Buck slid his eyes away from
the gun and looked at the boy. The kid was still alive
but from this distance Buck could now see that most of
Marcus's fingers on his right hand were gone, sheared
off at the joints, the stubs all bleeding heavily and dripping onto his shirt. He did not feel any sympathy. Yes,
they had an almost familial connection, most of the real
Gladesmen from the Ten Thousand Islands did. But it
wasn't enough in these modern times. The world had
gone small. People bumpin' up into people now that
they would never have known even existed before.
People grabbin' for what they considered their share.
Buck had seen men turn on their own before over

greed. He'd seen white supremacists shiv one another in prison. He'd seen black gang members rape other blacks. If he had to put a .45 round through the kid to take out the man behind him, he would.

"But what you don't realize, sir," Buck continued, "is that there is a still a cop and his partner inside that there storage bin of yours. Now, I'm sure you don't want him or her surviving to let on about your stash of cocaine or pot or meth or whatever the hell it is you got in there. And considering we're two armed against them unarmed, maybe we could come to some kind of a share and share alike understanding?"

The man in the jacket still said nothing. Maybe he was pondering the offer. Maybe there was some hope to the situation. Then the man nodded his head as though he'd come to a decision.

"There's nothing Mexican about this standoff, my friend," Harmon said, his voice tired but succinct. "It's just humans being humans." Then he pulled the trigger and the powerful, small-patterned shotgun blast ripped Buck Morris's leg off just above the knee.

Harmon wished he was home. He wanted to be sitting in his protected den, reading his books, enjoying the quiet air-conditioning provided by his generator and sipping a cool drink and mildly gloating over how he had beaten nature this time. Instead he was in the middle of a bloodbath.

Harmon did not trust nature and this was exactly why. The whole way out here he'd looked down to

see homes and cars and buildings and roadways all
skewed off balance. At two thousand feet you couldn't
see the details but everything in the wake of the hurricane looked different, the colors gone dirty, the normal flow of things stopped cold. At first it had almost
seemed a relief when the landscape turned watery and
open; then they'd found the cabin they were looking
for and even in its own backyard nature couldn't be
trusted.

As the pilot hovered and Harmon had waited for
Squires to touch down on the deck, he had chuckled a
bit at his partner's instant reaction to pull his weapon
and sight the corners like they were going into Beirut
again. But Harmon also noted the odd damage at the
roofline of the simple shack: some missing tin panels
and splintered wood that looked more like damage
from a hungry animal than from the wide slap of a
wind gust or falling limb. He was nervous when he
slid down the fast rope and landed on the balls of his
feet. When they'd unhooked, Harmon had given the
pilot the high sign and then bent and pulled the electronic lock switch from his bag.

"OK, partner. Let's check out the inside of Crandall's
mystery hole and then get the hell back out of here,"
Harmon said. They started for the south side of the
building and the instant he punched the button on
the switch an unholy scream seemed to fill the air and
Harmon looked stupidly down at the button like he'd
done something wrong and could turn it back off.

Suddenly they were confronted by the sight of a

young man, his face in agony, coming around the corner at them with an outstretched arm like he was offering them a bloodied portion of the devil himself. All
manner of their mercenary past boiled up in Harmon's
memory and he could only think now in retrospect
that Squires must have relaxed his weapon when he
realized the bloodied kid was unarmed because they
were both staring at the boy and wincing at the pitch of
his wailing when another voice erupted behind them.

This time Squires tensed and swung, his gun at the
ready, and when he saw a second young man come
running around the west corner with a shotgun, the
big man fired two quick rounds, dropping the assail-
ant in his tracks. Harmon watched as the boy pitched
forward and, almost without thought, he stuck out
his foot and stopped the shotgun as it slid across the
wooden deck by stepping on its barrel. For a moment
there was silence, the crack of Squires's pistol sucked
out into the humid air around them. The only reason
Harmon was not stupefied by the series of events was
that he had never been stupefied by the actions of his
friend or those of people in bad places and he now realized that's exactly where they were: in a bad place.
Just as automatically as he had pinned the sliding shotgun, he crouched and searched the immediate area. He
and Squires were not unfamiliar with flanking military procedure. So when his friend turned at an angle
and shouted: "Don't move, asshole!" with his gun still
raised but pointed down toward the water, Harmon
was not surprised that another unfriendly was in sight.

He looked past the big man's legs at a bearded, scruffy-looking guy whose arms were now raised in surrender and without taking his eyes off the threat of the big handgun in the new player's lifted hand, Harmon reached down for the shotgun.

It was when he felt for the wooden stock of the gun that his fingers touched an uneven surface of warm goop and when he shifted eyes to his feet he realized he was touching the back of a bloodied hand, the digits cleaved off like a rack of short ribs, the white stumps of bone glowing through the red syrup and the intact thumb still twitching as it tried to grip the shotgun stock.

"Jesus," he heard himself say. And the gunfire began again.

I was inside the cocoon of the closed room but there was no mistaking the sound of gunfire outside. I heard Marcus's screams and already knew I was responsible. The image of those severed fingers on the floor will be in my dreams. But then came some indecipherable yelling and two quick reports. A medium-caliber handgun, I thought. Not Buck's big .45. And then I felt more than heard something or someone tumble onto the deck just on the other side of the wall and the sound of something metal skittering across the boards. I was standing, the generator inside was humming, the air-conditioning clacked on, the computer indicator lights started popping on, glowing red and green. I took a step toward the window that showed damage from Buck and his crew's attempts last night to get in but then flinched at the sound of another shot. This time it was the .45 and it repeated itself twice more and there was another thud that vibrated the floorboards. I crouched down in exasperation. There was carnage of some form going on ten feet away from me that I couldn't see, could only hear, but I knew instinctively that its outcome was going to determine my fate and Sherry's.

Again there was silence, and I was afraid to move but then I remembered the open hatch in the corner and sneaked to it, my ear to its edge, hoping to hear, to get some clue what the hell was happening outside. Taking a chance, I moved my head into the opening, but the sunlight outside was still so new that very little penetrated under the raised decking and I could see little more than a black shimmer on the top of the water. When I strained, I heard nothing but a high-pitched keening like an animal in deep pain.

"Max?"

Sherry was trying to get up. She had somehow risen to a sitting position on the bed but her leg was locked straight and I needed to move to her, but hesitated. She tried to swing her damaged leg over the side and was just about to fall so I made a decision. I flipped the metal port closed with a clang and rushed to her side, catching her before she tumbled to the floor.

"Was that music that I heard, Max?" she said in a delirious whisper. "Are we home, Max?"

*   *   *

While the skinny peckerwood with the missing leg writhed around on the deck, Harmon let go of the boy and stepped over to kick the big .45 over the edge and into the swamp. He then looked down at the man who now had his stump of a knee in both hands and was kind of spinning on one hip like one of those break dancers on TV, though they didn't leave a smear of blood behind when they did it. He stepped over to his partner, who appeared to have lost part of the side of his head. Harmon had seen dead men before and you didn't have to take a goddamn pulse to tell. He did not mean to be callous. He and Squires had been through a lot together. But after what had been nearly a lifetime of war and violence, Harmon's nature was to care only about family. Squires was not family. He picked up the big man's Mk23, checked the load, and then realized, hell, he hadn't even taken his own Colt out of his pocket yet. He took two more steps and looked down at the kid who had come sliding around the corner yelling, "Marrcussss!" until Squires shot him. The kid's skin was already going pale. Chest wounds will do that. Harmon shook his head. Neither of these boys was older than his kids, sitting in their dorm rooms at Notre Dame, probably having a party while the campus got it together to enjoy the weekend.

He avoided the blood pool and went back to the older hick, who was now emitting a high keening sound of serious pain. Harmon thought for a minute about what the guy had said about unarmed police officers being

locked inside the shack. Why the hell would he make
something like that up? Then he thought about the idiot
claim that there were drugs inside. The company didn't
deal in drugs. They dealt in oil, which was much more
lucrative, though sometimes the way they obtained it
and bargained for it and set prices for it wasn't any
more legal than the way drug suppliers did the same
thing. In fact, Harmon had been working the company
angle on this trip since the minute he'd gotten off the
phone with Crandall. No doubt this place was clandestine as hell. Harmon knew enough about the business to understand the company was always looking
for supply. They had ways of studying deep rock for-
mations, ways of setting off subterranean explosions
and then measuring and tracking the echo effects and
movement of sound waves to tell them where the oil
and natural gas deposits were. That kind of shit went
on all the time all over the world. It's just that in most
of this particular part of the world, in an environmen-
tally designated part of the Everglades, such exploration was illegal as hell. That's why you need security
to check out a lonely outpost after a hurricane. That's
why you would be ordered to check its infrastructure
and report if it had been seen or uncovered by anyone.
He stood and looked across the deck. That's why you
clean up after yourself.

The older peckerwood was still crying when Harmon heard the clank of metal on metal. It seemed to
come from under him and he felt the vibration in his
shoes. Was that a door? Was it proof that this asshole

who had just killed his partner was telling the truth?
Were there more men inside?

Harmon stood still for a moment, listening, assessing. He couldn't divide his concentration now. He was alone. You focus on one situation at a time and if you can eliminate a distraction, that's what you do.

With no more thought than that, Harmon stepped forward and shot the older man with the blown-off leg through the back of the head with Squires's pistol. The end of the annoying whimpering. The fingerless boy took it easier. He was still wrapped up around his disfigured hand when Harmon put a round into his ear hole. Those chores done, he carefully walked around to the entrance of the cabin, noted the crowbar blade under the door, and used a single blast from the shotgun to blow away a six-inch hole around the metal tip. The hinges creaked as the door swung free and he entered at a crouch, weapon at the ready. No one greeted him. The place smelled of jerky and antiseptic, sweat and wet wood. One bed was partially disassembled on the opposite wall. A cooler and some trash were over in the corner. Sunlight was leaking through a rough opening in the roof, the damage he had seen from the air. Someone might have dropped through it, but there was nothing near it to indicate a man could have climbed unaided back out. There was no place to hide.

On the western wall he studied the door to the adjoining room. The red light was glowing on the electronic lock, and in all the confusion, he'd forgotten where he left the remote switch. He noted the damage around the door frame where attempts had been made to break in, unsuccessfully. The company was hiding its secrets well. Harmon tried the latch. Then he actually knocked.

"Hello?" he called out at the door, and even he realized how stupid he sounded. "Is anyone in there? This is the DEA, federal officers. Is anyone alive in there?"

CHAPTER 27

I was still at Sherry's side, easing her back onto the bed, repeating to her, "It's OK, baby. It's OK. We're almost out of here, Sherry. We're almost home."

Her eyes were open but the way they were twitching in her head, the irises never stopping long enough to absorb the light, made me wonder what she was seeing or what those images were telling her. I didn't think the pain was even registering anymore. She'd forgotten the leg, I thought. Now she was struggling with another demon and the only thing keeping her from it was her own internal strength.

Two more small-caliber gunshots sounded after I'd clapped the porthole door closed and both made me flinch. Then I heard the roar of the shotgun next door. But who was firing. Buck? Wayne? Was Marcus coming to pay me back for taking his fingers?

When I heard someone twisting the knob on the door, I pulled my knife and moved to the hinges. They'd have to come through here. I might wound one; everything else would fall from there. My face was close to the metal when I heard a stranger's voice identify himself as a DEA agent.

"Is anyone alive in there?"

I let him wonder while I tried to sort out the possibilities. This place was obviously not a drug storage bin. Buck's dreams were just that, a small-time thief's dream of a big score. So why the hell would DEA be out here two days after a hurricane? It might have been a good flush technique, but I wasn't going for it.

"Do you know Jim Born, the agent-in-charge for the Broward office?" I said, loud enough for him to hear it. There was a hesitation on the other side of the door.

"Yeah. But I just transferred in from Virginia. Look, you need to come out there with your hands raised, OK?" the voice said, exasperated. "If you're armed, you need to throw your weapons out first. Understand?"

Jim Born was an FDLE agent I'd been introduced to by Sherry. He hadn't worked for DEA in several years.

"Fuck you," I said. "There's an officer from the Broward sheriff's office in here so why don't *you* come in *here* with your hands up and toss the shotgun and the handgun in first." I was guessing the weapons based on the last sounds I'd heard. It might throw the guy, wondering how I knew.

Would some of Buck's shithead friends have joined him on their merry looting party, maybe even started a shootout to cut down on the number of shares in the proceeds? That'd be a lot of homicide for a little profit. Or was this another group altogether? I didn't have time to wait the guy out. Sherry was dying next to me.

He didn't know that. But I wasn't taking the chance of having him come through the door with backup behind him. I'd be outflanked again. So I worked out logistics, coveted the high ground, and took a gamble. If it was someone with the ability to help us, friendly or not, I'd have to take the chance.

"You already know you can't get through these windows. People have been trying to chop into them all night.

"And you probably also know there's one other entrance. The escape hatch through the floor in here. So here's the deal. You go below. I open the hatch. You show me some kind of identification. I let you come up."

There was silence. A whispered discussion? A plan being prepared? I was flying blind but if I minimized the space, made it impossible to be rushed by bodies and force, I might at least be able to put more information together than I could through a door. I was hoping this guy was cagey enough to be thinking the same thing.

"Yeah, OK," the voice said. "The surveillance intel shows that hatch. Open it and I'll toss my badge up."

I listened as intently as I could, heard one set of solid footsteps move away. The sound of the air conditioner drowned out anything once the voice moved to the outside. I got up, found the switch, and turned the machine off. I had not registered the coolness in the room until then. The chill in my skin had started with the first sound of gunfire and had stayed. I now moved to the hatch and yanked it open so I could at least hear or maybe see the ruffle of the water when one or three men sloshed under the decking. When I peered in over the edge there was already a telltale swirl, some kind of eddy on the dark surface that seemed to have been pushed up from the bottom. Then I heard the slosh of someone lowering themselves into the swamp.

"OK. Where's this hatch?" The man's voice echoed up from the porthole.

"West side. In between the last two stringers," I said. There was more movement on the surface, expanding arcs of water like rings moving away from the plunk of a rock.

"Look. Tell me your name, friend. Let's make this easier," the voice said, loud now as if he was already in the room, his tone booming from the space between water and wood like it was coming from a wet basement.

"Freeman," I said. "Max Freeman."

"You're a cop?"

"No. Private investigator working with a cop," I said, maybe giving too much away if they were drug hunters following a rumor.

"OK, Freeman."

Looking down through the circular hatch at an angle, I caught a glimpse of fabric.

"Here's my ID."

I sneaked another look. He only showed a forearm and hand, holding a wallet. I noted it was his left hand. Most people are righties. His gun hand was hidden.

"Toss it up," I said.

He underhanded it high but I did not follow its trajectory and instead watched the circle of water. The man's face, ruddy, middle-aged, slipped into the space and we made eye contact. If I'd had a gun I would have had the muzzle over the edge pointing down. I hoped that didn't give him courage.

I moved around in a half circle and picked up the wallet: Edward Christopher Harmon. Florida private investigator. The photo was similar enough to the glimpse I'd just had. The lie about DEA didn't surprise me. Admitting it did.

"So now we're on the same field," Harmon said from below. "Two PIs doing a job. You yours. Me mine."

"It doesn't exactly make us brothers, Harmon," I said. "What's your job and what the hell happened out there?"

I heard him slosh. But I'd been down there myself. There was no way to suddenly leap up off that mucky bottom. I was tall enough to reach up and just get my fingers over the edges. Unless he was seven feet, he wasn't coming up until I let him.

"Your friends, I'm afraid, got a little trigger happy. Probably jumpy after that boy came screaming around the corner with half of his hand gone. I'll assume that was your work, Freeman. Maybe he wasn't your friend?"

"Never was," I said.

"Won't ever be now," Harmon said.

"Since we're assuming, let me take my turn," I said.

"Everybody out there is dead. Or everyone except your team?"

"My partner got his face blown off. He's gone," Harmon said and the tone was actually somber, like it meant something to him. "It's just you and me, Freeman. Or is your cop alive?"

I looked up at Sherry, concentrated on her chest, thought I could see it rise and fall, but for a second I didn't think I could truthfully answer him.

"What's your job?" I said instead and again I heard him, or something, slosh in the water.

"My company owns this research facility. They sent me out to secure it after the hurricane, make sure it was still standing."

"It's illegal as hell to have a drilling field in this part of the Glades," I said. You didn't have to be an environmentalist to know that spoiling the Glades and threatening the water supply was a raw nerve in Florida. The profiteers would get a foothold any way they could. The computer systems behind me, the plotting desk, the seismic charts, the security lock on the door. No other explanation made sense.

"No one's drilling that I know of, Freeman. You see a drill up there? Fucking thing would have to be six stories high on a metal platform. You know anything about oil drilling?"

"Yeah," I said. "You set some charges down in the substrata first, doesn't take a big drilling operation. Then you fire off explosions that no one hears or sees and you measure the underground reaction, sometimes with lasers and the sensitive kinds of computerized equipment you've got up here in your little den, Harmon. And that's illegal too."

This time the voice took a long break. Making a decision. Or making me think he was making a decision.

"OK. OK, Freeman. We can debate all day. It's a fucking job for me and it ain't worth this much shit. My partner's dead. All the assholes who started firing on us when we came to check out a company project are dead. I have no knowledge of the legal status of this place. But I do have a satellite phone and I'm gonna call my pilot, have him do a pickup and I'm outa here.

"You wanna go with me or sit up there with your cop friend, who I'm assuming is a corpse by now or he would have said something. What I'm not going to do is stand here in this fucking soup any longer."

This time I was the one hesitating. This guy might be our last chance. He leaves, Sherry dies. I'm certain of it. There's not much of a choice left.

"Toss up the guns," I said. "I'll help you load your friend's body."

This time there's no discussion.

"Stand away so you don't think I'm trying to shoot you," he said, and an over-under shotgun came up, stock first, and he pushed it hard enough for the gun to clear the opening and clack onto the floor. I dragged it away. Then an Mk pistol flipped up out of the space and clattered to the floor.

"That's what I got," Harmon said.

This time when I peered over the edge he was standing in full view, empty palms raised, fingers spread wide.

"Give me a hand," he said.

I braced myself on either side of the porthole and reached down. He locked on with a grip on each of my wrists and I did the same. It was an old climber's technique I learned long ago and it surprised me that he knew it.

"OK," he said and I yanked him up and over the edge of the hatch. While he was still on all fours I picked up the Mk23 and held it loosely in one hand. He stood and did not seem to care that I was now armed. He was a man of medium build, probably in his early fifties but in good shape. His grayish hair was matted from the moisture, his clothes soaking wet. He first looked me in the face, seemed to study my eyes until he'd made some kind of assessment, and then scanned the rest of the room, nodding, like it was familiar and he was pleased that everything appeared to be in shape. He stopped when he sighted the cot and Sherry behind me.

"How's your officer friend, if she is indeed an officer?" he said.

"She needs help," I said.

"Then it's a good thing we made a deal."

"Did we?"

He refocused on my eyes. It is an old cop trick that was probably taken from the art of magicians. Most people, even shy people and especially criminal people, will try to be brave and look you in the eye when you first start talking to them. And if you are engaging, with a smile and a purpose, you can hold their attention for the second it takes to do the sleight of hand you need to do.

"Actually, I'm going to have to take a little time here to do some documenting. Simple tasks like pulling some computer memories and such," he said, turning just slightly to his right, but with his feet still planted, a solid foundation. His move might have even worked if his jacket had not been so wet, the heft of the soaked fabric pulled just hard enough to expose a hard edge in his right pocket, and when I saw his shoulder raise to slip his hand inside I shot him.

The round hit him in the hip and must have made solid contact with bone because he spun, just a quarter turn, but when he stepped back to gain his balance, he put his foot directly into the hole of the open space of the escape hatch and went down. Trying quickly to straddle the void, he landed with one leg hanging and the other spread out at floor level. His rib cage and right underarm scraped hard against the inside edge of the hatch and then came to a hard halt. He was wedged in the hole, looking suddenly like a human pair of scissors, doing a painful split. He was awkwardly stuck; his right arm pinned and left one flailing. I changed position and circled. I had to give the guy credit. He hadn't cried out, though I knew it had to hurt, both the bullet into bone and the fall. I looked down at him and his lips were pressed tight into a hard line. Might have been pissed, might have been pain. The look said either. Through the space between his back and one edge, I could look down and see the lump in his pocket was still there, hanging heavily, and impossible for him to reach.

"Is that a pistol in your pocket or did I just shoot you for trying to get a two-pound pack of cigarettes out of your jacket?" I said.

"Fuck you, Freeman."

The strain in his face increased. His breathing started to go ragged. He might have broken some ribs going down, possibly punctured a lung. But still his eyes were flashing left and right, trying to figure a move. Guy like him had probably saved his own ass a dozen times and was still confident he could do it again.

I heard Sherry moan behind me, the first sound she'd made since Harmon started banging on the door, and we were wasting time.

"OK, Harmon. Now you've got a reason to work with me here. You gotta get to the hospital, my partner has to get to the hospital," I said. "You tell me how to call back your helicopter pilot and all three of us fly out together."

He looked up and saw me pointing the gun in his face and thought about the alternatives for less than ten seconds.

"Out in my bag on the deck there's a satellite phone. Pilot's on the same frequency. Get me up out of here and get the phone. I'll make the call."

I had to give him credit; he was still working the advantages for himself, slim as they were.

"No, I'll get the gun out of your pocket. Then we'll get you up," I said.

With the doorway jammed, I knew the only way to get outside now was through the hatch. I figured I'd have to get him up and tied securely to a stanchion before I could climb down and get to the phone. Then I'd be calling Billy. His pilot's job was over. I circled him again, kept the Mk in my hand, and then knelt down.

"I'm going to reach down into your pocket, Harmon. You move, I'll put a round through the back of your head. It won't make a difference to me. You're out of my way regardless."

I went down on the floor behind him, my face next to his back, and I could see the stain of blood spreading down the side of his pants where I'd shot him. I was hoping that I hadn't hit the femoral artery, but the bleeding was already extensive enough that droplets were falling into the water below.

I extended my arm down and with a little trouble found the pocket opening and reached inside to touch the hard metal of a short-barreled pistol. I came up with a new-looking Colt revolver and slid it across the floor toward Sherry's cot.

"All right, Harmon," I said, standing. "Now I'm going to get you under the arms here and lift you up. From the looks of it you're gonna bleed out if I don't get you out of there now and get a patch on that wound. So don't fuck with me. I'm the only one left here to save your ass."

He grunted once and then said: "You think I'm afraid of you, Freeman? Don't flatter yourself."

"No. I doubt you're afraid of anything," I said and meant it.

First I put the Mk in the waistband at the small of my back and then bent behind him, got him under both armpits and started to lift. He seemed surprisingly light at first, and I had his rump almost over the edge of the hatch when he suddenly got heavy and his eyes got suddenly big and the man who feared nothing started to scream.

They call them prehistoric, the alligators of Florida. And they have survived so many thousands of years because they are nature's superior predators in their world. Their jaw muscles are machine-strong when they are biting down and weaker but much quicker when they are opening the mouth. It's the quickness that's astonishing.

The first yank pulled Harmon back down through the hole and I almost followed him. Over his shoulder I could see one black eye, like a shiny marble, mounted on the rumpled, gray-green snout. Unemotional, limbic, it stared up at me with no recognition that a man's leg from the knee down was in its mouth. The other eye was missing, the socket where it should have been was a bloody hole, as if it had been drilled or merely gouged out by the shaft of a sheared-off golf club. Then like a whiplash the gator flashed its tail and threw its thousand-pound body into an S shape and Harmon went down through the hole like he'd been flushed. I heard the crack of bone and snap of ligament over the man's deep-throated scream and tumbled back, landing on my ass. I scrambled back to the edge only in time to see that classic roll of the big reptile's spin, showing its light-colored belly and black, mottled back as it pulled its prey down under the water where it cannot breathe and will soon give up. It is all very natural. And nature is sometimes a terrible thing to watch.

CHAPTER 28

They were all dead. Arms folded at impossible angles. Clothing unnaturally empty and stained in dark amber colors that they never would have worn for themselves. Human bodies are diminished by death. In a movie some alien called us bags of water and in death our life leaks out.

I stepped around Marcus, let my eyes skim over the head wound but they stopped on the outstretched hand, the missing fingers I was responsible for. I moved on to a jump bag, one I hadn't seen before and assumed was Harmon's. Inside I found the phone he'd spoken of before the gator took him away in pieces. I turned it on and dialed Billy Manchester's number. He would be the one person I knew would have the technological ability to take the call even if the power and the cell towers were down in West Palm Beach. He was my friend, my attorney, and since I often worked for him as a private investigator, he was also my boss. He listened as always in absorbed silence until I was done describing where Sherry and I were and the GPS coordinates, her medical condition, and a quick synopsis of the carnage lying around me.

"I will be on a med flight in thirty minutes, Max, with a crew and an evacuation basket," Billy said. "I will also inform the Broward sheriff's office of the situation. Are you OK?"

"Yeah, Billy. Just get here."

I punched the off button and stepped out past the hand with one thumb. Buck was facedown, the ripped left leg of his jeans was empty. Farther along the deck was the body of a big man I did not recognize. As I walked around him, I glimpsed a clump of bloodstained gristle against the nearby wall that I barely recognized as an ear. At the corner was Wayne, lying on his side, his arm extended out in the direction of his friend as if offering the four fingers he had left from an accident long ago to match his partner's lonely thumb.

The sun was partway up now, smoldering behind an overcast sky, dimly glowing. A humid wind stirred and blew through the broken Glades trees and ferns, momentarily sweeping away the stink of blood and cordite and humans. Sometimes nature cannot stand us. And sometimes we cannot stand our own nature. I carefully made my way back inside to Sherry's side and waited for the sound of a rescue.

EPILOGUE

We are through the hurricane season. It is January in South Florida and the tourists and winter residents are leaking back down from up north to seek out the sun now that it is safe and the chill of winter is pushing them out of their own homes. It is nice to avoid the inconveniences of nature if you can afford to.

I am avoiding them myself by spending most of my time at Sherry's home in Fort Lauderdale. After she was released from the hospital, I built a ramp from her driveway up onto her back deck, which overlooks the pool. I installed a new set of stainless steel handles that let her ease herself down into the water, and although that was their immediate purpose, she has taken to using them for doing "dips." It is an excruciatingly difficult exercise she learned in rehab that is like an inverted pull-up and works the hell out of one's shoulder and triceps muscles. I've tried to match her repetitions and failed. She calls me a wimp but concedes that she is only pressing the weight of her body minus one leg. I kept telling myself I was there to help her but I have not yet returned to my river shack. I think perhaps I'm there to help myself. Being alone in the wilderness has lost some appeal. Being with someone you need and needs you is, well, natural.

When Billy's privately arranged medevac helicopter arrived at the Everglades shack, a rescue jumper and an emergency medical physician winched down and immediately took control of Sherry, inserting IVs, stabilizing her leg, administering who knows what antishock drugs. They strapped her into the basket and pulled her up into the chopper and I followed. While they worked on her, a flight nurse was trying to open another vein in Sherry's right arm but had to pry her hand open to loosen a muscle, and in her palm she found a necklace with two stones, an opal and a diamond. Sherry had not let loose of it since ripping it off Wayne's neck. The nurse handed it to me and I put it in my pocket. The flight back to West Boca Medical Center took such little time it caught me off guard. We had been so close the whole time, barely twenty miles away.

I was kept in another room of the emergency center, treated for cuts and abrasions to my face and hands, and proved to be an uncooperative patient until Sherry's doctor checked back with me to update me on her condition. She would recover, he said, after the amputation of her infected leg. Later, when she was lucid, I stood by her hospital bed and then laid my head on her chest, listening to her heart and promising that we would do together whatever it took to make her whole again.

Billy, the stoic and always-in-control attorney, left the room and I suspect he used one of those silk handkerchiefs he always carried in his suit pockets to dry his tears. When he'd arrived in the helicopter he had deferred to the others and stayed up in the aircraft. Later he told me that he had taken several digital photographs of the area, including shots of the four bodies and their positions on the outside deck. The Broward sheriff's office homicide unit would take over the investigation with interagency help from the Department of Natural Resources and the Palm Beach and Collier County sheriffs. The illegal drilling exploration station would of course be exposed.

Billy made sure his photographs got to the right reporters at the right newspapers. The environmental folks took the fuel and ran with it, demanding that the state's attorney general get involved in an investigation of other possible operations. In time the equipment and computer files at the station were confiscated and tracked directly to GULFLO.

The oil company of course would be publicly stunned that, due to the misreading of a survey map, they had made a mistake in operating the research station in an area off limits to such work. They would also disavow any knowledge of a "so-called" security team. They paid a fine. They were sorry. But Billy had kept his feelers out, investigating on his own the identities of Harmon and Squires and although Squires's portfolio remained thin and scattered, Billy would eventually flag an obscure civil suit brought by a woman in Coral

Springs who claimed to be Harmon's wife, which she had filed against GULFLO. The suit was asking for five million in compensatory damages for wrongful death. Billy was watching to see how long it would stay on the docket before being settled out of court.

Billy had often schooled me on the past and present way things work in Florida; two centuries of people flowing to the sunshine had brought with it the spoiling of big business, corruption, money, and crime.

"Nature knocks it back every once in a while, Max," Billy said. "But the nature of men, I'm afraid, will always prevail."

I did not believe I'd gained much insight into the ways of nature or the nature of man. The bodies of the boys would be returned to their mothers, and Buck Morris would be buried alone in a pauper's grave.

Sherry and I would recount to the homicide detectives our days since the hurricane struck in as much detail as possible, as many names as we could, estimated times, conversations as close as we could recall, number of shots fired. The days we spent at the Snows' fishing camp leading up to that night, we kept to ourselves.

After she was home, when it seemed right, I tried to return her necklace. I held it out in my hand, the chain still broken. She stared at it for a time then asked me for a tiny wooden box from her dresser top. She placed the necklace inside and then tucked it deep into a bottom drawer she used only for keepsakes and memories.

For now she swims. She is researching prostheses

and has already subscribed to a Web site detailing the training involved in wheelchair marathons. The park ranger checks my cabin regularly and said its traditional Dade County pine construction weathered the hurricane with nary a damaged stairstep or busted window. When he asked when I planned to return, I had no answer.

How about, I said, we let it take its course.

Acknowledgments

As always the author would like to acknowledge the excellent work of the folks at Dutton, especially Mitch Hoffman and Erika Imranyi, who succinctly debunk the statement that editors don't edit anymore.

I also wish to thank Philip Spitzer without whom there would be no Max; my early reader, Lillian Ros Martin, for her insight and Spanish lessons; and Joanne Sinchuk, who spreads our work and without whom so many Florida mystery writers would simply be broke.

National Bestselling Author
JONATHON KING

A Killing Night

Max Freeman is no longer content to keep hiding in his secluded shack deep in the Everglades. So when his onetime girlfriend Detective Sherry Richards asks him to help nail an ex-cop she suspects of killing several young women in South Florida, he's ready to lend a hand. Until, that is, he discovers that her suspect is the ex-cop who once saved his life. Caught between his loyalty to Sherry and the debt to his former brother in blue, Max begins to dig in to his fellow officer's shadowy, troubled past—only to come face-to-face with his own....

Also Available:
Shadow Men
A Visible Darkness
The Blue Edge of Midnight

Available wherever books are sold or at
penguin.com

Penguin Group (USA) Online

What will you be reading tomorrow?

Tom Clancy, Patricia Cornwell, W.E.B. Griffin,
Nora Roberts, William Gibson, Robin Cook,
Brian Jacques, Catherine Coulter, Stephen King,
Dean Koontz, Ken Follett, Clive Cussler,
Eric Jerome Dickey, John Sandford,
Terry McMillan, Sue Monk Kidd, Amy Tan,
John Berendt…

You'll find them all at
penguin.com

Read excerpts and newsletters,
find tour schedules and reading group guides,
and enter contests.

Subscribe to Penguin Group (USA) newsletters
and get an exclusive inside look
at exciting new titles and the authors you love
long before everyone else does.

PENGUIN GROUP (USA)
us.penguingroup.com